D0863896

WHERE CRIME NEVER SLEEPS
MURDER NEW YORK STYLE 4

An Anthology of Crime and Mystery Short Stories from the New York/Tri-State Chapter of Sisters in Crime

Edited by Elizabeth Zelvin

ISBN-1-947915-00-2
978-947915-00-8

The Dames of Detection
d/b/a Level Best Books
18100 Windsor Hill Dr.
Olney, MD 20832
www.levelbestbooks.com

This is an anthology comprised of works of fiction. Any references to historical events, real people, or real locales are used fictitiously. Other names, characters, places, and incidents are the product of the authors' imaginations, and any resemblance to actual events or locales or persons, living or dead, is entirely coincidental.

Trade Paperback
ISBN-13: 978
ISBN-10:

Manufactured & Printed in the United States of America
2017

FOREWORD

Has any other city in America inspired half as many songs and stories as New York?

East Side, West Side
All around the town . . .

That's where this book takes us: from Staten Island to Queens to Battery Park. From Coney Island to Rockaway Beach. From penthouses overlooking Central Park to Gracie Mansion. In these pages, you can visit Astor Place, be charmed by the butterfly collection at the Bronx Zoo, explore the Museum of Modern Art and Rockefeller Center, get a glimpse inside the National Arts Club, or walk the Brooklyn Bridge. My husband's a native New Yorker, and we lived here for several years. I set my first series here, but I still haven't visited some of the places that fired the fertile imaginations of Sisters in Crime's New York/Tri-State authors. Whether scam artists, whistle-blowers, beleaguered civilians, or career criminals, their characters have used poisons, knives, guns, and even a gorilla to get the job done. After all, as they say, New York, New York really is one hell of a town!

— **Margaret Maron**

Margaret Maron is a founding member and third president of Sisters in Crime. Named a Grand Master by Mystery Writers of America, she was inducted into the North Carolina Literary Hall of Fame in 2016.

INTRODUCTION

What makes New York New York? What are its iconic attractions, its don't-miss events, its hidden treasures? And what makes a New Yorker a New Yorker? Is there such a thing as a typical son or daughter of New York? Some transplants consider themselves the "real" New Yorkers. As a New York native, I'm bound to take the opposing view. As we say when comparing humans to even the best programmed GPS, there's no substitute for local knowledge. The city is our briar patch. It's home, and we negotiate it with ease, whether we're exploring its history, developing its real estate, visiting its museums, beaches, zoos, and parks, drinking in its bars, running in its famed Marathon, or murdering our fellow citizens within its boundaries. The characters in these seventeen stories do all these things with panache.

This volume is the fourth in the Murder New York Style series conceived and written by members of the New York/Tri-State Chapter of Sisters in Crime. The first, titled simply *Murder New York Style*, captured the flavor of mystery and mayhem in the five boroughs, the metropolitan area, including Long Island and New Jersey, and bits of suburban and upstate New York. (An e-sampler was later reissued as *Deadly Debut*.) The second, *Fresh Slices*, challenged contributors to set their stories in New York locations that would *not* be familiar to most readers: a Brighton Beach strip joint, the scuzzy side of Long Island, Alphabet City before gentrification. The third, *Family Matters*—everyone knows that family and murder are kindred spirits.

Our original intent was to devote MNYS4 to New York attractions: landmarks and events that draw visitors to our city, perhaps with visitors as the protagonists, victims, and killers in the stories. Our storytellers had other ideas. You will read about the Brooklyn Bridge in these pages, along with the Museum of Natural History, the running track around the Central Park reservoir, and Carnegie Hall. But the characters who inhabit these places and breathe life into these stories are New Yorkers. To them, the iconic places of New York are not attractions to be gawked at, but the places where they go about their lives. So we went with what we got, and our theme became the infinite variety of New Yorkers and the uniqueness of New Yorkishness.

The term "New York attitude" is overused, and not enough is said about what it really is. Forget the caricature of crude pugnaciousness, the New Yorker as nihilist giving the rest of the world the finger. I think the real attitude is the New Yorker's ease in her skin (or his), a way of being thoroughly at home in his (or her) New York world—or worlds, because New York consists of hundreds, thousands of worlds. The authors of these stories have given us a glimpse into a few of these many worlds. What constitutes the look, the sound and smell and taste of New York? It all depends on the senses of the individual and which New York that person currently inhabits.

Inevitably, these worlds intersect. It is said that, psychologically, Americans require eight feet of personal space around them, more than any other people on earth. In a crowded subway car at rush hour, they're lucky if they get eight inches. And crowding leads to conflict and drama—perfect for stories of crime and murder. In each of these stories, the most unlikely characters rub elbows with one another. Mansfield's "An Actor Prepares" features a devotee of Stanislavsky, a bunch of "hormonal and over-caffeinated" high school kids, and a gorilla. Ebenstein's "Me and Johnny D" throws together a Rockefeller Center tour guide with a PhD and a school of executive sharks with harassed underlings nipping at their tail fins in "the profitable world of schlock TV."

New York is the city where crime never sleeps. Neither do public transportation, food delivery, drug stores, convenience stores, or the world's most interesting people, some of whom are working, playing, solving crimes, and writing or reading mysteries at any given moment.

Some of these stories are multilayered, rewarding readers who take the time to tease out the various threads. Is Siegel's "Levitas" about art, gender inequality, or how far New Yorkers will go for an affordable apartment? What disturbing reality to which the ten-year-old narrator is oblivious lies beneath the surface of the Rockaway vacation idyll in Page's "The Cousins?" Is the menace we sense in Bell's "Prey of New York" approaching from the present or the past?

You'll find betrayal and revenge in these pages, the need to keep a secret, all the usual motives—love, money, convenience, and dire necessity—as well as a couple of oddball motives that make perfect sense to the killer. Don't forget that coming up with unusual ways to kill people is mystery writers' favorite topic of conversation over a convivial dinner. So if you overhear such a conversation in your favorite restaurant, please don't call 911— unless the participants split their infinitives and end every sentence with a preposition. If they do that, they can't possibly be crime writers, so it's safe to say they must be thugs.

Some of the protagonists in these stories investigate the crimes, others commit them. You may not empathize with or approve of all of them. We hope, however, that they will intrigue and entertain you, that you will care about their fate, and that these stories will give you many hours of reading pleasure.

— Elizabeth Zelvin, Editor

Elizabeth Zelvin, Editor, has been nominated twice for the Derringer Award and three times for the Agatha Award for Best Short Story. Her stories have appeared in *Ellery Queen's Mystery Magazine, Alfred Hitchcock's Mystery Magazine,* and all three previous volumes of the Murder New York Style series. Both her mystery and historical adventure series include short stories as well as novels. Before turning to fiction, she worked as a reference book and textbook editor for many years.

A note about the New York/Tri-State
Chapter of Sisters in Crime

The authors of the stories in this anthology are all members of the New York/Tri-State Chapter of Sisters in Crime: sixteen sisters and one "mister sister" who are proud to be part of a flourishing thirty-year-old national organization whose mission is "to promote the ongoing advancement, recognition and professional development of women crime writers." The Foreword to the volume was written by **Margaret Maron**, one of Sisters in Crime's most distinguished "goddesses," as past presidents of the organization are affectionately called.

Stories

AN ACTOR PREPARES

NINA MANSFIELD

If you've never taken a group of twenty-two hormonal and over-caffeinated fifteen-year-olds to the Bronx Zoo, I don't recommend it. And if you do, for the love of Chekhov, don't confiscate their cell phones in the name of theatrical inquiry, because God forbid you stumble across a dead body in the Congo Gorilla Forest.

Why, you might ask, would a Moscow Art Theater-trained drama teacher such as I take her acting class to the Bronx Zoo? Year after year, my principal would ask me the same thing.

"A field trip, Ms. Slut-skaya, must have some sort of educational purpose."

Mr. Dower was a man in whom every creative instinct had been smothered at birth.

"It's pronounced Slooz-Kaya," I would remind him for the five hundredth time, and then launch into my impassioned monologue. I'd let the remnants of my Russian accent loose and allow every ounce of my soul to fill his depressing little office until each football trophy trembled.

"Zee animal exercise—first pondered by zee great Stanislavsky, and brought into being by zee renowned Lee Strasberg—teaches my acting students zee power of keen observation, of fine detail. Vhile I vas a young acting student, I spent many, many hours at zee Moscow Zoo. Zee horrors zat filled it made me veep for all animal kind—zee three-legged lion, zee vhimpering hyena, zee terrible steel bars. Truly scenes from a Humane Society nightmare. But I digress."

At this point in my presentation, I would usually drop the accent, lower my voice, and attempt to connect with him, educator to educator, colleague to colleague, human to human.

"This exercise has been an important part of the drama curriculum for many years. Oh, sure, these days students could watch their apes and antelopes on YouTube, but one cannot truly become the animal unless they live, walk, and breathe with the animal. It is in this way the young actor can capture the essence,

1

the spirit of the beast."

I would choose this moment to channel the crane—that beautiful, sad, caged bird that had become a part of my soul all those years ago at the Moscow Zoo. I would draw back my shoulder blades, stand on one leg, and affect a vacant hopelessness in my eyes.

At this point, Mr. Dower would always reluctantly sign the necessary paperwork.

This year, however, he surprised me.

"I would love to join you, Ms. Stut-skaya."

I was oddly disappointed I wouldn't have the pleasure of performing my yearly monologue for the man. I'd no doubt have to sit next to him—and smell his gag-inducing cologne—on the nauseating school bus ride to the Bronx.

"What a pleasant surprise," I said. "I would love for you to come."

While I had no desire to spend more time with Mr. Dower than necessary, I did not expect the hostility I encountered from my darling student actors when I informed them he would be joining us.

"No way, Sloozy," they yelled.

"He's evil!"

"He sucks!"

"He scares me!" Even shy little Alice had joined in on the discussion—if you could call it that. At least they were all projecting their voices.

"Children, please, settle down. First of all, you will refer to me as Ms. Slooz, not Sloozy, is that understood?"

I try to keep things somewhat formal during class time.

Some grumbled, but I held a menacing gaze until there were contrite nods all around.

"Now, please tell me, why all this vitriol?"

"I hate that man!" Anthony let out a primal scream that did credit to my teaching. "He's not letting me audition for the musical next week."

For a moment, I thought he might throw a chair. Had he shown such passion in his audition for our fall drama—my existential contemporary adaptation of *Macbeth*—he might have

2

received a part larger than the Porter. Anthony is a former football player. After his third concussion, his parents made him drop the sport, and he landed in my drama program. He's only a sophomore, but he has such potential.

"No, Anthony, let's be clear about this. You are not allowed to audition because you decided to show up wasted to the Spring Dance last week, and you puked on Ms. Cloretta. Mr. Dower was just following school policy."

"So give me detention. Suspend me for a day, a week. Don't take the musical away from me." Anthony punched a theater block, and it skidded across the floor.

"Mr. Dower made me change my clothes like five times this year," Aurelia said.

"Aurelia, darling, while I abhor a dress code that unfairly punishes young ladies, rules are rules, my dear girl. You'll have plenty of time in your life to wear what you want. Just don something that covers your navel when we go to the zoo and we shouldn't encounter any problems with Mr. Dower."

"But it's like, he goes out of his way to hunt me down each day to see what I am wearing! I swear, that man will chase me down anywhere."

The truth was Aurelia was impossible to miss. She was a girl with true star potential. When she played Lady Macbeth for me last fall, I could taste the blood on her hands. She could act all "out damned spot" over a real-life disappointment too. Last summer, for example, she'd had the opportunity to study in London at the Royal Academy, but alas, the cost of tuition had been out of her reach. "I would have killed to go," she'd said. Always the drama queen. But she'd often been unprepared at rehearsals. Sure, she could improvise brilliantly, but she was impulsive and lacked discipline. She knew she had talent, and she thought that should be enough.

"If you are going to pursue acting, Aurelia," I told her time and time again, "you must do your homework. You must learn to prepare. An actor prepares!"

"Now, does anyone else have a complaint they wish to voice?"

"He's the reason—"

"Yes, Abe?" I asked.

Abe mumbled something and ran his long, thin fingers through the sandy hair that hung perpetually in front of his eyes.

"I'm sorry, Abe, but you are going to have to speak up."

Abe Rafferty was a very slight, quiet boy. He had the soul of an artist, but he hadn't learned to express that soul on stage yet. He spoke as if he were afraid his voice might actually make noise, and he had never even auditioned for one of our school productions. Sometimes I wondered why he had enrolled in acting class at all. Somewhere inside him, there burnt a red hot passion, but I had yet to see it.

We looked at Abe expectantly.

"I just don't like the guy," he whispered.

"But your mom sure does!" Victor, our class comedian, muttered audibly and the class broke out in titters. "She sure seems to like the Dowster a whole lot."

Abe's face turned a most unappealing shade of red.

"There will be none of that! I will not tolerate rumor mongering in this room. Now, if there is nothing more, I will ask that you be respectful to Mr. Dower. You do not have to hang out with him or sit with him on the bus. He is a chaperone—there to ensure your safety, and that no mischief is made—and that is all. And speaking of chaperones, Abe, please tell your mother we would be thrilled to have her accompany us again. Now, I don't want to hear another word about this. Is that understood?"

The class groaned their collective assent.

"Quite frankly, I am pleased our administration is taking an interest in the arts."

000

The day of the field trip arrived. Risa Rafferty, Abe's mother, brought candy for the students.

"Ooh, this is going to be fun," she said, as she handed out little bags of Skittles and M&Ms. "I just love the Bronx Zoo!" She adjusted her blouse, which revealed a little more cleavage than one might recommend in an educational setting.

"You're awesome, Mrs. R.," Victor proclaimed.

4

He slung his arm around Abe.

"You know, your mom is really something."

The words themselves seemed harmless, but his tone was lascivious.

Abe pushed Victor away.

"Victor!" I said in my sternest teacher voice.

Risa Rafferty was a dear for volunteering for our field trips, but the students could have done without a sugar high first thing in the morning. They were incredibly loud on the bus ride down to the Bronx from our sleepy suburb. The trip was rather nauseating as well, and by the time we reached the zoo, I was more than ready to de-bus.

"Why don't we start at the Butterfly Garden," I said, consulting my map.

The zen of those beautiful little creatures flying about was sure to alleviate some of the pain in my brain.

"Do we all need to walk around together?" Aurelia asked. "Can't we just split up and find our animals?"

"We could, but we won't," I answered. "How else will we be able to provide proper critiques if we do not experience each other's animal? Besides, Aurelia, we are starting with your butterfly, so why complain?"

At the entrance to the glass structure that housed the butterflies, a sign warned: "Removal of butterflies or moths is prohibited and a violation of the Plant Pest Act."

"Seriously? Plant Pest Act?" Victor pointed to the sign. "I mean, why would anyone actually steal—"

"You'd be surprised," a zookeeper interrupted. "The Lotis Blue, for example, which we've recently acquired, had been considered possibly extinct. Some people would pay quite a bit for such a rare creature."

While the zookeeper went on about endangered butterflies and the zoo's conservation efforts, Aurelia moved around the enclosed garden. She took her time looking at the various butterflies before choosing a petite, bluish, almost violet specimen.

"Notice how it holds its wings when it lands," I said. "Let the movement come from your spine. The center of gravity for a butterfly is very different from your center of gravity. In fact, it is almost immune from gravity, is it not? Try to capture its weightlessness."

Aurelia arched her back and waved her hands gracefully up and down.

"I'll capture it, Ms. Slooz," she said calmly.

The actor needed her space, and I gave it to her.

"I'm pleased to see that young woman dressed appropriately today," Mr. Dower commented.

Like a pleased parent, he watched Aurelia glide about. It was true. Aurelia wore an uncharacteristically baggy sweater.

"Perhaps you've made an impression after all, Mr. Dower," I said.

"Perhaps," he said, scowling, and I wondered if I'd allowed any sarcasm to creep into my tone.

When Aurelia announced that she had mastered her butterfly, we headed to the giraffes.

"Anthony, you cannot rely solely on your height to become the giraffe. You must transform your shoulders, your legs, the very core of your being to catch the essence of this animal."

It was this essential core that seemed to elude him. The peacefulness of the giraffe was obscured by an anger in his eyes.

Elephants and zebras, polar bears and camels. We took two separate trips on the Asia monorail.

And at long last, we found ourselves in the Congo. Several students had chosen primates to observe—the mandrill, the monkey—and I was surprised that quiet Abe had selected a gorilla.

"Your class is really helping Abe to come out of his shell," Risa Rafferty whispered.

Abe was pressed up to the glass, watching a husky silverback lumber up a hill.

"He has seemed rather morose of late," I said.

"It's the divorce," she said suddenly. "He's angry with me. But he doesn't understand that— "

It was then that Alice—shy little Alice who could rarely project her voice more than two feet, however hard she tried in class—screamed a scream that might have awoken Stanislavsky himself.

The silverback dragged the body of a man behind him.

6

"Whoa, that totally looks like the Dowster!" shouted Victor.

"James. Oh, my God, James!" Risa Rafferty started banging on the thick glass that separated us from the gorillas.

"Who's James?" Victor asked.

As the gorilla flung the man's body over his shoulder, I realized "James" was Mr. Dower.

I became so entranced with Risa Rafferty's fists, and whether or not they would break through the glass, that I did not hear Anthony at first.

"Slooz, Sloozy!" he yelled in my face. "Phone. I need my phone!"

The phones had all been bagged and left on the bus. I fumbled for my own phone, but it was completely swallowed up by the teaching detritus that covered the bottom of my bag.

Security guards had come running the moment Alice screamed. More zoo officials appeared on the scene once they realized the gorilla was involved. A crowd quickly gathered around. Visitors shot footage of the silverback tossing Mr. Dower's body around like a rag doll. I couldn't have told you when the police showed up. Somehow, time ceased to move forward at all. Throughout the ordeal I began to question my reliance on sense memory as an actor, because in truth, I think my senses ceased to work.

Eventually, we were ushered into a back room of the Crane Café, where we sat for hours. One by one, students were questioned by the police.

"How long are they going to keep us here?" Anthony asked.

"Murder is serious business," I said.

"Murder?" Victor spat out the Snapple he was sipping. "Who said anything about murder?"

"Yeah, this was all just an awful accident!" Aurelia glanced down at her hands as if she didn't know what to do with them.

"They didn't kill the gorilla, did they?" Abe asked, his voice shaking. "They just stunned him, right?"

"Abe, how can you be worried about the gorilla at a time like this!" Risa Rafferty cried, mascara running down her face. "I just don't understand how he got in there. I mean—it's not like he could have fallen in. They're behind glass! He was right here with us and then—this is all my fault."

"Mom, you need to cut it out."

"But if it hadn't been for me, he would have never—"

"Mom, stop! Just stop it!"

Abe grabbed hold of his mother's shoulders and pushed her down into a chair. He had already managed to channel the gorilla. As his acting teacher, I was proud. As one who empathizes strongly, I was concerned.

Risa Rafferty, stunned silent for only a moment, continued to weep and wail with renewed vigor. She was not crying like a concerned parent who had just witnessed a gruesome death. She was mourning like a woman who had lost a lover.

Suddenly, Abe's transformation made sense. His parents' divorce and his mother's all too conspicuous relationship with "the Dowster" might have finally brought forth the animal in this quiet boy. I've always believed anyone could convincingly portray a murderer. But could someone like Abe really have been driven to kill?

"Abe, chill out." Anthony put a comforting arm around Abe's shoulders. "I know you hated the guy."

But Anthony hated him too. And he certainly had the strength to break Mr. Dower's neck, if that was indeed what had happened. Considering the way his head had flip-flopped when the silverback tossed him about, this seemed likely. Maybe the gorilla was innocent of any crime.

"They can't keep us here all night, can they?" Aurelia whined.

"I hope not," I said.

But I knew that if foul play was suspected—and surely it was—we would be held for as long as the police deemed necessary. I tried to recreate the Congo Gorilla Forest in my mind. Risa Rafferty was right. There was simply no way a visitor could fall into the gorilla habitat by accident. The parts that weren't enclosed by glass were surrounded by a fence. A deep ravine served as additional protection for visitors and gorillas alike. I didn't know how Mr. Dower had ended up with the gorillas, but I knew it was no accident.

I've always thought that great actors would make the best detectives. After all, we are keen observers of human nature. It is our mission to put the truth on stage. So many times, while I was studying at the Moscow Art Theater, my teacher would yell, "I do not believe you!" There is no place for lies on the stage. If we are not fully committed to our actions, it could ruin the theatrical illusion. So I did what I do best. I observed.

The room was warm, but Aurelia had not taken off her bulky sweater. Anthony paced the room, squeezing his fists. Victor had fallen asleep with his head on a table, a little puddle of drool collecting near his mouth. Alice braided a stray lock of hair. Abe had made peace with his mother and silently held her hand.

Risa Rafferty was not acting. Her grief was genuine, as was her son's outburst of anger. But Abe had remained with us the entire time in the Congo. He had been pressed against the glass studying his gorilla. I had watched him watch.

But someone had been missing, if only for a short time. It seemed the only plausible solution. He or she had somehow managed to avoid zoo staff and slip into a restricted area. A skilled improviser might have been able to pull that off. This person had forced Mr. Dower to follow, or perhaps he had been lured to do so of his own volition. An argument may have occurred, a struggle of sorts. Or Mr. Dower may have been taken completely unaware, struck with a blunt object perhaps. He hadn't yelled out once he'd been pushed into the gorilla enclosure. Whether he'd been unconscious or dead by the time the silverback got to him, we might never know. But who would do this? Who was to blame? I looked about the room.

Who was it that I did not believe?

000

Mr. Dower's death made the news on all of the major networks. But only one small online paper reported the disappearance of the rare Lotis Blue from the Butterfly Garden.

We were in the middle of our warm-up the next day in acting class when the police arrived.

9

"Aurelia, I think they would like to speak with you, darling."

She was dressed like her old self today—like a girl who wanted the paparazzi to follow her around. Like a girl desperate for fame. Like a girl who would truly do anything to get what she wanted. She wanted RADA: the Royal Academy of Dramatic Art in London. A rare butterfly could have paid her way.

If only Mr. Dower hadn't caught her stealing it.

"Me? Why would they want to speak with me?" Aurelia asked, her eyes ablaze with innocence.

The class held its collective breath as the police walked toward the stage.

Aurelia looked down at her hands.

When she looked back up, I knew she had prepared for this performance.

Nina Mansfield is a Connecticut based author and playwright. Her stories have appeared in *Ellery Queen's Mystery Magazine*, *Mysterical-E, Kings River Life,* and *Fast Women and Neon Lights: Eighties-Inspired Neon Noir*. Her first novel, *Swimming Alone*, a young adult mystery, was published in 2015 by Fire & Ice YA. Nina's plays have had close to one hundred productions throughout the world; they are published by Smith and Kraus, One Act Play Depot, YouthPLAYS, and Original Works. She is a member of Sisters in Crime, Mystery Writers of America, International Thriller Writers, the Society of Children's Book Writers and Illustrators, the Short Mystery Fiction Society, and The Dramatist Guild.

PREY OF NEW YORK

RONA BELL

"We are hawks," my father said. "We select the highest point in any city wherever we buy property. The highest point."

He still talked as though he were driving, even holding out his hands as though gripping the wheel. These were the same hands he placed flat on the windshield when I was growing up, letting the heat from his body melt ice.

But I was driving now.

"In New York City," he said, "the highest point is in Fort Washington."

"I know that," I said. "You told me that when I was four years old and you took me to the new lots where we tore the buildings down in a single day."

My father gave out a laugh, a great laugh that exploded for a few seconds before he sucked it back in. Even a laugh was too much for him, a loss of control he could not allow. I knew that.

"Dad, I appreciate what you say. I take my children to the museum, and I hear your voice in my head. All the layers of facts float to the surface."

He looked at me sideways.

"I thought that we might find the bones of George Washington, but I would have settled for one of those stubby pipes."

"I wanted bones too," I said. "But remember we found one of those pipes. Or you took it from someone."

"That was a long time ago. Never found the bones of George Washington. Found a lot of gold, though." He laughed again, then took it back.

"Where should we go now?" I asked.

The car felt low to the road, the leather seats deep, sighing as the car shifted. Dad's cars were always black. Like black animals, Dad's cars moved most at night.

I played in the back of the black cars then, drawing with my tiny finger on the fine cover of dust. We'd head out to the bare lots where he was building, putting it all together, conquering New York. I remember my mother in the front seat. Even late at night, the streetlights would catch her diamond earrings. To me, she was beautiful, dressed to go dancing though she never left the car.

"You remember the name for it?" he asked me.

"For what?"

He turned, and in the light it seemed to me that his face followed him, his skin catching up to his bones. This was what disease did. Disease started from the inside. I wondered, did disease look at cells and know which were honest, which were sick, which were hiding something?

"Damn it, kid, you are lost in space. I am asking you, do you remember the name of that kind of pipe? Yes or no?"

"No," I said, staring at the dark road ahead.

"Your mother would have known the answer."

I kept driving, moving the car as though it were a panther, hungry but cautious, the two of us resting in the silence of it, neither one of us speaking for a while.

"The thing that makes a man," he said finally, "the absolute thing that makes a man of character is that when he is coming to the end, he knows it."

"You got years to go, Dad. Years."

The car rumbled with its own language.

He let out another laugh, and I waited for him to take it back, and he did, as though he would need those laughs soon, in another world.

"There is one thing I am afraid of," he said. "One thing I think about."

"What's that?"

I took my eyes off the road and looked over to him. I saw the line of his jaw, sinking toward the black leather seat as though it could slide down to join up with the leather and I wouldn't be able to tell the difference.

Then his hands were up in front of his face, as though he saw something coming that only he could see.

"You okay?" I asked.

"I am afraid that my enemies got to heaven first," he said. "They will be waiting there to have things out with me."

"Your enemies are not in heaven, Dad. Do not worry."

I did not take it back, I let it fill the car. I let it go as if to energize him and give him life and maybe even years he didn't have.

"Your enemies are waiting for you in hell," I said. "Not heaven."

I expected him to laugh, ready to have it out, ready to give me something to remember. But he was not laughing. He just sank down further and stared through the window.

We turned onto Park Avenue.

"I never bought anything with a Park Avenue address," he said. "I always wanted to. I always wanted to be part of the club here. But I never got in. Your mother never let me forget that."

"Didn't you hear my joke, Dad? You might be going to hell and I might join you there."

His hands slapped at the leather seat.

"Never. Never."

Then his head tipped back, cushioned. This was where he was most comfortable in the entire world. This was where he rode at night, alone with my mother, with her decked in jewels, a diamond necklace blinking around her neck. I knew she wore bracelets under her sleeves. I could hear them but never see them.

I believed that if I closed my eyes, the car would take the lead, knowing the way to all the places in the city that he had tried to buy but stolen instead.

"You know where I want to go now," he said, his voice quiet. "Take me there."

"Back to the highest place?"

"No. You know the place."

He bumped against the door as though he would leap out of the car.

"Mama's grave?" I asked.

"No." That laugh again, fast and taken back. I thought of her diamond necklace. Who had that necklace now?

"Take me to the lowest place in the city. Right on the river. Your grandfather used to say that the river is always working."

I drove. I took him all the way down the FDR, the great winding path that seemed to go back in time, past the seaport with

13

the old ships, like skeletons come to be admired.

"You see," he said. "You know. You were in the back seat, but children learn like migrating animals."

And I did, the place where Wall Street falls off into the river, where the water takes over for the land. And there we stopped.

I helped him out of the car.

"Amazing," he said. "That in this city there is a place where you can just pull up, empty the trunk, and the river takes over from there."

He lifted his arm, with effort.

"Do you see those tugboats?" he said. "Your mother loved tugboats. They are like women, she always told me. You cannot believe how much work they do when you look at their size."

She had said that to me too. She, the sole woman in a family of all boys. A mystery. No one to look through her closets. No one to steal her things.

"What happened here?" I asked.

My father did not answer for a moment.

"All bad guys do this," he said then, looking into the dark of the river. "We come back to the scene."

We stood there for ten minutes, twenty, almost an hour, waiting for dawn, watching the birds fall from the sky, land on the river, and be carried away.

"Not much time left," he said. "You will do fine."

His hand was on my back, burning through my jacket with the last embers of his life.

"No need for *you* to graduate from the bad guys school," he said.

Too late, I thought. I already had, and he knew it.

He looked at me in a way that he never had before.

"Well, Dad, it is not as though you wanted me to be a senator, a doctor, or anything like that. You never even brought it up. You spent your life driving around in black cars. I do the same."

He squinted down at a rock like the hawk that has spied the mouse from a thousand feet and just needs an assist. I went to pick it up, but he stopped me.

14

"Don't," he said. "If you pick up that rock, I might smash your face."

It was a startling admission, but it was a fact. Even in his prime, he was so close, so very close to violence with me. My mother, he treated like a loving pet. Once, when his fist had gone through the door, I saw her look up from her chair, the magazine on her lap. I heard her say to him, "You scare your children. But no one else. No one else."

That wasn't true.

He went to her, like all men who smashed their fists into doors. And behind the broken door, he cried.

"What do you need done when you are not here anymore?"

I believed he was waiting for that question. I needed instructions, I needed something. I thought that was what he wanted.

But that question turned into a knife before my eyes, and he was on me.

"No, Pop."

I threw a hand out to stop him. His weight, all the muscle that I remembered, wanted to believe was there, was gone. I caught him as though we were dancing. I was holding onto bones that slid back from me. For a moment I believed that he would splinter into a skeleton.

But he gathered whatever strength he had left. That old knife that his father gave him was in his hand. At my neck.

"I could take you out right now," he said, his breath in my ear, his voice trembling, his hand trembling.

I reached around and pushed his arm down. It was like feeling an elevator move, as though his whole body was something I controlled.

We were still at the river's edge, and the lights on the other side, Long Island City, were our audience.

"This game is not for the old." My father sighed. "I remember that with your grandfather. I remember the same thing, the same thing as now."

I took the knife and led him back to the car, opened the door, and guided him in, folding the skeleton in. He breathed out and barely seemed to breathe in.

15

"Let's go see your grandmother," he said after a moment.

I moved the car along the river's edge and under tunnels to the apartment house where Giaconda Brown had lived, to where she had run the world.

"You know that your grandfather had a temper that attracted money," he said.

I slapped the steering wheel, and we laughed together, the sound of laughs bouncing off one another, that was our sound.

"Coffee would be good," my father said. "Coffee cures everything."

"Giaconda Brown said it just that way," I said.

He fingered his seat belt, as though he might pick a fight with it.

"People were afraid of your grandfather," he said. "They paid him to stay away. I never had that talent and I didn't want it for you. But Giaconda Brown was a queen."

I turned the car down an alley tucked in near the Brooklyn Bridge, a tiny alleyway where he'd parked with me when I was young and riding in the back seat.

This was the place where he said he had always felt safe. I saw him relax, put his head back, and dream, probably of money.

I once asked him, "Do you think New Yorkers can smell money?"

"No," he said, "but they can taste it."

The car itself seemed to settle too, to lean into the space. There was a garbage can off to the side. Years ago my father would have gotten out, lifted the lid, stood back and peered deep inside. He needed to know, to see everything. Now he saw the garbage can and I could see him calculating the energy it would take to launch himself out of the car and look into it, too much. Instead, he sat there and I knew he was thinking about coffee and his mother, Giaconda Brown, and the coffee beans she ground herself and how she would bring the coffee to him with her hands wrapped around the coffee cup. Asbestos hands. That is what she called them. She fed him coffee from the time he was an infant.

"I always looked in the rear view mirror to see you," he said. "And now I just look to my left. You're in the goddamn driver's seat."

16

I didn't know what to say to that.

"I am remembering Giaconda Brown," he said. "I never called her mother. I never said *mother* until you were born. And then it was grandmother. I think she must have asked for that."

"I always remember her in the kitchen," I said, "walking the ten paces back and forth. And I remember the telephone ringing, always ringing."

And then there was the laugh again.

"Your grandmother ran the world from her telephone," he said.

I felt the alley closing in. I could have sworn the walls had moved a fraction of an inch and were squeezing my lungs.

"I remember her cooking," I managed to say. "I remember the carrots she made. She burned them, one at a time, but the sweetness that came from those carrots."

My father's hands were on me, the bare hands that had wiped away the ice from the car in the middle of a storm. But now his hands were light. I knew he was not fully himself. The energy that had nearly stabbed me with a knife, nearly smashed me with the rock, was gone.

"Your grandmother," he said, "ran girls."

"What?"

"Wait," he said. "Your grandmother ran ten girls at any time. She did it all from the kitchen. She did it without ever stepping out of the house. And what is more amazing, without ever raising her voice."

I could hear the voice of my grandmother, Giaconda Brown, how she lifted the telephone to her ear, bent down, turned around. I closed my eyes and saw myself at her kitchen table with the coffee and how she said drink it, that it would make me grow up strong. And other words, the whispered words I could never hear.

"I remember, Dad," I said. "I remember that she spoke very low into the telephone and she never spoke for long."

"She didn't need to."

Far away, the early cars on the Brooklyn Bridge sailed over us.

"I knew," he said, "but your grandfather didn't know."

17

"I want out of this alleyway," I said, the rats itching around us, the darkness closing in. "It doesn't mean the same thing to me as it does to you."

But there was his hand on my hand again, the waiting, the patient way that poison drips into the blood.

"Can you roll down the window, son, can you let some air in?"

"It lets the grit in too," I said.

"I have to tell you about your grandfather," he said. "There will be no one else who can tell you this story."

I wanted the story. I could taste it. In some way I had always wanted the story, a story that I didn't know.

"Your grandfather never really made money. Yes, he attracted it. Somehow he got money, some, but it was never regular. You have to be brilliant to work on the other side of the law and still have steady income. You understand?"

"Yes," I said. "Yes. I went to law school."

"You didn't graduate," he said.

"But I went," I said.

"Your grandfather could not do anything that truly started a fire. But your grandmother was a queen! When I told her that, she would say that she was one arm of a queen, a toe of a queen. But without her, nothing would have been possible."

As we sat there, the grinding steel sound of the cars grew louder. A stray cat padding past the car looked up at us with weary, half-lidded eyes. A tremulous whisker with one drop of water bulging at the tip glinted in the light.

"I loved her, grandmother Giaconda Brown," I said. "She made me eggs with onions that had been soaked in coffee. Burnt worms I called them, and they filled me up for hours."

My father leaned against the car door. "I'm getting out."

He started to open the door, but I leaned over him and pulled it shut, the way I did with my own small son.

"No. I was hoping on this car ride you would tell me your plans for after you are gone. What do you want me to do, Dad? What the hell do you want me to do with everything you've acquired?"

My voice rang out beyond the car and echoed in the canyon

18

of the alleyway.

"Did you ever wonder how your grandmother died?" my father asked.

I remembered Giaconda Brown's funeral. I was eight. I remembered thinking about whether those mysterious women in the back of the funeral parlor, the aunts, knew how to make the coffee cake with the bits of chopped coffee beans covered with chocolate. I remembered thinking that it wasn't something I should be thinking about.

"I need air," my father said and banged against his door again.

"Okay, Dad."

I held my father's arm firmly as he eased out of the car.

"Ah," he said. "The air is fresh now."

"Your grandmother was brilliant," my father said. "She figured it all out from a tiny kitchen, with the children right there, and the world at war somewhere. To know that her husband, my father, could never really provide for the family. She never held it against him. She just knew that it was no use to ask him to do things that he could never do."

My father was panting a bit.

"Did you take your medicine this morning?"

"I don't know. Never mind that now. I am telling you a story you need to know."

"I need to get back, Dad," I said. "I cannot drive around all night. Men have to be at home. Everyone knows where everyone is. It is a different time."

We stood leaning on the car. He seemed to gain some strength from the car holding him up.

"Your grandfather finally found out what your grandmother was doing to keep the family together."

"I wish I could have heard that conversation," I said. "Did he ask her how she was paying the rent on the rooms the girls used?"

The sky was lightening and then darkening, as if deciding whether or not to come together for another day.

"You are smart," he said. "That should have been the end of it."

19

"But?" I said. "What happened?"

"Your grandfather killed Giaconda Brown."

I remembered the flavor of coffee, the ground bits covered with chocolate, the worship of coffee that she spoon-fed to me and my smallest cousin, and I remembered how that little boy spit it out and Giaconda Brown held his fat hand down and fed it to him again and again.

"Aren't you going to say something?" my father asked.

At that moment I knew that he had been fed that way too, forced to eat, forced. Times were different then.

"I am not going to cry for you, Dad. Is that what you are looking for here?"

"I want you to know that he killed her."

"So now I know. It was so long ago. No one ever knew, the cops, no one, right?"

"Just the neighborhood. We had an apartment where every child had a bedroom. Unheard of. Never happened. But we had one. Your grandfather hadn't known where the money came from."

"So? They all did what they had to."

"Your grandfather—he was a regular at Giaconda's girls."

"Oh."

"I blame the girl."

"Which one?"

"All of them! Especially one, who told him it was so nice that Giaconda Brown paid her extra when he showed up."

I remembered the funeral, the cups of coffee in the back, and the soft laughter. As my father talked, I lifted my eyes to the Brooklyn skyline, changing all around us. I saw the great cranes like elongated hawks at the top of buildings, waiting for the day to begin. I saw the exchange of money that would cover up all of our sins in the promised land that was America. And I saw the buildings that my father had owned for a short time and lost and dreamed of again. I saw all of that as he spoke to me.

"Your grandfather stormed into the house, he came crashing through the door, yelling that Giaconda Brown had made a fool of him. And she said that he had made a fool of himself and that it was she who had picked up the pieces for a lifetime—and

20

that she was done.

"Then Giaconda Brown rushed into the hallway, and in sight of all the neighbors, who opened their doors to watch, she crumpled to the ground. It was all very fast. It was even beautiful, this strong woman deciding that her life was over. If her husband could not love her anymore, then she would die like a queen. And she fell to the floor and was dead."

"Is this true?" I asked.

My father shrugged.

"It is true enough," he said. "It was true enough for no police ever to be involved. It was true enough that we could have a funeral. We buried her like a queen."

"I have to get you home," I said. "And I have to go home too."

"I want to go like Giaconda Brown," my father said. "This is my great wish right now. I want to decide the time of my death."

We pulled out of the alleyway.

"Now you know the truth," he said.

"I think it is the truth that you wanted to tell me," I said.

"It is a terrible thing," he said, "to have something like this in the family. And I am sad to have to leave you with this. But I am ready to go."

"We are not ready for you to go. We need you to guide us. What do you want done with what you have? You have never spoken about it."

I headed up onto the Brooklyn Bridge. His breathing was slower now.

"There are dead bodies under the Brooklyn Bridge," he said. "This very bridge. It was such a monumental effort that when people died they were just like one more brick in the structure. And it stands. It is magnificent."

I guided the black car to the topmost point of the bridge.

I half expected him to jump out then. To leave this earth with his family stories, told and untold, true and untrue.

"You have been a good father to me," I said. "I want you to know that when you are ready to tell me about what you have and what you want me to do with it, I promise that I will take good care. We are far from the world of Giaconda Brown. She was our

21

history, but she is not our future."

"Take me back to the highest point again," he said.

"Too late," I said. "Too late and too early. Another time."

"There won't be another time," he said.

I drove in silence all the way up toward where the cliffs began on the Jersey shore across the Hudson, and I pulled in to a spot where I knew he liked to look down toward the barges that floated toward Manhattan.

"Look at that," he said.

We watched a ship glide on the river.

"Let's talk about the fortune," he said.

Finally. This was the place to do it.

"It is gone," he said. "There's nothing. I have left you with no money and a secret about Giaconda Brown. I have left you with both, with nothing."

"Nothing? Nothing, Dad? *Nothing?*" I screamed.

"I wish I was a hawk," he said.

Later, I told my children he died in his bed, and then I took them to a museum. That is what you do when you want to hurl yourself back to something normal. And we came across the head of an Egyptian queen that the museum called a fragment of the head of a queen. Fragment is better than a piece, I thought. I will say fragment when I talk about Giaconda Brown. Was that all you ever got, fragments of things, fragments of truth? Still, I thought, it was a good word for secrets that took generations to be buried.

Rona Bell is the pen name of a New York business executive who has published (under other pen names) in the *North American Review*, the Akashic Books *Mondays are Murder* series, as well as such publications as *The New York Times*, *Washington Post*, and *Business Insider*. She is a graduate of the University of Rochester and received a graduate degree from the University of Michigan. In addition, she is a singer with the Oratorio Society of New York, founded in 1873, the second oldest cultural organization in the city. She has always been interested in the concept of opposites and the possibilities for story between those two extremes. She believes that crime fiction is the ideal lens to explore opposites through a character's eyes and is a proud member of the Crime Fiction Academy in New York, led by Jonathan Santlofer. She is based in New York City.

DEATH WILL FINISH YOUR MARATHON

ELIZABETH ZELVIN

My friend Barbara has talked me into doing some crazy things over the years, but running the Marathon was right up there. Run twenty-six miles? Without getting paid to do it? And neither the law nor bad guys breathing down my neck? Yep, it was one of those unexpected gifts of sobriety that makes everybody laugh when you complain about it at an AA meeting.

My best friend Jimmy, who can always find a consoling historical tidbit, said be glad I wouldn't have to wear armor like Pheippides, the guy who ran the original Marathon.

"Oh, yeah?" I said. "What was his story?"

"He ran from Marathon to Athens to tell the Athenians they'd won the battle."

"And how did it turn out for Pheippides?"

Jimmy's square Irish face got a little pinker than usual, and his eyes rolled upward and to the left, where the guardian angel left over from his Catholic childhood sits.

"Come on, dude, full disclosure."

"We-e-ell, he dropped dead at the end of it."

"But he got there," Barbara said. "Don't listen to him, Bruce."

It's usually best to let Barbara have the last word.

"It's only the New York Marathon," she said. "Nobody's going to die."

ΩΩΩ

If you've never been on Staten Island, you must be a real New Yorker. If that isn't on a T-shirt, it ought to be. Marathon Sunday, the ungodly hour of 5 AM, my first trip ever across the Verrazano Bridge. Jimmy drove, with Barbara beside him in front so we couldn't accuse her of backseat driving and me in the back with my eyes closed so I didn't have to watch the terrible effort it took her not to anyway.

24

"Weather's looking good," Jimmy said.

"It was a gorgeous day the time I came out here with the psyching team," Barbara said, not for the first or the fortieth time.

"I hate pep talks," I said. "I don't need a counselor to psych me up. I'd rather listen to that still small voice within."

They both glanced around to see if I was kidding. They've been dying to know if I have a Higher Power ever since I got sober. I'm not telling.

"I didn't pep talk," Barbara said indignantly. "I did a little deep breathing and meditation with the anxious ones before the race, that's all. We could do some together if you want, Bruce."

"If I need any help breathing, I'll let you know," I promised.

The sun was beginning to light up a cloudless sky when Jimmy dropped us off.

"I'll see you at the finish line," Jimmy said.

It took pull to get anywhere near the finish line in Central Park, but Jimmy's boss was one of the sponsors of the race.

"Cindy will be at the finish line too," I said. "She'll be working, but you might get lucky and spot her."

My detective girlfriend was one of the three thousand cops working the Marathon. Since she normally wore plain clothes, it would be a rare opportunity to see her looking fetching in uniform.

Cops and Marathon officials were shooing droppers-off away. Barbara and I headed toward the sea of white tents pitched on a vast grassy field under a dome of cerulean sky. There didn't seem to be any way out of the race short of jumping off the Verrazano Bridge.

"Don't forget to look for the Ancient Marathoner," Barbara said.

"Here? He can't be running," I said. "He needs a cane to make it around the reservoir track."

The Ancient Marathoner was a legendary runner who had finished strong in the first New York Marathon in 1970 and many subsequent Marathons until old age had overtaken him. They called him the Ancient Marathoner because he dominated a park bench by the South Gatehouse at the Central Park reservoir, telling his stories to passersby, whether they wanted to hear them or not,

25

like the Ancient Mariner in the poem.

"At the finish line," she said. "When he ran, the runners would touch Arturo for luck before the race. Now they do it at the end."

"Touch him?"

"Yeah, the guys would pat his arm or shoulder, slap him on the back. The women would give him a hug or kiss him on the cheek. Whatever. He's a famous New York character, so he gets to stand with the dignitaries. Text Cindy to look out for him."

"Why would you need luck after the race? You've already finished."

"It's so you'll run again next year."

"Whew! I'm glad you told me. I'll stay far away from him."

"Bru-uce. Don't be like that! Everybody loves Arturo."

But somebody didn't. The blow was perfectly timed: the moment when everyone without exception was looking at the approaching runners—when the two men in the lead, a Kenyan and an Ethiopian, were neck and neck, fighting over the last hundred yards. When the Kenyan, exhausted but triumphant, stumbled across the finish line, he tripped and fell across the body of the Ancient Marathoner. It could have been a heart attack. But as the Medical Examiner's office discovered soon enough, it wasn't.

ꝋꝋꝋ

I never did get to see Cindy in uniform. In fact, I didn't see her at all for a couple of days, since she had been transferred to the Central Park Precinct's detective squad six months before and caught the case along with her partner Natali. You'd think with all those spectators, all those cops on high alert—since the bombing at the Boston Marathon in 2013, they'd included Special Response teams armed to the teeth—and all those cameras rolling and cell phones clicking, someone would have seen Arturo's killer. A couple of cameras caught an unidentifiable crouched figure in a dark hoodie hovering behind Arturo as he lurched forward and fell. The murder weapon was a thin blade applied with force from behind, maybe the kind of knife used for gutting fish or one of a similar shape.

"Tell Cindy she's got to talk to runners who listened to Arturo's stories," Barbara said, bouncing up and down with excitement the way she does. "Like me!"

"She's way ahead of you, Barb," I said. "Every runner in the city was right there on the scene. She and Natali and their team are interviewing runners as we speak. I'm sure she's hearing all about his stories."

"There must be some way we can help," she said. "I feel so sad. Who would kill Arturo? Everybody loved him. He was a wonderful old man."

"Maybe you're not supposed to be investigating, pumpkin," Jimmy said, "just feeling the loss."

Barbara wasn't the only one mourning Arturo. His many friends, ropy-muscled runners ranging from youngsters fresh from their first Marathon to graying veterans, gravitated to the bench where Arturo had held court. Flowers, candles, Marathon caps and T-shirts—finishers' wear, not souvenirs anyone could buy—and even prized Marathon medallions appeared, turning the bench into a shrine. Every day Arturo's admirers plastered more clippings and photos on the grate over the gatehouse windows: news articles from *The New York Times* and the *Post*, computer printouts of blog posts, photos of Arturo shaking hands with public figures, and many more that showed him grinning with his arm around ordinary runners, not only the elite, and families of unmistakable tourists.

We stood gazing at the wall of memorabilia one afternoon a few days after the murder along with half a dozen others. Marathoners traditionally slack off once the big race is over, but a lot of us were running the reservoir track, rather than the longer Park loops, in tribute to Arturo.

"Arturo loved being a New York character," Barbara said.

"He sure did." The tone of the voice at my right ear was wry and not particularly admiring. "He loved the limelight, all right."

The speaker was a short, wiry guy dressed in a performance tank and shorts and very expensive running shoes. He was slightly hunched with age but still extremely fast. I knew because I had just seen him circle the reservoir three times to my two.

"Oh?" I cocked my head and tried to look like a therapist.

"He was a publicity hound," the guy said. "All those news guys buzzing around him. It was like he was the only one who'd been around a long time."

Barbara beamed at him and moved in, holding out her hand.

"That is so interesting! I'm Barbara Rose."

She cast a meaningful look at me, like a mother who wants her child to say thank you. I got it, I got it.

"I'm Bruce Kohler. And you are—?"

He had no choice but to shake and tell.

"Ben Parker."

"It's good to meet you, Ben," Barbara said warmly. "We saw you making great time out on the track. You must be one of the elite runners. This was our first Marathon. Have you been running them since the beginning?"

"You bet," he said, "and the Boston Marathon before we had it in New York. I *was* elite. We all get older. But I can still run! No cane for me, but I don't tell stories, so nobody's ever heard of Ben Parker. Stories! Who knows if they were even true?"

"I guess you knew Arturo for a long time," I said.

Barbara gave me a kick on the ankle that I *think* was meant to convey approval.

"Yeah, yeah, we were buddies from way back."

"So you didn't dislike him?" Barbara asked, all innocence.

"Of course not," he said. "He was just a bit of a blowhard. I told him to his face. Everybody loved Arturo."

"Tell Cindy," Barbara said as we left the park later, "to interview Ben Parker. Even New York's Finest can't make contact with all forty-five thousand Marathoners, and if they did already talk with this one, I bet he told them he didn't even know Arturo."

"You did good, Barb. I'll tell her."

"Shrinks and sleuths," she said. "Two sides of a single coin."

"Yeah, yeah," I said. "The flippin' queen of the probing question."

Arturo's memorial gathering at the main entrance to the reservoir drew a huge crowd. The speakers were all runners who'd heard Arturo's stories many times over the years.

"Hey, everyone. I'm Rosie Spitzer."

I'd seen her hanging out with Arturo, a tall, lean woman with frizzy hair and a Rosie the Riveter T-shirt.

"I'm proud to say I was Arturo Delgado's friend, like many of you here today. You could say that Arturo collected friends."

A murmur of assent and appreciative laughter from the crowd.

"I'll never forget Arturo's stories. Remember the one about Jackie Kennedy Onassis?"

A ripple of nods, like sports fans doing the wave.

"She lived right around here, and she used the track so much they renamed the reservoir after her. Arturo would watch her go by every day. He'd wave and smile the way he did to everyone, but he never let on he knew who she was. He said she deserved her privacy. Then one day, he was running the track, and she fell in beside him. They circled the reservoir side by side without a word. After that, they were friends. They would run the track together whenever she was in town."

"He hardly ever changed a word," Barbara whispered. "Jimmy says that's the way storytellers in preliterate societies invented history."

We were standing with Cindy and Natali. They were working but blending in, just another couple of civilians.

"Delgado wasn't illiterate," Cindy said. "He came from a middle-class Puerto Rican family."

"I didn't know he had a family," Barbara said.

"She thought he sprang fully shod in Nikes from the forehead of Fred Lebow," I said.

"The founder of New York Road Runners," Barbara said, in case Natali didn't know.

"He went to college as a pre-med," Cindy said, "but he dropped out to be an activist."

"Like Che Guevara," I said.

"Except when he got to New York, he found running."

29

"Imagine if Che—" Barbara said.

I was waiting for her to get to "But I digress," so I could say, "You always do," but Natali shushed us. He was writing down each speaker's name and scribbling notes.

"I'm Laurel Canio. I loved the way he told his autobiography. He would say, 'I was born in a tiny fishing village. It had a population of more pigs than people and aloe growing along the sides of the dusty pink road. I could have been a simple fisherman. But I wanted more. I wanted to see the world. Then I wanted to heal people. Then I wanted to right wrongs and save the world from evil and stupidity. Then I wanted to follow the love of my life to the ends of the earth. Then I wanted to run like the wind. And now here I am, an old man on a park bench.' How many of you heard him tell it just that way?"

Hands went up all over the crowd, and people laughed and clapped.

"Love of his life," Cindy murmured. "That's new. We've only been looking for living relatives—haven't found any yet."

"I'm a terrible runner," Laurel said. "I do about a fifteen-minute mile, and every time I passed him, Arturo would wave and smile and say, 'Looking good!'"

Everybody laughed again.

The emcee, a guy named Roberto Curcio, said, "Arturo told us all that we were looking good, and you know what? He'd mean it. He used to say, 'In my simple way, I make a lot of people happy.' You sure did, Arturo. Wherever you are, God bless you."

"Bandanna," Barbara said.

I handed over a nice big red one, and she snuffled into it.

"How many people can say that?" The woman on Barbara's other side regarded her with sympathy. "It's much easier to make people unhappy."

Barbara beamed at her through her tears.

"That's what made Arturo special. Barbara Rose." She held out a paw. "Are you a runner?"

"Gilda Herrera," the woman said as they shook hands. "No, I'm writing a book about the ordinary people who decide to run twenty-six miles in the company of forty-five thousand strangers."

"I'd love to read it."

30

Barbara took the writer's card as the next speaker cleared his throat.

"I'm Jay Clayton." Add wings to his cap, and he could have been a fleet-footed Hermes carved in ebony. "Arturo Delgado. I loved that old man. I grew up in the hood a sports-crazy kid, except I was too short, too scrawny, and my eyesight sucked. I was fast. But what was I gonna do with fast but run from the cops to the gangs and back again? Arturo showed me what when he taught me to run. He set me free."

ρρρ

Cindy drew her legs up onto the park bench, crossed them, and lifted her face to the sun, breathing in the spicy scent of fallen leaves and the equally enticing aroma of a pastrami sandwich from her favorite deli. Beside her, Natali groaned as he unwrapped the healthful mix of mashed black beans, hummus, nooch, and arugula on multigrain bread that his wife had tucked into his backpack that morning. She had gone vegan—and evidently delusional about the odds of Natali being pleased.

"Have half of mine," Cindy said. "It's huge. Why don't you just tell her you'll get your own lunch? Nicely."

"Do you know the stats on cop divorce?" Natali said. "Of course you do. Besides, the baby's teething. I don't want to add to her load."

"I've been thinking," Cindy said. "What if the Delgado murder has nothing to do with running? We need to take another look at the papers we took from his apartment. And let's go talk to the neighbors."

"Uniforms already did that," he said.

"Yeah, but they didn't get anything of interest," she said. "Everybody liked him, nothing out of the ordinary. And the super wasn't around. Let's go ask different questions. Let's find the super."

The super was a barrel-chested Puerto Rican named Oscar Robusto. Curly salt and pepper hair twined along his burly arms, crept out of his shirt collar toward his thick neck, and curled around the bald patch on his bullet head, which reddened when they displayed their shields. A wrench in one hand and a mop in the other, he gripped them more like weapons than tools of his trade. The building was the shabbiest on a block showing signs of gentrification.

"Have those bastards been complaining about me again?" he demanded. "You go talk to the landlord. He'll tell you. I run a good building. I don't do nothing but what my boss tell me. Those bastards don't got nothing to complain about. Look at this neighborhood. It was a slum. Now it's all, whaddaya call 'em? millennials, and these losers keep whining when they're still paying pennies in rent."

"Mr. Robusto, whoa!" Natali broke into the flow. "We don't know what you're talking about. We just need to ask you a few questions about Arturo Delgado."

"Him!" Robusto's eyes blazed, and his face got redder. "That troublemaker! He was the ringleader. Without him, it would never have come to this."

"To what, Mr. Robusto?" Cindy asked in her good-cop voice. "We can't help if we don't know what you're talking about."

"Rent strike!" he spat.

ooo

When Cindy told me Arturo had organized a rent strike in his building, she seemed annoyed that the other tenants hadn't mentioned it.

"It would have helped if they'd pointed a finger at the super or the landlord as Arturo's enemies."

"It's obvious you've never been a striking tenant, Ms. Law and Order. Rent strikers walk a fine line between outrage and fear of eviction. They want publicity if their complaints are just, but they're also vulnerable. What *were* their complaints?"

"Heat and hot water not reliable with winter coming on. Elevator broken half the time. Front door lock broken for months. That one he'd fixed—he had to unlock it to let us in. But the tenants said he'd promised them keys, and they're still waiting. They have to call and walk down the stairs to let each other in.

32

Once they knew we knew about the rent strike and weren't interested in their status as tenants, they couldn't talk fast enough. They said they think the landlord wants to sell the building, and if he can get them out by making it unlivable, he'll be able to make a bundle selling it vacant."

"That's a New York story I've heard as many times as any of Arturo's," I said.

"The landlord denied it," she said. "Pompiano Brothers Realty. I talked to George Pompiano. He said no one gives up an apartment in Manhattan at a rent way below market, all the complaints were about temporary conditions they were in the process of taking care of, and that he had no intention of selling any of his buildings. He agreed with the super that Arturo was a troublemaker and said now that he was dead—and I quote, 'may he rest in peace'—he expected to see the rent checks in the mail any day now."

So Arturo still had a bit of activism left in his heart. I didn't think a landlord would go as far as killing a tenant to end a one-building rent strike, especially since it wasn't his only building. But what about the super? Maybe he wasn't following the boss's orders. Maybe he was skimming somehow. If the landlord blamed him for problems that interfered with rent collection, he could be out of a job. Cindy said she'd check up on Mr. Robusto's finances and whether Arturo's building was his only source of income.

Cindy didn't bother telling me not to share all this information with Barbara and Jimmy. She knew nobody could stop Barbara from sleuthing, and Jimmy and I were putty in her hands.

"The part of Arturo's story I'm interested in," Barbara said, "is how he followed the love of his life to the ends of the earth."

"Why is that, petunia?" Jimmy asked. "Because it's romantic?"

"Give me some credit, Jimmy!" Barbara bounced indignantly. "Love is one of the most common motives for murder."

"Yeah, but that's all we know about it," I objected. "You know how Arturo was. His stories were always the same. 'I could have been a simple fisherman, but I wanted more. I wanted to follow the love of my life to the ends of the earth. And now here I am, an old man on a park bench.' That's all he ever said about it."

"He *did* say more," Barbara said, "to me."

"Arturo varied his story? He told you *more?* How on earth did you make that happen?"

"How do you think?" she said. "I *asked.*"

"She's got a point, Mr. Jones," Jimmy said.

"She is good at asking questions, Mr. Bones," I said.

"Everybody was so busy," Barbara said, "stoking the legend of Arturo the storyteller, who always told the same stories, that nobody *listened* to him anymore. 'Tell the one about Jackie Kennedy,' they'd say. Or, 'Tell the one about the woman who wrote a song about you.' It got so nobody even had to start him off. He liked to make people happy, and he knew that was all they wanted to hear."

"Tell us, pumpkin," Jimmy said. "What did he say about the love of his life?"

"She was an American photographer. She worked for National Geographic. His village was on the southwest coast, not far from some of the bioluminescent bays where you can see all the aquatic life glow in the dark. He was a student, but he was home for the summer, working as a fisherman. She was older, but you know how charismatic he was."

"We do?"

"Oh, come on, you think all those people loved him by *accident?* Do you think if you sat on a bench by the track every day for a year and said, 'Looking good,' to every runner who passed, hundreds of people would turn up at your funeral? Well, actually, I think both of you are charismatic in your own way, but that's beside the point."

"Yes, dear," Jimmy said, eyes twinkling. "Go on."

"He must have been a hunk as a young man. Gorgeous. He wasn't a runner yet, but I'm sure he developed his muscles fishing, and what with all that sun, and I doubt that Puerto Rican fishermen wear shirts when they work—long story short, they fell in love."

"Wait a minute," I said. "Go back to 'gorgeous' and elaborate, please."

"Men! He wasn't always ancient. You never listened, and you never looked. He had the most beautiful craggy bone structure:

cheekbones like cliffs, aquiline nose, soaring eyebrows. Did you ever notice Arturo's eyes? Of course you didn't. He had the most unusual eyes: one brown, the other hazel."

"You can't fault us for that," I said. "Straight guys don't gaze into each other's eyes. It's not part of our culture."

"You hug at AA meetings," she said.

"Yeah, but—Jimmy, do we close our eyes when we hug other sober guys?"

"Never mind," Barbara said. "Do you want to hear the rest of the story?"

"We're all ears."

"He followed her while she photographed nature all around the world until she died in a diving accident. Then he settled in New York. He'd left a girlfriend behind in Puerto Rico, but he never went back. Tell Cindy."

Barbara would have liked me to call Cindy then and there. But there was a fine line between being helpful and being a pest, and although Madam Sherlock couldn't always detect it, it was crucial if I didn't want to lose the love of *my* life.

Besides, it sounded like a dead end. When I did tell Cindy, she agreed.

"It's a sad story, but NYPD can't fly a detective down to Puerto Rico to scour the coastal fishing villages for a lead. Arturo's village might be a booming metropolis or resort by now, or it might not exist anymore. We don't even know the abandoned lady's name. Anyhow, she's probably long dead."

That was before they found the letter in Spanish, the ink smudged with tears, the single sheet crumpled as if Arturo had meant to throw it out and then changed his mind. In it, she told him she was pregnant and begged him to come home. Cindy told Barbara about that piece of evidence herself, because she had a question that only Barbara could answer.

"What *exactly* did Arturo say about the girl he left behind?" she asked. "Bruce says he told you he had a girlfriend back in Puerto Rico. Is that what Arturo said? Girlfriend?"

"He said *novia*," Barbara said. "*Novia* is girlfriend."

Jimmy, our resident geek, got to Google Translate before the rest of us could take a breath.

"Yeah, girlfriend. Also fiancée and bride."

Who knew what she had told her kid about his father? She had signed the letter only with an initial, so it was still a dead end. The police had every scrap of paper Arturo had kept. If traces of the story—names, pictures, a trail to follow—had existed, they would have found them.

"Outside of cheesy movies," I told Barbara, "I don't think sons nowadays are brought up on a cold dish of revenge."

We were all together, as it happened, when the break in the case came. Cindy, Jimmy, and I had just come out of an AA meeting, and Barbara had come out of the Al-Anon meeting next door, complaining, as usual, that AA was more fun than Al-Anon, she could hear us laughing through the wall, and it wasn't fair. So we went to Starbucks, where she could complain that alcoholics got to drink caffeine whenever they wanted even when they got sober, but she'd be awake all night if she drank anything stronger than herbal tea at this hour, and it wasn't fair.

We had just settled down with our drinks when Cindy's cell phone rang.

"Natali," she said. "Gotta take this."

We all pretended not to listen, but our figurative ears were up and quivering.

"The sister? Good work. Sure, if the ME is willing. Why the rush? Oh, I see. Sorry, it's noisy in here. Got it. Staying with a niece in New Jersey. Sure, tomorrow morning is fine."

"Cindy, wait!" Barbara said.

She grabbed Cindy's arm. You don't grab a cop, off duty or not. I saw Cindy's other hand go for her gun and check in midair.

"Cindy, listen to her," I said.

"Hold on a sec, Natali. What?"

"Ask him if he's got the niece's name and address in New Jersey."

Cindy repeated the question into the phone and scribbled Natali's answer on a napkin.

"Okay, Miss Marple. Now what the hell was that about?"

"First let me see what you got."

Cindy had written Arturo's sister's name, Adriana Delgado, and a New Jersey address that started *c/o Herrera*. Barbara reached into her bag and laid a card on the table next to the napkin. It was Gilda Herrera's business card, at the same address.

"Arturo didn't have a son," Barbara said. "He had a daughter. When I met her at the memorial, I thought she looked vaguely familiar, but it didn't make sense. Now it does. She had a feminine version of the cheekbones, the eyebrows, even the nose. I didn't notice consciously that her eyes were two different colors, but I bet when you look again, you'll find they are. She wasn't writing a book. She'd gotten her revenge, and she came to gloat. Arturo's sister will be able to confirm that Herrera was the name of the woman he abandoned. Gilda probably grew up in that fishing village hearing over and over how he'd wronged them, running off like that without them. I bet she gutted fish to earn money every summer all through school and hated it. But she knew her way around a fish knife. And when the time came, she knew how to use it."

Elizabeth Zelvin is the author of the Bruce Kohler Mysteries, a series set in New York that began with *Death Will Get You Sober*, and the Mendoza Family Saga, historical adventure fiction that includes the Amazon bestselling *Voyage of Strangers*. Both series contain both novels and short stories. Liz's work has been nominated twice for the Derringer Award and three times for the Agatha Award for Best Short Story. Her stories have appeared in *Ellery Queen's Mystery Magazine*, *Alfred Hitchcock's Mystery Magazine*, and all three previous volumes of the Murder New York Style series. Another of her stories was listed in *Best American Mystery Stories 2014*. Before turning to fiction, Liz authored two books of poetry. She is also a psychotherapist and, as Liz Zelvin, a singer-songwriter with an album of original songs, *Outrageous Older Woman*. Her author website is www.elizabethzelvin.com.

VINCENZO'S HEAD

JOSEPH R. G. DeMARCO

The grisly severed head told Detective Sammy Gallo that this would be one of those days. As he watched, the head tumbled from the top of the Alamo, the gigantic cube sculpture that dominated Astor Place. Rolling like a bowling ball, it came to a stop on the pavement near the lectern where the mayor was supposed to speak later that day. Screams and gasps ripped through the small crowd admiring the newly reinstalled Alamo cube. Astor Place hadn't been the same while it was being refurbished. As soon as the cube returned, so did the gawkers. Like many onlookers before him, a guy in the crowd had placed a hand on a corner of the cube to spin it gently as it was made to do.

That's when the head rolled to Sammy's feet.

Sammy gawked. When the head, trailing jagged bits of torn and bloody flesh, came to a stop, its eyes stared right at him. But that wasn't what knocked the breath out of Sammy. Fact is, it wasn't just any head. It was Vincenzo's head. A guy Sammy had grown up with and had, later on in life, expended lots of energy arresting without any results. All those futile arrests flashed through Sammy's mind as he stared at Vincenzo's bruised and battered face. Sammy couldn't believe the guy was dead. He leaned down, hands on knees, and took deep breaths.

"Hey." Detective Buck Gwent elbowed Sammy. "You all right?" The towering, barrel-chested officer had been Sammy's partner since both had made it to the ranks of detective several years before.

He and Buck had been assigned to secure Astor Place ahead of the mayor's speech about public artwork, reclaiming outdoor spaces, yadda yadda yadda. They were on scene to clear the place for hizzoner, a blowhard if ever there was one, as far as Sammy was concerned. There'd been threats against the mayor, and the mayor had demanded that two detectives from the Special Investigations Division be tasked with protecting the venue. Sammy cursed his luck at having drawn the assignment to keep the big man safe. This protection detail was work for a pair of uniforms, not for two Detectives Second Grade, even though Sammy knew that Astor Place wasn't an easy venue to protect and needed the benefit of experience, which Sammy and Buck both had.

The wide open space of Astor Place, surrounded by tall buildings with sunlight glancing off their shimmering glass façades, was already a big headache for the protection detail. And then Vincenzo came rolling onto the scene and blew things to hell.

Sammy turned to him. "No. I'm not okay."

"It's just a head," Buck said. "We seen lots of 'em, right? I'll call it in, get homicide involved and—"

"It's not just a head."

Sammy pulled out his handkerchief and mopped his forehead. There was a chill in the air, but his sweat glands were working overtime.

"What is it, then?"

"It's him."

"Him who? The mook people say lives in the cube? An' only comes out at night?" Buck laughed, a phlegmy sound. "Listen, you jamoke, they just cleaned up this piece of junk. Don't you think that anybody livin' in it would'a been cleared out, too? Unless maybe he heard they was gonna clean it and went someplace else until now."

"You don't recognize him?"

"I don't. And I don't understand how some boombats could even try to live in such a thing. There ain't no room in this whatchamacallit."

"The Alamo."

"Yeah. The Alamo." Buck paused. "How'd they give it the same name as that place in Texas anyway? Ain't there a monuments registry?"

"I'm telling you, Buck, I know that guy."

"You know this head?"

"Not just the head. The whole guy."

"Okay, smartass, who is it?"

"I can't believe you don't remember him. That's Vincenzo."

"Vincenzo who?"

"Vincenzo! Vincenzo!" Sammy said, as if repetition would bring enlightenment.

"You sure you're okay? You look pale and sweaty."

"I'm fine." But Sammy did feel queasy. "He goes by one name. Like Madonna. Don't you remember him now?"

"Don't ring no bells."

"He was a go-between for hitmen and clients. But we could never nail him on it."

"Oh, *that* Vincenzo. This is him?"

"The last time we tried to collar Vinnie was more than a year ago. He gave us the slip in Chelsea. You remember that?"

"He looks so different. But I guess you get your head lopped off, you ain't gonna look the same. I remember the dirtbag now."

"I've been wanting to take him down since I don't know when. And now somebody did."

Buck, head cocked to one side, peered at Sammy. Sammy knew that look. Buck was chewing on something he wanted to say but didn't know how.

"What?" Sammy snapped. "What?"

"You holdin' out on me?" Buck asked.

"What do you mean?"

"You and Vinnie," Buck said. "He was a ball-buster. He made you crazy."

"He did," Sammy said. "Now he won't anymore."

"Yeah, that's what I mean," Buck said.

His face took on creases that only appeared when he was thinking about something he hated considering. His expression asked questions he didn't want to voice.

"Come on, Buck. You can't think I did this."

"I don't wanna think it, Sammy. But somethin's up with you. You're halfway between happy and ready to throw up your guts."

"I'm fine," Sammy said.

"No. You ain't. Now spill."

Sammy massaged his temples. He felt a headache coming on. Buck was right. Sammy *was* having a hard time facing what really bothered him about all this. Vinnie was dead. That should have been satisfying. And it was. Except it wasn't.

"It's complicated."

"Try me."

"It's like you have this thing," Sammy said. "I don't know. It's like something you want but you don't know exactly why you want it or how you're gonna get it. Didn't you ever feel that way?" Sammy waited, but Buck said nothing. "And you've been chasing this thing a long time. Nobody else thinks it's much, but to you it's huge because it's been occupying your mind forever."

"Yeah, okay. So?" Buck said.

"For me, that was Vinnie. I could never get him outta my mind."

"Now somebody did him for you. You should be happy."

"I am. Well, I'm not happy somebody's dead, that wouldn't be right. I'm happy he's not gonna be a problem anymore. But—"

"What? You're not gonna tell me you feel sorry for this bum."

"No. I feel empty. Somebody took away that thing I've been chasing all this time. Vinnie was my white whale. Now somebody went and harpooned him. After all my planning. Right under my nose, somebody does it for me. It should'a been my collar."

"You're weird, y'know?"

"I've gotta call this in," Sammy said, feeling his head begin to pound. "Let Homicide take over this scene. We can get back to the precinct." Sammy pulled out his cell phone. "The mayor's not gonna be happy."

"Shit!" Buck snapped his fingers. "We gotta call the mayor's office, too. Let 'em know about this."

"Too bad. It'd be fun to let the blowhard come down and step in this shit himself," Sammy said. "That'd be something to see."

"Yeah. Then the next thing you'll see is you and me on the unemployment line," Buck said with a chuckle. "I'll call the mayor." He glanced around. "Look at this crowd. What? They never saw a head before? When you call Homicide, ask for some backup. We'll need a few more unis."

They both hunched into their calls. When they were finished, Sammy told the two unis who'd been assigned to Astor Place with them to set up traffic barriers and roll out crime scene tape to keep onlookers from trampling the scene and whatever evidence there might be for the CSU to collect.

"The mayor's a dick," Buck said matter-of-factly, pocketing his cell phone.

"Like you didn't know that? What'd he do now?"

"He was swearin' up a storm in the background. Said we should'a known about this earlier. That it wasn't supposed to happen. Said his speech was important. Cursed like a sailor, too."

"He's a prima donna."

"Didn't sound like he was only mad about not givin' his speech."

"What, then?"

"He told his assistant to ask me why the head was on the cube. Like I know?" Buck laughed. "The guy's nuts. I swear I heard him say the head should'a been someplace else. Like some killer is gonna accommodate him."

"He's pissed about missing a photo op."

Sammy had had encounters with the ego-driven mayor. None of them pretty.

"Could be. From what I could hear in the background, he wanted to know how that head got to the exact same place as he was supposed to speak."

"Yeah, right. It's always all about him." Sammy looked at the gathering crowd. "I called it in. Sullivan from Homicide will be here any minute. And CSU."

"They'll probably send a gang. Lots'a territory to cover. They love this crap." Buck chuckled.

"I told them we needed techs to process the Alamo, and the guy on the desk thought I was pulling his leg."

"Don't people livin' in this town know what we got here?"

"I still can't believe somebody wasted Vinnie like this," Sammy said. "You want to kill a guy, you kill him. But mutilating him, sticking his head in a public place?"

"Who'd want him dead anyway?" Buck asked. "They say he ran a service everybody wanted. Everybody. The big and the small."

"The people he associated with are not the type you wanna turn your back on."

"So, you're sayin' anybody could'a killed him?"

"Not just anybody," Sammy said. "Look at this mess. Who'd go to all this trouble? The killer either especially hated Vinnie or he wanted to send a message."

"Maybe one of Vinnie's clients just went haywire," Buck said.

"Nah, Vinnie ran a tight ship. He was a great organizer. Nobody would know from nothing about who did what."

"Word is, he ran his business like them dating sites," Buck said. "Except he matched up clients with hit men. Dangerous business."

"That kinda business, anything could happen. But Vinnie was good at it. Doesn't make sense that his clients would turn on him."

"The old days, people wanted a hitman, they went out and got a hitman. They didn't need no middleman who could maybe come back and bite 'em in the ass. Could be that's what happened. Or maybe Vinnie thought there was somethin' more he could get outta one of his clients."

"I don't think so," Sammy said. "Vinnie wasn't stupid. He knew how to keep a secret. One of our informants said that Vinnie never let anybody know who was who. Names were never used. Everything was cash and dead drops. I'm not sure even Vinnie knew who he was dealing with."

"Don't believe that, you chooch. Vinnie was too smart to keep everything anonymous. I'll bet he knew exactly who everybody was. Clients and killers. Otherwise he could'a been dealin' with undercover cops. Then he'd find his ass locked up before he could say jack shit." Buck nodded sharply for emphasis.

"Even if he did know all the names, he'd never reveal anything."

"There's always a leak. Always."

"Then how come we never found anything to nail him with?" Sammy asked.

"We never looked hard enough," Buck said.

43

"You're kiddin' me, right?" Sammy snapped out the words. "I busted my balls for years trying to get that douchebag. Don't tell me I didn't try hard enough."

"Okay, okay, so you tried. But we came up empty."

"Well, maybe we should try again," Sammy insisted.

"Why? Vinnie's dead. It don't matter. What're we gonna do, arrest his head?"

"Just because he's dead doesn't mean we stop. We can't get *him*, but looking into his business could be the way to find his killer."

"Maybe." Buck didn't sound like his heart was in it. "But this ain't our case. We're not Homicide."

"That's not gonna stop me from looking for Vinnie's killer. After all these years chasin' him down streets and alleys, I'm not gonna stop now. Besides, we're Special Investigations. That'll cover us for a while."

"The brass ain't gonna like it. You could be in deep shit, and you'll be draggin' me down with you."

"Not if I solve this. Sure, I'll ruffle feathers. But if I collar the guy who did this, what? They'll complain?"

Buck's cell phone jangled. After listening a moment, he looked over at Sammy.

"What?" Sammy asked.

"Know the Wall Street Bull, the big bronze one down on Broadway?"

"Who doesn't?" Sammy said. "Don't tell me. Another head?"

"No, but I'm thinkin' it might be another piece'a Vinnie," Buck said. "Well, look who's here. Homicide's finest. How ya doin', Sullivan?"

"Fellas." The silver-haired homicide investigator nodded as he approached. "I guess this is all mine now. Lucky me."

"We may have more for you," Sammy said. "Buck just got a call about body parts at the Wall Street Bull."

"Gimme what you've got before you guys take off," Sullivan said.

Sammy let Buck fill him in before they hopped into the car.

"Traffic's a bitch," Buck said as their car crawled down

44

Broadway. "Look at that bastard blockin' the box."

"Let it go," Sammy said. "I'm in no hurry to see more body parts. Especially Vinnie's body parts."

"Who'd kill a guy that way?"

Buck spat out an obscenity at someone crossing on a red light.

"That's what we've gotta find out. All I know is, in his line of work, Vinnie probably didn't make a lotta friends."

"Made some mean enemies." Buck edged his way through the clog of cars. "He must'a ticked somebody off real good."

"Vinnie was always a piece of work."

"Yeah? You know the bum a long time?" Buck asked, his eyes on the snarled traffic.

"Since we were kids," Sammy said. "Vinnie was always hungry for what other people had. He put together a gang of tough kids who beat up other kids. Then Vinnie offered protection, for a price."

"Swell guy."

"I could never do anything to stop him. I think that's when I got hooked on wanting to catch him."

"Long time to carry that," Buck said.

"I put it aside when I went to college. Whenever I came home to visit, there was Vinnie, dressed to kill. Made me feel like a slob. But I could tell the poor bastard felt inferior even though he had more of everything than anyone else. Better cars, expensive clothes, and lots of women. Didn't stop Vinnie from feeling inferior."

"No excuse for him goin' the route he did," Buck said.

"No arguments there. Easy to see he was headed for no good. Rumor was he'd built an organization that provided services for local mobs. Every kind of mob there was. Italian, Russian, Albanian, you name it."

"Funny how you could never catch the mook," Buck said in an offhand way.

"Not like I need reminding. Vinnie was a criminal genius. Covered his tracks better than anyone I've ever chased. Kept two steps ahead of me."

Sammy let out a sigh. He'd built a large network of

45

informants to keep tabs on Vinnie's doings. But they never came up with anything solid on the guy. Now, though, whatever Vinnie'd been involved with had caught up with him big time.

They arrived at Bowling Green Park in the Financial District, where the polished bronze Bull was located. The huge, aggressive creature, permanently crouched, displayed a lethal set of horns and was ready to lunge. His smooth lines, all muscle and sinew, heaved with life and power, his tail lashing the air behind him. Flaring nostrils added a fierce belligerence to his already angry face.

A young officer approached them. Newly minted, he seemed uneasy.

"Detectives. My sergeant thinks you'd be interested in this. Said you found something similar elsewhere."

"Let's see what you've got," Sammy said. He was amazed at how fast word of their earlier find had gotten around.

The officer led them to the huge Bull and around to its magnificent golden-bronze head.

"Looks fine to me." Buck said. "What's to see?"

"The wreath."

The young officer pointed to the uncommonly large decoration made of greenery and bright flowers. The wreath's open U-shaped design fit nicely around the Bull's head.

"So what's the problem?" Buck said. "People always put wreaths—holy shit."

"What's the—" Sammy's mouth dropped open.

Someone had wired a few extras into the innocent-looking decoration: two hands. Real hands, each grasping several hundred-dollar bills. Interspersed down the sides of the wreath were more hundred-dollar bills, each splattered with blood, each folded into horrific "flowers" hiding amidst the real floral work.

"Vinnie's hands?" Buck asked, staring at the gruesome decoration.

"That's what I'm thinking," Sammy said. "The lab will have to confirm that."

Sammy arrived at work early the next morning. Visions of Vinnie's head and hands had floated through his mind all night. Even so, he felt energized and ready to find Vinnie's killer. The coffee he'd brought with him increased his focus.

Buck lumbered in a few minutes later. The man's outsized frame made his swivel chair groan and lurch back when he sat.

"Couldn't get the damned body parts outta my mind last night, and my wife made me sleep on the couch. Said I kept shoutin' in my sleep." He groaned. "You saw that couch. I lay down and half my ass is on the floor while my legs hang over the armrest. Sometimes I think she likes torturin' me."

"For what it's worth, I couldn't sleep either."

"Only thing that's gonna help is we catch the bastard who gave me nightmares."

"That's the plan," Sammy said.

The aroma of coffee wafted toward him, and he took a slug.

"You got a real plan?" Buck asked, crankiness coloring his voice. "Because just sayin' 'that's the plan' don't make it a plan. We gotta have a real plan."

"How about this? We talk to our informants, see where that gets us. Then we hit some of Vinnie's boys."

"Lab report come in yet?" Buck asked.

"Only preliminary. Head and hands are the same person. The full DNA profile could tell us more, but that's gonna take a while. So we might as well make the best of what we've got. Which is not much. No prints on the body parts. No helpful trace around the Alamo or the Bull. Outdoor venues," he scoffed. "Anybody and everybody was touching things." Sammy tossed the report to Buck. "See for yourself."

Buck waved it off.

"So that means we got bupkis."

"We've got pieces of Vinnie. We'll catch the butcher."

"Pieces is still bupkis," Buck said.

Sammy shrugged on his jacket.

"Let's see if we can scare up somebody who knows something."

"Who you got in mind?"

"Marty Two Fingers."

"He was Vinnie's main man once," Buck said. "No more."

"Don't let him fool you. Marty may inform for us, but he and Vinnie were still thick. Stevie, the pothead on Houston, keeps me up to date."

"Little Stevie knows a lot—for a pothead."

Their car chugged along like an old coffeemaker. It was shabby, but Sammy knew it'd been freshly tuned up. Since they were headed for who knew what, he wanted to be sure they could get out quickly if necessary. Sammy pulled the car into Marty's garage on Ninth Avenue. The smell of car oil reminded him of his father's old auto mechanic shop. Marty Two Fingers was bent over the engine of an ancient Chevy.

"Marty!" Sammy called out well before they reached him.

Marty was never without his gun and, despite his moniker, always able to fire it, a feat that had to be seen to be believed. The skinny man was up like a shot, one hand diving into his overalls, ready to pull his gun. When he recognized Sammy, he relaxed, but not much. He slowly removed his hand from his overalls and raised both hands, showing them empty. His right hand sported two fingers and a thumb. He smiled, showing gaps where teeth had been.

"Officers," Marty said.

"Where is everybody?" Sammy looked around.

"They on strike?" Buck asked.

"Business is slow. I gave 'em the week off."

"Chop shop business is slow?" Buck marveled. "You gotta be kiddin' me."

"This ain't no chop shop. I run a legit business."

Sammy let the lie slide.

"Got a question for you, Marty."

"Maybe I got an answer, maybe not."

"You know Vincenzo, right?" Sammy asked.

"Yeah, I knew the guy," Marty said.

There was a slight flicker in Marty's eyes, and Sammy caught Marty's use of the past tense. Sloppy talk, or did he know Vinnie was dead?

48

"Seen him lately?"

"S-seen him?" Marty's voice was low. "Naw, not in a long while."

"And yet, you seem to know he's dead," Sammy snapped, figuring it was worth a shot.

"Ye— no! Vinnie's dead? Shit, I just—"

"You was gonna say?" Buck loomed over Marty.

"I wasn't gonna say nothin'," Marty countered.

"That double negative says otherwise." Sammy grinned.

"Huh?"

"Listen, Marty, we have a proposition for you."

Sammy backed the mechanic against the car he'd been working on and got face to face with him. The guy's breath was stale, garlicky.

"Y-yeah?"

"Yeah. You tell us what you know about Vinnie and—"

"I told you, I don't know—"

"Hey, chooch." Buck muscled in to squeeze Vinnie between them. "We talked to people who say you and Vinnie was thick as thieves. You gonna lie to us?"

"Let him lie all he wants, Buck. No skin off my nose," Sammy said. "I don't have a chop shop to lose. Or a dozen flatbeds with products that fell off the back of a truck. Or a whole lotta—"

"Okay, okay." Marty relented. "V-Vinnie was here a couple days ago."

"When exactly?" Sammy flipped open his notebook.

"Two, three days ago. Was it Tuesday?"

"You tell me. Was it Tuesday or what?" Sammy growled.

"T-Tuesday, I g-guess."

"And?"

"And that's it. He was here."

"You're telling me he came in, stood here and stared at you?" Sammy said. "He didn't make a peep? Didn't ask how you were doin' or how your family is?"

"W-well, sure. He asked and I answered. But that was it." Marty's gaze shifted from one side to another.

"I know Vinnie was a quiet guy, but what you're describing doesn't sound like him at all."

49

"Well, it was him. He don't ever say much." Marty's voice was a whisper.

"So he's here standin' around, but he don't tell you he's in big trouble?" Buck asked. "He don't tell you there's a guy who's gonna chop him up in little pieces and sprinkle them all around Manhattan?"

"Ch-chop him up?" Tears filled Marty's eyes, ready to spill down his cheeks, but Sammy didn't think they were for Vinnie. "No, he didn't say nothing like that."

"But he said something?" Sammy nudged. "Like one of his clients had it in for him?"

"Couldn't 'a been a client."

"Why's that?"

"They needed him."

"What about—"

"The o-other ones? Them, naw, they liked the money he got them. Didn't even mind the cut he took."

"You seem to know a lot about this mook and his business," Buck said, shifting his bulk, making himself a threatening presence without much effort.

"No, no! Whaddayou saying? I only know what he told me. Who knows if it's true? Could be a load, but Vinnie's always been straight with me. So I believed him."

"He never said nothin' about bein' afraid? Never said he was worried about somethin'?" Buck asked.

"H-he might'a been. I don't know," Marty said.

And Sammy saw it again, that little flicker in Marty's eyes. The quaver in his voice was also back.

"You know more than you're sayin', you skinny ass prick," Buck said.

"N-no. He never told me t-things like that." Marty's voice was thin and low.

"Who was he afraid of?" Sammy snarled.

Marty was silent. His two-fingered hand twitched and shook.

"Give us a name, Marty. We ain't goin' away anytime soon."

Buck pushed the mechanic until there was nowhere for him

50

to go but through the wall.

"I can't." Marty's voice was hoarse.

"But you gotta, or all this will go away." Sammy, pressing closer, swept his arm around, indicating the garage and everything that went with it.

"H-he'll kill me. Y-you s-say Vinnie w-was c-chopped up?'

"In little pieces." Buck dragged out the words.

"But we won't let that happen to you," Sammy promised.

"You're too valuable," Buck said. "You help us, we help you."

"C'mon, Marty," Sammy urged. "A name. Nobody's gonna know it was you."

"Except him. He'll know. He knows things."

"Okay, Buck. Call the station. We gotta report what we found here," Sammy said, backing away.

"N-no! Wait!" Marty said.

"Yeah?"

"J-Jim—Jimmytom." Marty whispered. His two-fingered hand twitched again.

ooo

The drive back to headquarters seemed especially long, now that Sammy had a lead.

"Who's Jimmytom?" Buck asked as he unwrapped a large Three Musketeers bar, sniffed it, then bit off half.

"Beats me," Sammy said. "According to Marty, Vinnie used Jimmytom for muscle, even for protection when there was real trouble."

"Marty was pretty scared 'a this Jimmytom. That ain't sayin' much, though. He was afraid of a lotta people. Why d'you think he carried that piece all the time?"

"Marty's something else," Sammy said.

"Poor slob looked shocked when we told him exactly how Vinnie was murdered. Don't get me wrong, Marty could be the one, but I don't think so."

"We'll find Jimmytom. See if he talks," Sammy said as he

51

parked the car.

Sammy shuffled through the pink message sheets on his desk.

"They're all from somebody named Shelby."

"What does he want?"

"We'll find out." Sammy tapped Shelby's number into the phone.

"Hello?" A woman's voice.

"Detective Gallo returning your messages."

"Finally."

"What's this about, ma'am?"

"It's about my Vincenzo."

"*Your* Vincenzo? Who are you, lady?"

"You'll find out when we meet," she said.

Sammy set up the meeting, then dragged Buck from his squealing swivel chair and got back out on the streets.

"She wants to meet in a café? In Little Italy? People watch too much TV."

"If she's got information, I don't care if she carries a falcon statue wrapped in old paper."

Buck drove, and for a change, traffic cooperated. They got to the ornate, gold-encrusted Italian café with time to spare and took a table facing the door.

A few minutes later, a tall, voluptuous woman, her dark hair pulled into a French twist, strolled in. Her gaze landed on the detectives. With the shadow of a smirk, she ambled over and took a seat.

"Ms. Shelby?" Sammy said.

She nodded and waved over a waiter to order an espresso.

Buck peered at her.

"You said you got some information?"

"Why else would I call you?"

Buck said nothing, but Sammy knew what he was thinking, and it wasn't polite.

"How did you know Vincenzo?" Sammy asked.

"We were lovers," Shelby said. "He was really sweet."

"You have any idea who might want to kill him?"

"Maybe. Vincenzo came to see me a few days ago. He was

in trouble. I could tell."

"How did you know?"

"He couldn't sit still. That was unusual. Didn't even want me to give him a hug. That was more unusual. And then, well, my Vincenzo never talked about his work."

"You even know what his work was?" Buck asked.

"Once he told me he was a broker. Real Estate. Something like that. But now I know that couldn't be true."

"Why's that?" Sammy asked.

"He was scared. Said it was because of work. But who gets scared about real estate?"

"He tell you what scared him?"

"Not in so many words. He just said he should never have gotten involved with his two latest clients."

"Did he name them?"

"One. A man named Jimmytom."

"And the other?" Sammy asked, barely able to contain himself after hearing the name of the first.

"He said the other guy was important. Big name, big position."

"He tell you anything else about this big name?"

"That he greased the gears in this city. That the town couldn't run without him."

Sammy furiously made notes.

Buck cleared his throat.

"This Jimmytom, you know him?"

"Why would I? He was one of Vincenzo's clients. I never mixed with Vincenzo's people."

"Any idea where we might find him?" Sammy asked.

"It was strange, but Vincenzo said the guy made him call a certain bar, ask for Jimmytom, and they'd arrange a meeting."

"You know the name of this bar?"

000

"You believe her?"

"We have a choice?" Sammy asked. "She gave us Jimmytom. That sealed it."

"By my count, Marty and the Shelby woman makes two leaks that Vinnie had. See what I mean?" Buck flicked lint from his suit. "There's always a leak."

"Wiseass." Sammy pulled out his cell phone. "I'll place the call and see what happens."

The bar was called Kiley's, and Buck knew it. According to him, it was a filthy dive on the edge of the Lower East Side, the kind of bar where you could get anything you wanted as long as you had the cash.

Sammy tapped in the number.

"Kiley's."

The voice was like rocks grinding rocks. Music in the background was loud and voices louder.

"Callin' to speak to Jimmytom."

"You got 'im."

Sammy asked for a meeting.

"What for?" Jimmytom growled.

Sammy explained, giving as few details as he could get away with, hoping it was enough to make the guy curious.

"Not interested, pal." Jimmytom laughed dismissively.

"Don't hang up," Sammy snapped. "I just want information."

"Yeah, right, and I want a castle in Scotland."

"Look, you stupid fuck, we know who you are. We can find you anytime we want. So why'd I call instead of just grabbing your ass off the street?"

Jimmytom grunted.

"Be at the Alamo sculpture on Astor Place in twenty minutes. We just wanna talk. Don't show up, we'll do a lot more than talk."

Jimmytom grunted again.

"He'll meet us in twenty. Let's haul ass."

Buck stepped on the gas. Traffic was less than accommodating this time, but they made it just a few minutes late.

From the flashing police lights and the crowd, Sammy knew things had gone to shit. He sprang from the car almost before it stopped.

"Let me through," he shouted.

A man lay sprawled on the pavement near the Alamo, his grizzled face the picture of pain and anger. His chest heaved with his effort to breathe. The spreading pool of blood under him suggested that he'd be dead soon. Sammy knelt next to the guy.

"Jimmytom." It had to be him. "Jimmytom, who did this to you? Damn it. Who—"

The man's glassy eyes focused on Sammy.

"Fuck. You killed me."

"Tell me who did this to you."

"Had... hadda be him."

"Who?"

"Vinnie's..."

"Vinnie's dead."

"Don't I know? I did the fucker. C-cut him. Real good."

"Why?"

"He paid more than Vinnie. Vinnie hired me but... he paid more."

"*Who*, Jimmytom!"

"Big man... government shit. Works. You find... Grace."

He inhaled raggedly, turned his head away, and was gone.

Buck dashed over to them.

"He's dead," Sammy said. "Did we do this?"

"By settin' up a meeting?" Buck groaned.

"Somebody wanted to keep him quiet." Sammy got to his feet. "They must've bugged his phone at the bar. Had to be."

"This would'a happened one way or another." Buck's voice was flat.

"The homicide detective here yet?"

"He's on his way. Nothin' more we can do. The unis have the scene locked down." Buck paced a few steps away, then back, took out his notebook and flipped pages.

"What's up with you?" Sammy asked. "You're on edge. Somethin' wrong?"

"Sullivan caught the case. And you're gonna have to explain to him how this is connected to Vincenzo's head." It wasn't a question or a request.

"I am?" Sammy didn't want to think about it.

"You gotta and you know it. There's gonna be

consequences. With any luck we won't come up smellin' too bad since we cracked the case and all."

"Then let's get back to the precinct."

Sammy's head was swimming as they drove back. He needed to talk, to sort things out.

"Jimmytom said he killed Vinnie. Said he cut him good." Sammy cleared his throat. "Can I believe him?"

"Why not?"

"He said someone paid him to do it. Paid him more than Vinnie's client."

"Could be," Buck said. "Maybe this other guy turned the tables on Vinnie. Knew he was a target. The only way to stop Jimmytom was to pay more."

"And since Vinnie would never reveal his client, Vinnie had to go. I agree. Killing Vinnie also makes a nice little message for the client to forget about the target."

"So? Wrapped up, right?"

"But do you believe a heavy like Jimmytom is gonna turn on somebody like Vinnie? And give up future jobs?"

"Depends on a lotta things. Money, for one. How much was the target offerin' Jimmytom?" Buck asked.

"Hadda be a lot," Sammy said. "Once he kills Vinnie, that's a big money stream gone."

"Maybe this new honeypot has even more money. A guy like Jimmytom wouldn't think twice about blackmailin' the idiot who paid him to kill Vinnie. Boom! New money stream."

"I'm still not sure." Sammy felt tired.

"Jimmytom wrapped it up in a bow for you. Deathbed confession. Nothing stronger."

"He may have butchered Vinnie, but somebody else gave the order. Jimmytom was clear about that."

Buck grunted his assent.

"Whoever gave the order to kill Vinnie also made sure Jimmytom was killed."

"Would'a been even better if Jimmytom gave a name," Buck said.

"Closest thing he gave to a name was 'Grace'," Sammy said. "He also said something about a big government shit. Know anybody in government named Grace? Somebody big?"

"Maybe he was sayin' something else? Maybe grace was half 'a the word," Buck offered.

Sammy fussed with the seatbelt chafing his neck. Half a word? Grace? A name? Maybe part of a name?

"Grace. Gracie?" Sammy said, and he could almost hear the tumblers fall into place, unlocking the answer. *Gracie Mansion*, he thought. He didn't want to say it aloud yet.

Buck inclined his head without taking his eyes off the road.

"You're not thinkin' what I think you're thinkin', are you?" Buck said. "Gracie Mansion is where the mayor lives."

"Moby Dick." Sammy chuckled. "I'm thinking Moby Dick. I have a new white whale. Bigger than Vinnie ever was. And even harder to catch."

He sat back and smiled, not feeling so tired anymore. If he could bring down the mayor, he'd be a hero to a lot of people.

He started mapping out his next moves and didn't mind the snarled traffic.

Joseph R. G. DeMarco is the author of the Marco Fontana mystery series: *Murder on Camac, A Body on Pine, Crimes on Latimer, Death on Delancey,* and more (Jade Mountain Books). His Doyle and Kord mystery series begins with *Family Bashings* (JMS Books). He is also author of the Vampire Inquisitor series: *A Warning in Blood* and *A Battle in Blood* (forthcoming). A number of his short stories have been published in anthologies including *Quickies* 1, 2, and 3, *Men Seeking Men,* and *Charmed Lives.* His nonfiction appears in *Paws and Reflect, Hey Paisan!, The Encyclopedia of Men and Masculinities, We Are Everywhere, Men's Lives,* and others. His work for the gay press includes *The Advocate, PGN, NY Native,* and others. He was Editor-in-Chief of the *Weekly Gayzette* and *NGL* and contributing editor for *Il Don Gennaro.* He is now Editor/Publisher of *Mysterical-E.* Learn more at www.mystericale.com and www.josephdemarco.com.

LEVITAS

ROSLYN SIEGEL

Anabell was standing in her bathroom, half asleep, staring at her toothbrush, when it slowly lifted itself from the glass on the sink. It hovered a couple of inches in the air, quivered a little, and then dropped into her hand.

Was it her imagination? She had been feeling weak and frail lately, and it would be nice to move things without any expenditure of energy. Levitation was a sweet surprise, but she had been practicing yoga for fifty years, and her ex-yoga teacher Helen had told her levitation was common. All the experienced yogis did it. She figured if a person could levitate himself, she could move a toothbrush. She deserved some positive takeaway from Helen. Helen of Troy, Irwin had called her. Helen Destroy was more like it.

So she levitated a piece of soap and a little later a shoe. Small things. But it was a start. She needed all the positive energy she could muster to look for a new apartment. It made her sick just to think of it. To lose her home. Her sanctuary. She had lived most of her life in a brownstone on the Upper West Side. Her husband had died there, and she had expected to as well. And then the owner informed her that he had sold it and she had to move. Now she felt like a stranger, walking painfully—arthritis forcing her to use a cane—up and down the suddenly unfamiliar gentrified streets: the cracked masonry and sagging steps on the brownstones restored and power washed; the former rooming house on Amsterdam Avenue, with its broken windows and door hanging off one hinge, now gleaming with stainless steel trim and glistening picture windows.

And she couldn't afford any of it.

But how could she possibly leave? How she loved the smell of real wood burning in a real fireplace. Sprawling across her double bed, her chin level with the window looking out on a small green garden. She had helped plant the oak trees that now lined her street. She had raised money for the girl who had been run over by a drunken driver. She had collected books for the street fair.

"What's your price range?" the skinny blonde real estate agent had asked her. "Try Queens. The Bronx," she told Anabell while she filed her nails.

She had looked at notices for sharing tacked up at the corner deli. She had answered an ad for a third floor walk-up but turned back on the second floor when her knee buckled.

And then she saw a boxed notice in *The New York Times* obituary section.

Patricia Rothman, 76. Painter. Survived by her husband, celebrated artist Irwin Rothman. Memorial Service: The National Arts Club, 15 Gramercy Park South, Wed. 2 PM. Proper attire required.

Patricia. Her arch rival. Dead at last! Patricia had left Irwin years ago and moved away. Irwin probably still lived at the Club.

The National Arts Club! Larry Rivers, Alfred Stieglitz, Louise Nevelson had all been members. How excited Anabell had been when they accepted her. She had only had a couple of exhibitions, but the ribbon one of her paintings won at the Greenwich Village Outdoor Show had impressed the Board of Directors.

It made her smile when she read the words, "Proper attire required." That stuffy old Victorian dress code was still in place. Women had to wear dresses or skirts. No pants. Men had to wear jackets in all the public rooms.

What were they thinking, she wondered, beckoning modernity with one hand and holding it back with the other? On the modern side, it was the first arts club that made women full members. To protect them, it offered a home away from home— subsidized rental apartment/studios—where they could live and work in a safe environment. Of course, what actually went on in those studios was not exactly what the founding fathers had in mind. The painting she had posed for, *Nude on a Park Bench*, had almost caused a riot when it was first displayed outside in Gramercy Park. And what went on inside had nothing to do with safety. She could still feel Irwin's arms and legs around her own, smell the sweet scent of perfume mixed with the sweat of feverish lovemaking.

Maybe she could leave the Upper West Side after all. Once upon a time she had called The National Arts Club home. The apartment at The National Arts Club had once been hers, and she would find a way to get it back.

ᴑᴑᴑ

Anabell walked through the heavy doors of The National Arts Club, her cane making little tap-tap noises across the marble floors with their thick red veins twisting through the brownish slabs like rotten meat. Crossing the ornate lobby, she remembered much of what she had wanted to forget. Helen. Irwin. Patricia. Voices hoarse with yelling. Jagged shards of crystal glistening in a pool of water on the bedroom floor, lilacs squashed in the corner.

She deliberately arrived late for Patricia's memorial, partly excited, partly scared to confront her past and the people she had long ago given up.

Especially Irwin.

She scanned the crowd searching for him, but she couldn't find anyone who looked vaguely like him. Was that tall, thin man in the third row Motherwell? Probably not, he looked too young. The woman with the walker and the long blonde hair. Could that be Helen? No. Helen had died years ago. Anabell looked up at the ceiling. She was sure there was something floating there. Then she heard the tinkle of Helen's laugh. It had to be her imagination! She covered her mouth to stifle her cry.

When she looked again at the ceiling, Helen was gone.

As soon as the service was over, she turned her attention to the exhibition of photographs that lined the walls of the meeting room. She paused in front of the first photograph—a young girl, her blonde hair flowing with abandon, her legs spread wide apart. It was not her nakedness that was surprising, not the boldness of the pose—an aggressive sexuality that insisted upon its right to exist. This kind of statement was old news to Anabell.

What surprised her was that the outdated Victorian dress code she had always despised—the insistence on covering up a real woman's body while extolling a naked body in a frame on the wall—suddenly made sense to her. She smoothed the pleats on her skirt. A skirt seemed to provide a bridge from the past to the present. A guide rail that prevented completely falling off the path of respectability.

The years began to roll off her shoulders as she made her way through the hallway and climbed the stairs to the apartment she had once called her own. Here she had flung her pink cardigan, there she had slipped and broken the heel of her silver shoe, there—and there—and finally—here.

She paused for a moment in front of the door where she had once lived. How would Irwin receive her? She was not even completely sure he still lived there.

She knocked. Softly. Then harder.

When there was no answer, she turned the knob of the door, and it swung slowly open.

The man with white hair did not stir when Anabell entered.

"Irwin!" she called out. "It's Anabell!"

"Who are you?" He scowled. "What are you doing here?"

He took one step towards her, picked up a fork from the table next to him, and brandished it in front of her like a sword.

"Anabell! Anabell! Have I changed so much?"

Of course she had changed. Her once wild auburn curls trapped in a gray bun, her full breasts and round hips shaved down by time. But Irwin—the same shabby corduroy jacket with the patches on the elbows—the same dark brown eyes with specks of gold—the patrician nose, the superhero chin.

And this space! The light pouring into the room from the huge windows, the nine foot ceiling. The battered herringbone floor, spotted with drips of paint like a Jackson Pollock canvas. Better even than she had remembered it!

"Patricia!" Irwin called out.

"Patricia is dead!"

"What going on there?"

The door to the bedroom opened, and a middle-aged woman in a wrinkled turquoise kimono entered.

"Patricia!"

Irwin ducked behind the woman, glaring out at Anabell like a frightened child.

"I'm an old friend," Anabell said. "Actually, much more."

The woman looked her up and down. Anabell could see the woman's breasts sway beneath her robe. Her hair, a homemade henna job, was flat from sleeping on one side. Who was she? Lover or caretaker? Probably both, Anabell concluded. She slept in his bedroom.

"What nyem you say?" Her voice was accented and cigarette rough. Probably Russian.

"Anabell. Anabell Klein. The lady in the painting *Nude on a Park Bench.*"

The woman smiled and took Irwin's hand.

"Anabell. She remember your painting *Nude on a Park Bench.*"

"Not *remember* his painting! I *am* his painting!"

"My painting! Mine!" Irwin shouted.

He plopped down on a hideous wing chair upholstered in a garish flower pattern that only a desperate Russian would choose.

But the sofa was hers. Deep blue velvet. The wine stain on the middle cushion as familiar as the cleft in his chin.

"Sorry. He don't remember you. He don't hardly remember much. What you want to speak to him about?"

Anabell felt her throat tighten. The air, once plum-juicy and lilac-glazed, was dry as stale bread. Her salad days held hostage! Hijackers! Both of them! She wouldn't let them get away with it.

"I've come to take back my apartment."

The Russian cocked her head.

"What you say?"

"Irwin and I were lovers. He promised to divorce Patricia and marry me. But he didn't. So I married someone else. Now he's dead too."

The Russian's eyes narrowed.

"What this have to do with this apartment?"

She picked up a scissors from a small table near the ugly chair and stared down at Anabell.

"It's mine. It was mine before it ever was his. I was the young, poor woman artist the club was founded for. Irwin was already successful when I met him. Successful and charming. Charmed the pants right off of me. And then he moved in and stopped painting."

62

"Mine!" Irwin shouted again. He peered out at Anabell and tugged on the Russian's kimono. "Make her go away!"

Anabell pointed her cane at Irwin.

"I posed for *Nude on a Park Bench* right there in Gramercy Park. Irwin sketched me, but I completed the painting. Irwin never did more than sketches after that. I painted everything. He just signed his name. It was okay with me. He was famous and I was not. We split the money."

The Russian moved closer to Anabell. She smelled from nicotine. She raised her hand with the scissors.

"I don't believe any words you say. You make mistake. You leave now."

Anabell banged her cane on the floor.

"The mistake is yours! Irwin always loved me! You live with a great artist and you have the taste of a cow in the field!"

The Russian aimed a mouthful of spit at Anabell's shoe. A shiny streak of saliva slid across the black leather.

"You are old and ugly! No man look at you now. Irwin love me!"

Anabell raised her cane and lunged at the Russian, just missing her hip. She had been such a fool! She had abandoned this glorious apartment in a jealous rage after she found Irwin in bed with Helen, her yoga instructor. He had tired of Helen within a week.

And Anabell? She had given up painting, married a dull man, and never looked back.

Until now.

"This apartment is mine," Anabell announced. "It's time Irwin went to live in an old age home."

The Russian squealed and waved the scissors in the air above Anabell's head.

"Po'shyolnahui! Mu'dak! Piz'du!"

Anabell retreated closer to the door. She cringed under the sheer force of the curses even though she didn't know what they meant.

It was clear to her that the Russian would not give up the apartment without a fight. Well, she was ready for a fight.

Straightening her back, Anabell turned on her heel, paused

at the door, and gave her the finger.

ǫǫǫ

She should have known a leopard couldn't change its spots. Irwin could never bear to be alone, not even for a day. Certainly not for a night. Now she had to figure out how to get rid of the Russian.

Back in her apartment, she levitated her cup of coffee all the way from the kitchen to her bedroom without spilling a drop. It took her three phone calls to The National Arts Club to find out the rules of membership. Hers had lapsed thirty-five years before. To rejoin, she would need to be sponsored by two members and pass an admissions interview. Three obstacles to clear. She had slept with Marvin Shapiro in 1964. He was a few years older than she was, but he was still alive and still a member. And there was Miranda O'Higgens. Anabell smiled when she thought of Miranda. Yes. She had experimented a bit with same-sex partners too. But she had to move fast. She didn't know how much longer any of them would last.

ǫǫǫ

"What? What is that you say?"

Marvin bent his shaved head closer to Anabell. He had been delighted to hear from her—too delighted, she thought—the old goat had already made a grab for her breast on the way to the bar at The National Arts Club. Anabell was wearing the required skirt and had even found a pair of low-heeled shoes in the back of her closet. Marvin wore a jacket, but the top two buttons of his shirt were open so he could display a gold chain with a skull.

If he thought this made him look young and sexy, he had made a big mistake.

"Come a little closer," he cooed. "What did you say?"

"I want to join the Club again," she shouted in his ear.

"What journey? Where are you going?" he asked. "Did I tell you how good you look?"

"I need a sponsor!" She waved the letter she had written in front of his face. "Just sign the letter!"

"A sponsor? Are you going into business?"

"For the Club! The Club!" She twirled around on the stool, reached into her bag, and fetched a pen. "Just sign here!"

"Why didn't you say so!"

Marvin grabbed the pen and began to draw his signature. The M was a flowery flourish. The S turned into a slinky snake. Marvin had been a well-known cartoonist once.

The signature took a long time. Anabell finished her drink and motioned to the bartender to pour her another. She felt a movement in the air above her. Was that the sound of Helen's laughter—or was it just the tinkling of the glasses at the bar? Had she slept with Marvin too?

When the letter was finally signed, she folded it carefully and put it in her purse. She needed to hold on to Marvin's arm to get down from the bar stool. He walked her to the door and put her in a cab.

"One down," she said to herself. "Two to go."

ooo

Miranda declined Anabell's invitation to meet at the bar at The National Arts Club.

"Bunch of snots and snobs. Always were. Moved out years ago. Can't fit on the bar stool anymore anyway. I just keep up my membership to irritate them."

They met a couple of blocks away at a small Italian restaurant. Miranda took up two seats on the bench. Her hair was a mass of white curls, but her face was unlined.

"Sit next to me, sweetie," Miranda said, taking her hand. "Amazing how you've kept your figure. You look great!"

"You look very healthy," Anabell said.

"I may be a big girl, but I keep fit with yoga."

Anabell looked up at the ceiling, but the air above was empty. Perhaps Helen only haunted The National Arts Club.

Miranda reached into her purse and took out her iPhone. She pressed a couple of buttons and then set it in front of Anabell.

"My kids. Jordan, Sage, and Sasha."

The light in the restaurant was dim. Anabell could make

65

out three kids in jeans in front of a pine tree. She could not tell if they were male or female. Miranda touched the screen again, and a smiling dark-haired woman appeared.

"Kim. We're married. How about you?"

"Widow. No kids. She's beautiful, your wife."

Miranda smiled.

"We were ahead of our time. Are you still painting? Not me. Became a social worker. Felt like doing something useful for a change. Work with gender issues."

She motioned to the waiter.

"They have the best lasagna in the city. We'll take two. My treat."

Anabell looked down at the table. She had no children. She didn't even have an iPhone. She thought the only useful thing she had ever done was to pose and paint *Nude on a Park Bench*. She hoped the creation of a beautiful object counted for something in the world.

"I haven't painted much lately," Anabell said. "Membership at the Club will get me going again." She ordered a bottle of wine. "My treat."

When the food came, Anabell found she had lost her appetite. Miranda happily puffed out her cheeks with noodles while tomato sauce ran down her chin.

Anabell ordered a second bottle of wine. She fiddled with her fork. Once she had embraced her own life with such gusto. Now it seemed stagnant and empty.

Well—that was about to change.

When dessert was served at last, she brought out the letter of sponsorship for Miranda to sign.

"Of good character."

Miranda read the phrase aloud and smiled.

"Further the values and mission of the Club?" She chuckled. "Promiscuity, sexism, and snobbery."

Then she picked up the pen and signed the letter.

"Don't be a stranger!" Miranda called after her as they parted at the door.

"Two down. One to go," Anabell muttered to herself as she got into a cab.

000

It was her meeting with Morris Bentley, the President of the Admissions Committee, that undid her. He was a performance artist with a one-man show running off-Broadway at 59E59 Theaters. His head was shaved on the sides, with a tuft of hair in the front plastered with product so it stood up like an erection. He had never heard of Anabell Klein. Their housing records, he told her, did not go back that far.

"*Nude on a Park Bench,*" she said. "There were headlines in *The New York Times.* Protestors blocked the entranceway to the Club."

"We give membership to artists, not artists' models," Bentley said.

"I *am* an artist!" Anabell said.

Bentley's thumbs flew over his iPhone. The sun shone through the stained glass window of the members' bar and made the top of his head glow green. She could see he was texting. A slender man at the bar returned the text and nodded in his direction. Bentley pushed some more buttons on his iPhone and muttered something under his breath.

"When was your last exhibition?"

Anabell unfolded a yellowed flyer and handed it to Bentley.

April 23-27, 1987. Anabell Klein, New Work, The Central Gallery, 175 Hudson Street.

"Membership is limited to working artists or those who can advance the programs and fund future expansion. As for obtaining an apartment, you need to be a member for three years, and then there is a lottery."

Bentley coaxed his hair tuft to a more perpendicular position and stood, nodding to Anabell in dismissal. Her audience was over.

When she got to the door, Anabell levitated his iPhone out of his hand and suspended it just out of reach over his struggling lock of hair.

Her only option now was to make a deal with the Russian.

Spring had finally arrived. Gramercy Park was restricted to those with a Gramercy Park address, but Anabell had found an old rusty key that still worked. She had even discovered the key to her former apartment in her jewelry box. Anabell inhaled the scent of the freshly cut grass. She reveled in the glory of the red and yellow tulips that lined the path. She wandered along the path leading to the infamous bench upon which she had posed for *Nude on a Park Bench*. It was rough with splinters and peeling paint. One of the slats was missing. When she sat, the petals from the cherry tree fell onto her lap. She levitated a dirty napkin from the ground at her feet into the trash can.

She had rarely looked out the window of her apartment in the Club across the street. It was Irwin's caresses and the flowing wine inside that excited her. His breath in her ear, his fingers in her hair. She had never even bothered to sit in the park after that one sensational painting was completed. She wouldn't make that mistake again.

She came back to sit on the bench and watch the Club every day for a week. The Russian maintained a predictable schedule, leaving every day at 9 AM, not returning until 5:30. In between those hours, Irwin was alone.

She sat, planned, and remembered. Once more the sweet tobacco-infused haze swirled around her. Purple-red wine stained her lips. Velvety chocolate caressed the inside of her mouth.

Bacis! The small Italian kisses, wrapped in slips of paper carrying messages of love. Irwin was addicted to them.

The next day she waited until the Russian left. When no one answered her knock, she inserted her key. It worked!

Irwin sat in the ugly chair, staring into space as he had on her earlier visit.

Anabell handed him two silver-wrapped chocolate Bacis.

"Bacis!" he exclaimed. His arthritic fingers scratched at the wrapper.

"Bacis!" Anabell said.

She knelt down and slowly unwrapped one chocolate. He stuffed it in his mouth and put the other in his pocket. She helped him up from the chair.

"It's time to go to work," Anabell said firmly.

He smiled then, the golden glints still vivid in his brown eyes.

"Come," he said, pulling her towards the bedroom.

Anabell was amazed to see dozens of charcoal sketches leaning against the wall: full-bodied nudes, their breasts falling to the side, flowers covering their vaginas. She had hoped for at best three or maybe four sketches that she could turn into a painting. In the corner was a patch of wood, gouged, battle scarred, and water stained, still glinting with tiny shards of glass, relics from her last fierce confrontation with Irwin and Helen.

"Yes!" Irwin laughed aloud. "It's time to go to work."

Anabell took the fresh paints and brushes she had brought out of her bag.

Irwin lifted a large canvas and swung it around.

"This one!" he said. "Do this one first!"

Anabell squinted at the sketch. Wild curly hair fell in ringlets around the model's face. It was Anabell herself at age twenty-five or twenty-six. She carried it back into the studio/living room. Irwin began to mix the colors.

She started to paint, slowly at first, her fingers stiff with arthritis. It helped that she could levitate the palette.

Irwin stood over her as she worked.

"More white over here. More blue."

She felt his breath, surprisingly sweet, on her neck.

She completed one canvas. Began a second. For lunch, Anabell found a can of sardines in the kitchen cabinet. They consumed them, heads and tails, wiping their fingers on the kitchen tablecloth. They entwined their legs under the table. Irwin laughed out loud at nothing, and so did she. She felt excited. Her plan was working!

By 4 PM, the two paintings were finished. Together, they leaned them against the wall to dry.

"You must sign them," she said.

She kissed him goodbye on the cheek and left. She returned the next day and the next and the next. She awoke each morning with more energy than she had had in years. Irwin was falling more and more under her spell. He no longer called for Patricia or anyone else. At the end of the week, she did not leave at four but waited until the Russian came back.

When she saw Anabell, she screamed, "What you do here? Go away now. I call police!"

But Irwin held on to Anabell now.

"Get out!" he shouted. "I don't like you!"

He grabbed a fork and plunged it into the air in front of the Russian.

"I don't think this is a matter for the police," Anabell said. "Haven't you figured out by now that Irwin's best paintings were the ones I painted myself? These have Irwin's signature. You can sell them for a lot of money."

The Russian stared at the paintings leaning against the walls. She moved closer and squinted at the woman's figure in one of the paintings.

"This me. Once he sketch me every day. Now the paint smell up my bedroom. I wonder what going on. For five years he do nothing but eat and shit. When he still a man, he leave me for whore. Now he too sick to leave. How much money this painting can bring?"

"*Nude on a Park Bench* sold for $60,000 in 1956," Anabell said. "It is in the permanent collection of the Museum of Modern Art. I will give you all the money. All I want is the apartment."

"I leave," the Russan said. "But first I sell painting."

000

The painting's authenticity was questioned, the style and subject matter no longer considered edgy and exciting. It eventually sold for $30,000 to a collector in China who never saw it. But the Russian moved out. Now it was Anabell's job to feed and bathe Irwin. She couldn't send him to a nursing home right away. She would have to bide her time in order to hold on to the apartment. She was repelled by his sagging flesh, his rambling talk, the odor of sour milk that emanated from his pores. But she was prepared to pay the price.

As time went on, his once strong hands knotted with blue

veins under a transparent skin, clinging to her as she scrubbed his back, created a new intimacy between them. She was surprised to feel a strange satisfaction in his utter dependency.

To pass the time, Anabell let it be known to the directors of The National Arts Club that the great Irwin Rothman had started to paint again. The directors became excited. An exhibition of Irwin's new work was scheduled to take place in the Club gallery within a few weeks. The media were contacted. A reproduction of *Nude on a Park Bench* and an article were to be featured in *The New Yorker* to coincide with the exhibition opening.

But inside the apartment, things were no longer going according to her plan. Two weeks after they started working together, Irwin picked up a paintbrush. It was the first time he had held a brush in fifty years.

"You sit there." He pointed to the flowered chair. "Take off your clothes."

Anabell chuckled.

"You have already drawn me." She pointed to the sketch she had been working from.

His fingers dug into her shoulder.

"No. I will paint you now. Take off your clothes."

She undressed and sat on the chair. Irwin touched her breasts. Positioned her shoulders. He put a pot of geraniums in her lap. And then he painted. Furiously. All afternoon. At 4 PM, Anabell dressed and put the canvas against the wall to dry.

The next day was the same. His hands seemed to grow stronger, more insistent every day. He spent more time arranging her body. His fingers, once curled with arthritis, became straight, graceful. He massaged her shoulders, ran his fingers down her spine, along the inside of her thighs. It was unseemly. Indecent.

She loved it.

She had plotted and planned to take the apartment away from him. She had never expected to fall for him again. They began to make love, slowly, beautifully, like their early days together.

But as time went on, she began to notice how tired she was becoming after every session of lovemaking. And even though she was no longer painting, merely lying there while he worked, she felt depleted. Only her concentration seemed stronger, more focused. Her ability to levitate objects kept increasing. One day, she moved a canvas a few inches to the right purely by the force of her will. A few days later, she moved a canvas across the room without touching it.

As the days passed, she became concerned about her health. Her skin was so pale. Her beautiful hair, still thick and luxuriant even though it was gray, was beginning to fall out. Two of her teeth felt loose. Her cheeks sagged. She had been sleeping on the sofa, but now he wanted her in his bed. As his desire for her increased, he began to spend less time painting. He no longer seemed to care about the coming exhibition.

Past and present flowed together. She had to act quickly. She moved up the date of the exhibition.

"Marry me!" she commanded one afternoon as he slowly undressed her.

Within a week they were married. Their wedding night left her completely exhausted, but her mind felt sharper than ever before. The next day she felt too weak even to pose. She lay curled up on the sofa. Irwin had stopped painting altogether. That night, he went out. It was the first time he had left the apartment without an attendant in five years. The following evening, he left again. When he returned, late at night, she smelled another woman on his crumpled shirt.

There was no time to lose. She pulled herself out of bed and used all her powers of persuasion with the Museum of Modern Art, which had agreed to lend *Nude on a Park Bench* for the exhibition, to deliver the painting two days early.

When the painting arrived, in a heavy hand-carved gold leaf frame, Irwin insisted on carrying it inside. The staff marveled at his strength. He surveyed every square inch of wall before making his choice.

"It will hang there!" he announced.

The framed painting weighed so much that special hardware was needed to hang it.

"It must hang straight!" Irwin called out.

Anabell watched and smiled.

She followed him as he instructed the staff of the Club

where to place his new work. He ran his fingers over the thick paint and called out titles.

"*Nude with a Geranium Plant. Lady with Lilacs. Woman Devouring Sardines.*"

Irwin went out again that night and had not yet returned two hours before the exhibition was due to open. Anabell felt stronger in his absence. She curled her hair with a curling iron so silver ringlets framed her face. She clasped a heavy silver necklace with a turquoise pendant round her neck. She slid six silver bracelets onto her arm. She wrapped a soft black belt with a hand-hammered silver buckle low on her hips. She flung a black silk scarf embroidered with blood-red flowers across her shoulders.

She went down to the exhibition hall. All the preparations had been made. The staff had left or moved silently in and out. She seated herself in front of *Nude on a Park Bench* and meditated for a long time.

When she opened her eyes, people were beginning to gather. Lights flashed. A photographer from *Art News* and one from *The New York Times* had arrived. Irwin showed up at last. He presented her with a bouquet of red roses. She was once more the Great Man's Muse.

When Anabell and Irwin entered the gallery arm in arm, Anabell thought she saw Helen floating over the crowd, her flowing blonde hair billowing out behind her. But Anabell needed to focus her mind on the painting. It would take all her strength. She stood in front of it, took a deep breath, and counted to ten. The painting moved ever so slightly.

"The painting is crooked," she said.

Irwin clutched her arm.

"No! It must be straight!"

He rushed over and gave the heavy frame a tug. With a loud grating sound, the painting shifted, then tumbled forward off the wall. Irwin's head hit the marble floor, bounced once, and was still. A stream of red oozed from his skull, matting his white hair. As the crowd watched, mesmerized by the sight in front of them, the blood circled round his head and spread in diameter until it reached Anabell's feet. She levitated herself over the puddle and looked out over the crowd. Yes—she was sure of it—there was

Helen, hovering just below the ceiling, smiling down upon her.

"I think we all can use a drink," Anabell said.

And she floated all the way to the bar.

QQQ

When the will was read, Anabell found that Irwin had left all his paintings to the Russian. There were a dozen more stashed somewhere in New Jersey. No wonder Anabell had gotten rid of her so easily. But she didn't care. She believed it was poetic justice that Helen the yoga teacher, who was responsible for her loss of the apartment, had played a role in its retrieval. She had gotten what she wanted, a rent-subsidized, light-filled apartment at the famous National Arts Club, and she spent many happy hours sitting on one particular bench in Gramercy Park.

Roslyn Siegel, PhD has held senior editorial positions at Simon & Schuster, Penguin Random House, *Consumer Reports*, the Literary Guild Book Club, and MJF Books, where she is currently Director of Acquisitions. Her articles and book reviews have appeared in *The New York Times, New York Magazine, The Village Voice, Cosmopolitan Magazine, Publisher's Weekly*, and other periodicals. She is the author of *Goodie One Shoes* and *Well-Heeled*, part of the Emily Place Mystery Series, set on the colorful Upper West Side of Manhattan and featuring spirited amateur detective Emily Levine, proprietor of the fashionista's favorite discount shoe store, where there are always shoes to die for. "Levitas" is her second published work of short fiction.

CHILD'S PLAY

KATHLEEN SNOW

The point is this: there *was* no family conflict. That's why I came back this year to my family in the peninsula town of Breezy Point, Queens, to celebrate July Fourth. You can see the glass and steel towers of Manhattan from here. You can also see the Fourth of July fireworks when they rocket up from Manhattan's East Side and then fall back to earth. Something else fell earthward that night.

The term "summer house" has a magic ring to it, doesn't it? We had come to this yellow saltbox-roofed two-story with the porch like a big lap on the western end of the beach every summer now for twenty years. I wondered again why Mimi (our mother insists we call her that), who professed to hate sea, sand, salt, and heat, came back year after year trailing a clutch of five daughters who arranged themselves at various points along the continuum of womanhood. The middle of these, my marriage having ended, was Margot: me.

With each July Fourth, of the five of us sisters, there was one who sat at the battered desk in the hall and read countless romances, another who teetered guiltily on a pair of beautiful legs, wore baggy shorts, and affected an undershirt, and one distant woman child (as I had been) who played and shoveled sand and never worried about being happy.

The problem was this: Mimi's Fourth of July party. Tonight. That meant guests arriving on the New York Water Taxi, thrilled to be let into our gated community where the "Dinks"— security guards in pale blue shirts—kept out the DFDs (the despised "Down For the Days"). Mimi expected us to perform for the guests, and I hated it. Mimi assured me that reading from my new book of poems would be the highlight of the evening. Of course that would only be because my older sisters, Claudia and Frieda, were not here. Claudia was studying in Europe this summer, and Frieda remained behind in Manhattan at the Juilliard School. Now there was just me and the little-uns: Sara and

75

Marietta. We were just the remnants of a family now. I pictured Claudia in her vintage petticoat and scuffed pale-pink ballet shoes and her "down and up and keep your fanny tucked under and down and up," punctuated by agonized screams whenever her toes cramped with too much pointing. And Frieda banging away at the piano, sometimes at 3 AM, and my deathlessly tragic poetry from Middle School. I remembered all the ballets and recitations and scanty orchestras that flitted through our summer house and were performed now with a piece of toast in hand before breakfast, now on the porch more formally in the evening before Mimi's guests.

But already now the first guests for tonight were arriving. The Fourth of July was here. There was noise: that specific human sound requiring a response. Midway through it, I escaped to the kitchen, pressing my two cold hands against frightened cheeks. The hubbub out on the porch grew. The rumble came low pitched, the ice cubes in the sorbet and vodka punchbowl painfully clinking. What were these old terrors that I had forgotten in the small hotel rooms and the quiet voice of my husband? I just had to hold a drink in my hand and smile and talk to the abstract expressionist and Mimi's violin teacher, and above all, not stumble over sandaled, red-painted toes or deck shoes, or against bare backs with dark moles, or flail wildly in the pressing movement of bodies around me. I found myself seated in my chair again, safe, and looked at the small, diminishing porthole that was the kitchen door, wondering how I had come down and across that long way.

"Is it so bad?" Mimi said, cupping my face between her two hands.

And I felt the avaricious touch and knew that I belonged to her again, and that I was warm and happy and loved again. Like Sara. And Marietta, whose ten pudgy fingers that could not even complete a sandcastle on the beach now drew sketches foreshadowing future art. Now Marietta emerged towheaded and sunburned into the Fourth of July's fading light and walked around the porch, charming guests with a cocked head, a sudden bright smile in no way insincere, a burst of giggles or vivacious gibberish. And I at Marietta's age—what had I been upon the summer beach? Armed with a rusty orange shovel, I had finished my sandcastle and then dreamt a crab as its king, feeding him on ambrosia and peanut butter. Licking sticky fingers, I had sighed for the fall of sandcastles and man from Eden, climbed upon a rock, and looked out to sea.

Having supposedly attained adulthood, I kept on writing poetry, but for a new purpose. Just as I had assumed I knew I would never be the bride in the long white dress, so I would never fall in love. But into my school-winter miseries drove my husband, who was somehow willing to love me. I thought he could never reach me within the softened, hazy substance that was my summer. But he did, driving all the way from Westport, Connecticut in his noisy muscle car, as they called it in his alien men's world. How strange it was to see a man at breakfast among my sisters' bright robes and Mimi's fuzzy slippers, his sharp cologne among the crystalline bottles in our bathroom, his heavy, blunt gold watch, his square hands moving among the gauzy curtains. He stood on the porch, two points of sunlight struck sharply from the prominence of his cheekbones.

So then I wrote poetry, not for myself, but to give him pieces of myself that I could never have given him by speech or action. We were married the next winter, and perhaps that was the first mistake, for everything that happened subsequently was a continuation of winter. I had wanted a never-ending summer with my husband, and not so selfishly, for I wanted to give him the magical quality of my own summers as a girl. When a marriage doesn't work out, there is nothing really to say. Arguments, accusations, and the slow, slipping loss of that intensity which had once ruled in the name of love were there. And suddenly, at a new and more critical stage of our slow death, he sought for any weapon that would hurt me, and so said things about my family.

"Why don't you ask Sara? She could tell you what's wrong with you and the rest of your family."

"Do not criticize my family."

"You should have seen it a long time ago. All of you think you're better that anyone else because you have some tiny little talent. The Big Art. You think yours is the normal, happy family and everybody else second rate. But your family can be ugly. Just look at what you're all doing to Sara."

"We love Sara."

"But Sara's different, isn't she, Margot? She's never a part of things. Poor little Sara isn't talented, is she, Margot? Or I should say she isn't a self-deluded *artiste* like your mother."

The Fourth of July had darkened. Now, at Breezy Point, out beyond the porch, we all watched skyward for the first fireworks. Our guests were sharing pictures of their children, letting drinks slide into sand, and wading and wallowing down at the Atlantic's edge. Marietta was splashing her reflection into splinters and darting at occasional gleams of shells. Then dripping, sputtering, she flung herself into the still-warm sand and steamed there for a brief while.

Then the lights were bright, and not just on Broadway. Cascades and chrysanthemums of color filled the sky. Everyone clapped. Thank God it's over, I thought.

"I made something this year!" Sara stepped onto the porch.

Her voice sank, hardly heard, into the renewed pouring of Scotch and white wine, the chatter, the flirtatious talk, and the splashing of the surf.

Now she screamed, "I made something!"

Everyone looked.

Sara drew herself up, caught for one last summer between childhood and adolescence. The calm placidity she usually wore was gone. She held up a clay model of a rearing horse, fairly large in size. Even at my distance I could see beauty in its lines. Sara stumbled toward the crowd of people, holding the thing up in front of her like a sacrifice. Her face flushed with the terror and pride of the one chosen for immolation.

"I made it," Sara said.

The silence that had fallen gave way to a rush of praise. Too fast, too forced.

"Why, Sara!"

"It's lovely."

"I didn't know you were an artist."

"How did you do it?"

Sara looked happy, and her face relaxed.

"No no no! Sara didn't make it!" Marietta, face reddened above her sand-covered pink dress, wrested the sculpture from Sara's hands. "I made it! I made it!"

Marietta threw the baked clay horse to the porch's hardwood floor. The horse shattered.

"Marietta. You promised."

Sara doubled over and then ran from the porch.

"Sara!" I turned to go to her.

Behind me, I heard Mimi's voice, as angry as I had ever heard it.

"I'm so embarrassed. Please forgive."

Our summer house was in shadow upstairs. I ran up the steep wooden stairs, gripping the railings on each side. Sara had collapsed in a heap of white eyelet on the top floor.

I touched her shoulder.

"I understand why you did it." I was crying too.

She looked up startled through her tears.

"Margot, I want to be like everybody else."

I folded her into my arms.

"You're my sister and I love you."

"But I want to make something beautiful like you and Marietta and Mimi."

"You can be just as you are."

"I can't!"

Soon the guests were gone, the sound of the water taxis fading away. Sara and Marietta were in their bedrooms on the second floor. I said goodnight to each of them. Marietta lay asleep in her bed. In her arms she clutched her Lambie, a once white stuffed toy, now more grey and beige. In her room, Sara lay on her back, studying the ceiling.

"We'll talk about it tomorrow," I said.

Near dawn, a thunderous crash brought me out of my room. Marietta lay sprawled on the floor, fallen to the bottom of the stairs. Her Lambie was almost within reach of her right hand, as if she had tried to go down the stairs to retrieve him. The plush toy was red with blood.

While Mimi tried to restart Marietta's breathing, I called 911. Then I looked up the stairs.

Sara stood at the top in her nightdress, and I ran up to her. Someone had tied a stout piece of twine between the two stair railings. Even as this registered, I saw Sara untying the twine from her end and rolling it quite neatly into a ball. She closed the ball within her fist.

"Did you—tie that across the stairs?"

I had never seen such a look of innocence on her face. But then she spoke, and it was the second time I ever heard Sara lie.

"No," Sara said. "I just untied it."

Kathleen Snow grew up near Gnaw Bone, Indiana. She headed for New York to commune with books and went west to research bears. Her two mysteries are *Night Waking* (republished in 2011 by Random House UK) and *Searching for Bear Eyes: A Yellowstone Park Mystery* (2016) from University of Montana Press. Nonfiction includes *Taken by Bear in Yellowstone: More than a Century of Harrowing Encounters between Grizzlies and Humans* (2016), Lyons Press. You may visit Betty and Veronica, grizzly girls, at Central Park Zoo and Kathleen's website at www.kathleensnowbooks.com.

TAKING THE BROOKLYN BRIDGE BACK

ELLEN QUINT

The police officer is staring at me. As I walk towards the narrow cut in the base of the Brooklyn Bridge that hides the stairs up to the walkway on the Brooklyn side, I find myself staring back at him, unable to turn away. Can he see the guilt dangling from my shoulders, arms, and head, like tinsel on a Christmas tree? As I am about to turn into the stairs, he smiles, and I follow his gaze behind me to a woman holding a baby with curly blond hair. I take a deep breath and quickly head up the stairs.

At the top of the stairs, the expanse of the bridge and the Manhattan skyline fill my vision—a familiar scene that always impresses me, like walking into an old-fashioned picture postcard. My eyes scan the crowds—mainly tourists on a Tuesday midmorning.

My eyes are drawn to a woman walking towards me. What makes her stand out from the crowd? She looks like she has stepped out of the set of a ten-year-old sitcom. Her brown hair is streaked blonde and cut to emulate Rachel from *Friends*. As she comes closer, I can see the details of her face. I stop, the air knocked out of me. I recognize that face—it's my face. The giveaway is the nose—my big, sharp nose, always too big for my narrow face. I have always hated that nose staring back at me from every mirror, from every photograph. The one gift from my mother—the nose.

"Character," my mother would say. "Be proud of that nose—it gives you character."

That woman who is me is wearing the extravagant three-hundred-dollar black slim-cut Ralph Lauren jacket I had saved up for, the one that made me look ten pounds thinner. The younger me looks directly at me and smiles as she passes, moving quickly to the stairway down to the street that I just climbed.

I force myself to keep going. So what if she looked like me from back then. That couldn't have been me. Now my hair is cropped short with gray patches around my ears. I didn't even

81

notice what I was wearing when I ran out of the apartment. I gaze down at my dirty navy blue sweatpants, the oversized sweatshirt, and the worn-out running shoes.

Deep breath. Take a deep breath. Get a grip. You just killed your mother. You took the extra pillow she used to prop herself up and put it over her crinkly, mean face and held it down over that big nose till she stopped thrashing. Done.

The autumn wind is blowing. I pass the tall stone towers on the Brooklyn side and look through the crisscross of cables towards the post-911 skyscape of lower Manhattan against the gray sky. But instead of seeing towers of glass and steel, I envision my mother's crooked, arthritic fingers grasping at my hands, her bony legs trying to move under the tightly tucked covers. I hear her muffled screams—the last of her voice: the voice that made me cringe with every word.

How did I end up in this state of nowhere with no one? Ten years ago, I was working as a paralegal in a large Manhattan law firm. I was making a good salary, occasionally dating decent men, and coming home to my one-bedroom apartment, where I made sure that everything was in its perfect place. I would have my first cup of coffee before I left for work, looking out the window to the Brooklyn Bridge and the Manhattan skyline beyond. The noise from the traffic and the crowds on the street pulsed with the energy and the excitement of the city outside. Sure, many Saturday nights, I would stand by the window and listen to the sounds of people heading towards the bridge for a stroll on the walkway and a night out, leaving me with that empty feeling that they were all on their way to a party that I hadn't been invited to. But my apartment, filled with all the little things that I had selected and perfectly placed, was my cozy sanctuary.

My father passed away unexpectedly five years ago. Or maybe what was unexpected was that he survived my mother's incessant nagging through over forty years of marriage. His name was Milton. My mother would always yell, "Milt do this," or "Milt do that." My friends thought my father's name was Mildew. That was embarrassing. I loved my Dad. He made me laugh. I would wait for him to come home from work to leave my room, where I would be hiding from my mother. I had no sisters or brothers. Dad was my only comfort and my shield from my mother's badgering. How did he put up with it all those years? I believe he hung on for me. But finally, his heart gave out. Then there was only me.

After that, every night, my mother would call to complain about things near and far—the apartment was too hot or too cold, the garbage man hadn't picked up the recycle, the President of the United States was an idiot. She would tell me about her neighbor, Mrs. Krupnick, bragging about her children and her grandchildren. Every call would end with my mother reminding me that I should be married and how I owed her grandchildren. I would put the phone down and let her talk and talk. That voice—her unbearably penetrating voice—I can hear her saying, "Mrs. Krupnick, she has a daughter she is proud of. What do I have?"

I come up to the middle of the bridge, where the twisted steel cables swoop down, providing an unobstructed view of Manhattan looking south and north. Then I see me again. I am weaving around a group of smiling tourists who have stopped to take pictures of each other with the skyline in the background. My big Farrah Fawcett hair is blown back from my face. I am wearing white sneakers with layers of brightly colored socks and a red suit jacket with outsized shoulder pads. That is me twenty years ago. I want to shout to me, "Don't believe him. He will never leave his wife. He's just using you."

If I had never gotten involved with that married bastard, would I be leading a different life? I think of him now—Nathan Levine, the junior partner I was working for when I first started at the law firm. Nathan Levine. How many times did I sing his name and search for him online, following his career moves and his two wives and his four kids? Back then, he was an almost handsome guy. His brown eyes were set too close, and his shoulders were narrow and hunched from working at his desk for long hours. But he would cradle my chin, tip up my face, and run his finger down my nose. That nose that I hated. He would say how beautiful my nose was, like it belonged on a finely sculpted classic Venus. He was the first guy who touched me like he thought I was special. The affair was a delicious secret. I had never felt that total enchantment with any man before. I've never felt it since. Finally, it was Nathan who left the firm and me. Three precious years wasted. Time down the toilet.

I've lost sight of that younger me. Where did she go? I want to tell her to give up the relationship, give up the job, give up the sneaking around life. I want to tell her, You are only getting part of him, and not the best part at that. He will leave you with nothing but memories you can share with no one. But back then, I never would have listened to anyone. Like a million foolish women before me, I convinced myself it would all work out. Of course, I lied to myself. I am good at that. I lied to my mother, who would blabber on about how I wasn't getting any younger and I needed to find a husband. I wanted to tell her I *had* found one—he just wasn't mine.

I pick up my pace as I come around the towers on the Manhattan end of the bridge. There I am. The young woman in jeans and a turtleneck is jogging towards me. My chestnut hair is pulled back into a ponytail that keeps time with the bounce in my steps. My rosy cheeks bookend that nose of mine, distracting from its sharpness.

Back then, in college, I had so much energy. What I didn't have were dreams. My mother taught me well.

"Be careful what you wish for," she would say.

Every dream, every wish was washed away by the fear of being not good enough, not pretty enough, not smart enough, not rich enough. So I learned to limit my dreams. And look at the nightmare that has turned into.

Last year, when my mother fell and broke her hip, she refused to go to a nursing home when they released her from the hospital. I had to give her my bedroom and move my stuff into the living room. What else could I do? It was supposed to be temporary—until she could get around independently and then she would move back into her apartment. It wasn't so bad at first, when the insurance paid for twenty-four-hour care. I could go to work. I could sleep through the night, even if it was on the pull-out couch in the living room. But rather than getting stronger, she seemed to get more dependent. Then coverage ran out. I had to cut back on my work hours and start paying a health aide to come in when I wasn't there to help my mother get out of bed, bathe, and dress. My mother detests these health care workers. She claims they steal from her, pinch her, ignore her when she asks for food, and bring her lukewarm tea. She complains that I treat her as badly as "those damn health care workers."

"You are useless," she told me this morning, when I had trouble lifting her from the wheelchair into the bed. Those were her last words.

I am nearing the end of the walkway when I see my mother. She is young, good-looking, thin, wearing a felt hat. She is holding my hand, pulling me alongside her up the ramp to the bridge. My long brown hair is in two braids that fall forward over my shoulders. I am wearing my favorite patent-leather Mary Janes with white socks. I am looking up at my mom, who is looking directly at the grownup me.

"I am sorry," I whisper to her. I look down to the little girl holding her hand. "I am sorry," I whisper to the little girl, who looks up at me and smiles.

My phone rings. I pull it out of my bag. The number on the screen is my home phone. It is our latest home attendant.

"Your mother just woke up," she says. "She's asking for you. She seems quite agitated. She insisted I call you to find out when you'll be home."

It feels like I just walked straight into a wall that I didn't see right in front of me.

"Tell her I'll be back soon," I say.

I turn to walk back over the bridge.

Ellen Quint, in her day job, trains and coaches professionals on how to succeed in their leadership roles. Her work takes her around the globe, but all roads lead back to Brooklyn, where she lives with her husband. Her short story, "Crossing the Line," was published in *Family Matters*, the previous Murder New York Style anthology. Ellen is a judge for the Audies, the annual awards for audio books, and her reviews can be found in *AudioFile* magazine. Visit Ellen on her blog, www.authorspottingnyc.com, where she keeps followers in touch with author readings in the New York area. Ellen is currently the Program Chair of the New York/Tri-State Chapter of Sisters in Crime.

fa

LOVE, SECRETS, AND LIES

CATHERINE MAIORISI

Responding to simultaneous pings, audible even over the wheezing air conditioner and the shouting match in the far corner, Detectives Jo Bradley and Ray Griffin reached for their phones. Grinning, Bradley looked up from her screen, extended her hand, and wiggled her fingers. Griffin shook his head and slapped a five-dollar bill into her palm.

"Jeez, Bradley, are you psychic, or do you have an in with God?"

For the last three months, Jo had won every one of their wagers. Just minutes ago she'd bet they'd get called out for a possible homicide today.

"No visions or pipeline to heaven, Griff, just woman's intuition."

"Yeah, yeah. Have you bought a lottery ticket lately?" He looked at the message on his phone again. "And does your intuition tell you where the hell Penny Park is?"

She touched her forehead as if conjuring.

"I see water. I see the Statue of Liberty. Oh, there, behind Stuyvesant High School. It's part of Rockefeller Park on the Hudson River."

"How do you know this, Jo Jo? I thought you only left the Upper West Side to come to work."

She turned away, hoping he wouldn't notice her flush. She hadn't come out to anyone on the job, so he had no idea she was seeing a woman who lived in Battery Park City. Or that she and Max often walked the path along the Hudson River and sometimes stopped at Penny Park to watch the children playing. But she wasn't ready to tell him yet.

"Have you ever noticed the whimsical bronze figures frolicking on the ceiling and floor of the subway station at 14th Street and Eighth Avenue?"

He looked puzzled.

"Can't say I have."

"I love them, so when I read that the artist had created an installation at Rockefeller Park, I went down to see it."

Though she hadn't finished her first coffee of the day, Bradley stood and tossed her cup in the wastebasket.

"Let's go."

Outside in the sunlight, they slipped on sunglasses and headed for their vehicle. Jo, the more confident driver, preferred to be in control, so, as usual, she slid behind the wheel.

"I didn't know you were into art," Griff said, fastening his seat belt as Jo started the car.

"Well, sweetheart, I do have my secrets."

Her eyes on the road, she drove out to West Street, which ran parallel to the Hudson River and would bring them to Penny Park.

"Ooh, so mysterious." He poked her with his elbow. "So, wiseass, is it Penny Park or Rockefeller Park?"

"Rockefeller. But neighborhood kids call it Penny Park because of the piles of large bronze pennies strewn around the cartoonish bronze sculptures of people and animals."

She slowed down for a group of runners and dog walkers crossing West Street, then picked up speed, marveling at the relative quiet of the city this Monday morning. This past week, the streets in Greenwich Village had overflowed with people in town to celebrate Gay Pride Week. And yesterday, hundreds of thousands of people, gay and straight, had attended the Gay Pride March. She and Max had watched the parade from the balcony of a friend's second floor apartment on Fifth Avenue. It had been festive and celebratory, as always, and the atmosphere resolute despite the fear of violence after the death of forty-nine people in a gay Tampa nightclub a few weeks earlier.

At Stuyvesant High, she made a right onto Chambers Street, then drove as far along the short block as she could, given the number of police vehicles and ambulances already there. At the top of the staircase overlooking the park, a uniform handed Jo the log and watched her enter her name, title, shield number, and time of arrival. As Griff signed in, Jo scanned the scene below: the body draped over what she knew was the two-foot-high bronze sculpture of a fist, the uniforms guarding the entrances to the small park, the

EMTs standing to the side, and the CSU donning their protective garb.

Jo and Griff trotted down the stairs, put on booties, then moved closer. *What a waste.* She closed her eyes, reaching for the distance she needed to do her job, took several relaxing breaths, then leaned in to study the victim. Even sprawled on his back, one arm under his body, the other thrust out to the side, his lifeless blue eyes staring at the equally blue sky, and his mop of curly black hair crusted with clumps of dried blood, she could see he'd been handsome. And had taken care with his outfit: an orange tank top, blue shorts, and matching fluorescent orange and blue sneakers. Nice. But having his blue shorts pulled down to his knees, exposing his genitalia, ruined the effect. A message? Or just the result of a sexual encounter gone wrong? And what about the rainbow flag wrapped around his throat and stuffed in his mouth? Had it been used to strangle him, or was it another message?

Griff tilted his head toward the victim.

"Hate crime?"

Jo's eyes drifted to the cloudless June sky, the sparkling water, the lush lawn rolling down to the river, and New Jersey across the Hudson. She inhaled the tang of the Hudson River and the freshness of the newly cut grass, heard the gentle clang of ropes slapping the masts of the boats moored nearby and the distant roar of a lawn mower. Had the young man sprawled at her feet ended up dead in this bucolic setting because he was gay?

"Could be."

"Damn it to hell, so many steps. Why do these people always die in the most inconvenient places?"

Jo recognized the voice of Ellen Dellinger, the Medical Examiner. Dellinger was near retirement and complained at every opportunity that her knees were shot from kneeling beside bodies left on concrete, in water and snow and mud. Huffing, she appeared next to Jo.

"Detectives," she said. But her attention was focused on the young man she'd come to see. Her voice gentled. "I'd hoped we'd made it through the Gay Pride festivities without any problems."

Dellinger pulled on gloves and knelt.

"Considerable bruising on the face and chest and

knuckles." She probed his chest. "At least three broken ribs."

She wrapped his hands to protect any tissue under his nails, then gently unwrapped the flag from his neck and pulled it out of his mouth.

"No ligature marks, so he wasn't strangled, and it looks as if the flag was stuffed in after death. Maybe it's a comment on his sexuality. The lowered shorts might indicate he'd had anal or oral sex with his murderer, so I'm going to wrap his penis, then take a liver temperature."

They watched her use a scalpel to make a small cut in his abdomen, then push a thermometer into the body. She recorded the temperature, then, after Griff helped her turn him over, she examined his pockets.

"No wallet, phone, or keys. But wait." She dug deeper. "Bingo."

She handed Jo a crumpled piece of paper.

Jo smoothed it.

"Harrison Sanders had dinner on MacDougal Street Friday night. Maybe he's our victim." She handed the credit card receipt to Griff. "See if you can use your charm to get an address from Amex."

Dellinger brushed the victim's hair aside, looking for the wound.

"Lots of brain matter mixed in with the blood. I won't know for sure until I get him on the table, but my guess is he died from a severe blow to the head."

She lifted the victim's head and studied the sculpture in relation to the wound.

"I'd also guess that it was hitting his head on this sculpture that killed him."

Dellinger's willingness to share her theories was one of the reasons Jo was always happy to see her at a crime scene.

Dellinger sat back on her heels.

"Based on body temperature, rigor, and lividity, I'd guess he's been dead eight to ten hours, but, as usual, I'll have better estimates of cause and time of death after the autopsy."

She waved the morgue techs over.

After Dellinger left with the body, Jo and Griff knelt to

examine the sculpture.

Griff pointed to an edge covered with blood and brain matter.

"Is it possible he smacked his head during sex?"

Jo closed her eyes and imagined the scene.

"A guy on his knees giving him a blow job wouldn't have enough leverage to knock him back. And if it was anal, he either was facing the fist or facing away from it with the guy behind him. Neither works for me. The flag and his pants pulled down say sex. The missing wallet and phone point to robbery. But the broken bones and bruising indicate a level of rage that doesn't fit with either. Could be an accident. Maybe he stumbled backwards and hit his head on the sculpture. But if the guy meant for him to die he could have taken advantage of the situation and smashed his head against the fist hard enough to kill him." She noticed the techs hovering. "We need more pieces to solve the puzzle, so let's leave the fist to the CSU."

It turned out Harrison Sanders lived three blocks from Penny Park, so they walked to his high-rise building. They flashed their shields at the doorman.

"Have you seen Mr. Sanders this morning?" Griff said.

"I haven't seen him or Ms. Fleming yet."

"Ms. Fleming is Mr. Sanders's . . . ?" Jo's tone invited the doorman to fill in the blank.

"Fiancée."

She'd assumed the victim was gay, but even if the credit slip wasn't his, they needed to talk to Mr. Sanders and Ms. Fleming. "Buzz her and let her know we're coming."

In the elevator Jo nudged Griff.

"Your turn to break the news."

"I was hoping you'd lost track."

Laura Fleming, a pretty blonde wearing a blue nightgown with a matching robe over it, threw the door open. Her voice shook.

"Do you have news about Harry already?"

"What do you mean already?" Griff asked.

"Well, it's less than an hour since I reported him missing." Laura sounded angry. She turned to Jo. "He's never stayed out all

91

night without letting me know ahead of time."

Jo touched her lips, signaling Griff that she would take over.

"Have you tried texting him?"

Laura pulled her robe tighter.

"I texted him about an hour after I got home last night, but I heard the message pinging and found his phone stuck between the cushions on the sofa, so I realized he'd gone out without it." Her face crumpled. Tears filled her eyes. "I'm afraid—"

Jo put a hand on Laura's shoulder.

"Can we come in?"

Laura swiped at her tears with her wrist.

"Of course."

As they followed her in, Jo surveyed the open-plan room: to her left a wall of windows and sliding glass doors led to a terrace overlooking the Hudson River; straight ahead a modern steel and granite kitchen was separated from the living and dining area by a counter with four stools; and to her right a table with eight chairs and a buffet. Her gaze lingered on the large painting of Laura with a handsome dark-haired man hanging on the wall over the buffet.

"Is that Harrison Sanders in the painting?"

"Yes, I surprised him with it after we became engaged." Laura extended her hand, displaying a large diamond ring.

Well, she had her identification. They sat on the sofa, facing Laura.

Jo hated this, but it was necessary.

"Ms. Fleming, I'm sorry to tell you that Harrison Sanders was found dead this morning in Penny Park."

Now Griff owed her two.

"Oh, God." She doubled over and covered her face with her hands as if seeking privacy for her sorrow, shoulders shaking and tears slithering between her fingers. Time seemed to drag in the silence punctuated by her sobs, but it couldn't have been more than a minute or so before she took a deep breath, lowered her hands and sat back. "I knew something was horribly wrong. Was he mugged?"

"It's too early in the investigation to say. Right now we're trying to get to know Mr. Sanders. Are you up to helping us?"

Laura dug in the pocket of her robe and pulled out a tissue. She dabbed her eyes.

"What can I tell you?"

"Where were you last night between nine and midnight?"

Her eyes opened wide.

"Am I a, um, suspect or something?"

"It's standard procedure to establish the whereabouts of everyone involved."

"I've been in Michigan for three weeks helping my mom recover from a double mastectomy. I'd planned to fly back this coming Wednesday, but mom's doing well, so I decided to surprise Harry and come back early. I got back about nine o'clock last night. When he wasn't here by ten, I texted him. That was when I found his phone. At midnight I gave up and went to bed."

"Did you talk while you were away?"

"Every night in the beginning, but not so much in the last week or so."

"What changed?"

Laura stared out at the wall of glass, at the water sparkling in the glorious sunshine.

"He was distant, which was unusual. He rushed me off the phone. When I asked if something was wrong, he was vague and evasive until I got angry and confronted him, then he apologized and said he was having problems at work. But after that we only spoke if I called him. And his few texts were brief and impersonal."

She shrugged as if it wasn't a big deal, but her fingers were shredding the tissue in her hand as she spoke. She stared at her hands.

"Did you suspect Mr. Sanders of having an affair?"

Laura's shoulders tensed and her hands froze.

"It crossed my mind, but he never paid attention to other women, so I didn't take it seriously. But I had no idea what was going on." A sob escaped. "And now I'll never know for sure."

Jo felt for the woman. It was horrible to be left wondering whether your lover was cheating on you. But she'd probably feel worse when she found out he was.

93

"I'm so sorry for your loss, Ms. Fleming."

"Thank you."

"We'll need to take Harry's phone with us."

Laura pushed herself up.

"It's on his dresser in the bedroom. I'll go—"

"Detective Griffin will get it. I need your mom's phone number so we can confirm you were there and your boarding pass or some proof you were on the flight."

Laura retrieved her purse from the kitchen counter. She handed Jo the stub of her boarding pass, gave Jo her mother's name, then referred to her phone to dictate the phone number. Griff returned with Harry's phone as Jo put her notebook away.

"Would you like us to call someone to be with you?"

"I called my friend Debra when I woke up. She's on the way."

Back at the station house, they went through Harry's phone, reading the many texts to and from Laura, the last, as she had said, at ten on Sunday evening. Though Laura texted him multiple times every day, sharing what was happening in Michigan and what she was feeling, Harry's texts dwindled over time and were brief, just *hi* or *too busy to talk* or *working late*. After listening to Laura's angry voice mail demanding to know what was going on with him, they moved on. In the past four months, Harry had exchanged hundreds of texts and phone calls with someone named Damon. Many of them indicated they were more than friends and mentioned meeting in Penny Park. However, Harry's last text to Damon, Sunday evening at 8:30 PM, was less than friendly.

"U lying prick. How cd u?"

A few minutes later Damon responded: "Meet me in Penny Park at 10."

"If the relationship soured, Damon could be our guy." Jo rubbed her forehead. "Is there an address for him in the Contacts list?"

Griff typed in D-a and selected Damon.

"Just the phone number."

"Okay. You compile a list of Harry's friends. I'll call Damon." She keyed his number. "Not answering."

"Maybe one of Harry's friends can put us in touch." Jo stood and stretched, more than ready to get out of the office. "So after Laura and Damon, who did Harry text most?"

"Graham Ford." Griff responded without looking at the list. "He has two entries in Contacts, a business address on Wall Street and a personal."

They'd waited twenty minutes for Human Resources to locate Graham Ford, but now he sat on the other side of the conference table in stunned silence, struggling not to cry. Finally, he wiped his eyes with his handkerchief.

"How did it happen?"

Jo leaned forward.

"How did you know Mr. Sanders?"

"We've been friends since junior high school."

"When did you last see him?"

"Yesterday. We marched together in the Gay Pride Parade." He rubbed his eyes. "I can't believe he's dead."

"Were you together all night?"

"No. Harry left before the parade ended. My partner Allan and I went to the dance on Pier 26, then to a party at a loft in SoHo. We got home about one-thirty this morning. Our doorman can confirm it. Have you talked to Damon?"

"Damon?" She wanted his take on the relationship.

Ford shifted in his chair, ran a hand through his hair, and straightened his tie.

"I guess it doesn't matter now. Damon was Harry's boyfriend." He cleared his throat. "Harry had always been attracted to men but couldn't admit he was gay. He convinced himself that as long as he protected himself, having sex with men didn't hurt Laura. However, he hadn't counted on falling in love with Damon, or any man for that matter."

Ford drank half the bottle of water the HR woman had delivered when she heard they were informing him of the death of a friend.

"Anyway, Harry and a small group of us marched in the Gay Pride Parade. He was really up, laughing and having fun, until we got to those religious fanatics from that church that shows up at every parade waving signs like 'Kill the Homosexuals.' Suddenly,

95

Harry went crazy. He left the parade and ran at them screaming, then started punching and kicking one of the guys holding a sign. We didn't know what was happening, but we pulled him away. Harry was hysterical. The guy he attacked was Damon. Harry was head over heels in love with him and was going to break up with Laura this Wednesday. He had no idea Damon was a closet homophobe. Harry was devastated and in such a rage that I wouldn't have been surprised if you'd come here to tell me he'd killed Damon."

He held out his phone.

"He texted this selfie of him with Damon the day before the parade."

Jo and Griff studied the picture of two beautiful young men, obviously in love.

"Do you know Damon's last name and where we can find him?"

Jo knew the police maintained files on the fanatics involved with that church, but getting the information from Ford would speed things up.

"No to both." He drank the remaining water. "Can you tell me how he died?"

"It's too early in the investigation to be sure. We need contact information for your partner and the people at the party last night."

Jo walked to the window and stared at the Statue of Liberty in the harbor while Griff took the numbers. It *would* make more sense if Harry had killed Damon, but people killed the people they claimed to love every day. She'd never understood it, and she probably never would.

As they drove back to the precinct, Griff made a few calls to get the department's file on the church, then, hoping the police video of the march had captured the fight, he arranged to pick up a copy. They watched the fight a half-dozen times. Harry dashed out of the march, his face twisted with rage. Damon looked stunned. He dropped his sign and raised his arms to ward off Harry's punches, but he didn't fight back. One of the religious guys jumped between the two men, then Graham Ford and another man dragged Harry away. Damon was bleeding, and he and Harry were both in tears.

Jo sat back.

"Wow, Harry must have felt sucker punched." She thumbed through the church file. "Our Lord Saves the Righteous Church is based in Mississippi but sends members to New York City to convert homosexuals to save them from eternal damnation. Damon Glass came here from Mississippi five months ago." She copied the address of the church. "Let's go."

They headed out to round up their number one suspect. Their only suspect.

The rundown four story in Chinatown didn't look like a church. The front door lock was broken, making it easy to enter. They checked the apartment listings in the lobby and walked up to the fourth floor. As Griff lifted his hand to knock on apartment 4B, the door swung open, and they were face to face with a bruised, swollen, and black-eyed Damon Glass, holding a suitcase.

"Um, can I help you?"

Several men watched from the shabby room behind him.

"Damon Glass?"

He put the suitcase down.

"That's me." He looked at Griff, then at Jo, obviously making them as cops, and fear flashed across his face. "Is this about the fight yesterday?"

Jo tilted her head toward the suitcase.

"Where are you going, Mr. Glass?"

He glanced over his shoulder at the men he'd left behind.

"I haven't figured that out, but I have to leave here."

Griff placed a hand on his shoulder.

"So how about you take a ride with us, and maybe we can help you with accommodations."

"I—do I have a choice?"

When they didn't answer, he sighed, picked up his suitcase, and walked to the stairs.

In the interview room, Damon put his elbows on the table and dropped his head into his hands. They observed him for a few minutes before entering.

"How did you meet Harry Sanders?" Jo asked.

Damon looked up, brushed his fingers over his bruised and

swollen lips, then straightened.

"Late one night I was feeling depressed about the work of the church. It seemed hateful and unchristian, so I went for a walk to think about it, and I ended up in Penny Park. Harry was sitting on a bench smoking. We got into a conversation, and after a while he suggested we stroll along the river. We walked and laughed and talked for hours. When we said goodnight, he invited me to dinner at his apartment several nights later. After that, we spent many evenings together." He chewed the cuticle on his thumb.

They waited, but Damon didn't continue. Interesting that he hadn't asked again why they'd taken him in to the police station.

"So when did you become lovers?"

Damon flushed.

"I was so happy to have a friend outside the church that I didn't recognize what was happening. In a matter of weeks, I was in love with Harry, and we got involved. My church believes homosexuals should be put to death, but I couldn't stop myself." He cleared his throat. "Then last week, Harry said he loved me and asked me to live with him. I decided to leave the church." He touched his swollen eye. "Harry needed a few days to clear up something, and we agreed to meet this Thursday at his apartment."

"Where did he live?"

"Fifteen MacDougal Street."

"Did Harry know that you were a member of Our Lord Saves the Righteous Church?"

He shook his head.

"I almost told him then, but the Gay Pride March is a big deal for the church and I felt guilty about deserting right before it. I decided I would leave right after and tell Harry once I was free." Tears trickled down his face. "Then Harry saw me holding a sign that said, 'Kill the Homosexuals,' and he went berserk, punching and kicking me."

"Why didn't you fight back?"

"I was stunned. I felt guilty that he had found out this way. I tried to explain that I love him and that I was done with the church, but he wouldn't listen. I should have told him in the beginning. I see now that he felt betrayed." His voice dropped to a whisper. "That I'd betrayed him."

98

Jo let him sit with that thought. His head drooped, and he seemed to go inside himself.

"So did you fight again when you met him in Penny Park last night?"

His head shot up.

"What? I haven't seen him since the march."

She shook her head.

"Come on, Damon, give it up. We have his cell phone, and you texted that you'd be in the park at ten."

He raised his hands in a defensive position.

"All these questions aren't about the fight, are they? Is Harry accusing me of something?"

"Give me your phone." Jo extended her hand. "I'll show you the text."

"I lost my phone yesterday."

"How convenient," Griff sneered.

Damon stared at him.

"I must have lost it during the fight, because I didn't have it when I wanted to call him afterwards. And I couldn't remember his number, so I waited on the stoop in front of his building all night, but he never came home."

Jo believed him. She'd be unable to call Max without her cell phone. So if Damon was telling the truth and he didn't send that last text, whoever had his phone could be their killer.

"Let's look at the video again."

They left Damon to his thoughts.

"Stop. Rewind just a bit." Jo pointed. "There. Damon's phone drops to the ground, and while he's watching Harry being hauled away, the guy with the 'Homos Burn in Hell' sign pockets it. Maybe he made the call. Play it again, and freeze it so we can see that guy's face. Interesting." She flipped through the church file and found his photo. "Wayne Harmon. Let's have him picked up."

They let Harmon stew in the interview room. He didn't have the phone on him, but that didn't mean he didn't have it. When they sat opposite him, he was sweating.

Jo clasped her hands on the table.

"So, Wayne, why did you meet Harry Sanders in the park?"

"Who?"

Jo slammed her hand on the table.

"Stop the bullshit, Wayne. We know you have Damon's phone, we know you love Damon, and we know you met Harry last night."

His eyes widened.

"You can't know—"

She slammed the table again.

"We can show you the video, and you can watch yourself pick up the phone when he drops it and then look at him like a lovesick puppy, but spare us, we've already seen it too many times."

His jaw dropped, his face reddened, and he looked everywhere but at Jo.

"As long as it wasn't possible, I hid my unnatural feelings for Damon, even from myself. But once I knew, I was overcome with jealousy and rage, so I texted Harry to meet me at the place they mentioned in their texts."

Jo gentled her voice.

"What happened when you got there?"

Wayne rubbed his temples.

"I accused him of leading Damon into sin. He laughed, and I lost my temper. I boxed when I was younger, and I'm bigger, so I beat him really bad. He could hardly stand, but when I left he was still cursing me and Damon and our church. Is he going to press charges?"

"What did you hit him with, other than your fists?"

"Nothing." He looked Jo in the eye. "Though I might have kicked him in the ribs when he was down."

Griff pushed his notebook over to Jo.

"Let's talk," he'd written.

Wondering what he'd remembered, she followed him out of the room.

Griff thumbed through the stack of reports on his desk.

"Ah, here. We have a statement from a man walking his dog on the street above the park. He saw a guy come up the steps and walk uptown, while another guy was cursing and yelling about religion down below in the park."

"It sounds like Harry was alive when Wayne left. Damn, we don't have enough to hold either Wayne or Damon." Jo ran her fingers through her already messy hair. "You get to tell Damon Harry is dead. I'll release Wayne and check in with the team at MacDougal Street. Then let's start from the beginning."

Griff went out for sandwiches, and Jo began rereading the reports from the interviews done so far. The first few were Harry's friends. Graham and his partner were the only ones who mentioned Damon. She scanned the results of the canvass of the buildings near Penny Park and the neighborhood around it. Nothing.

She picked up a loose report. Ah, she'd forgotten she'd tasked someone with contacting Laura's mother to ask what Laura had said about Harry. Jo was surprised at how much intimate detail Laura had shared with her mother.

"Laura was worried. Harry had lost interest in sex, often drifted off in the middle of a sentence, and frequently came home late. Once she was in Michigan, it got worse. Their phone conversations were brief and distracted. And when Harry stopped calling her every day as they'd agreed, Laura was sure he was having an affair. She flew home early to confront him."

A little different from Laura's version, but close enough. She pulled over a stack of reports that had been dropped off a while ago. Halfway through the pile she found one from a neighbor who'd arrived home somewhere between ten-thirty and eleven. He hadn't seen Harry, but he had seen Laura. She seemed dazed and had not responded to his greeting, which was unusual since she was always friendly.

Griff dumped her sandwich and coffee on her desk and dropped into his chair. He ate his while skimming the reports on his desk.

Jo checked her notes, then leaned back in her creaky swivel chair and put her feet up on her desk. Laura had said she hadn't left the apartment after she got in at nine, yet her neighbor claimed to have seen her closer to eleven. Could it be? Laura came home early because she was angry and suspicious. In that state of mind, once she found Harry's phone, how could she resist reading the texts to confirm her feeling that he was cheating? Jo imagined Laura's rage, thinking the lovers were together just a few blocks away.

"I like Laura for it," Jo said and ran through her scenario.

"My money's on sex and robbery." Griff waved a report. "Someone used Harry's Visa and Amex cards overnight."

Jo smirked.

"Ready to put a fiver on it?"

It was late when they knocked on Laura's door. She answered wearing what appeared to be the same nightgown and robe.

"Have you found the mugger?" Her voice was flat, her face drawn.

Jo felt a stab of pity. Did Laura feel that way because her fiancé was dead or because she'd killed him? Or maybe both.

"Please get dressed. We'd like you to come to the station house."

Laura tensed.

"Why? Do I need a lawyer?"

"We need a written statement from you. If you feel you need a lawyer, you can call when we get there."

Laura glared at Jo, then walked to the bedroom.

Forty-five minutes later, they settled into an interview room. Happily, Laura hadn't mentioned a lawyer again.

Jo took the lead.

"Please go over what happened from the time you arrived home Sunday night."

Laura gnawed on her thumb.

"I arrived about nine. Harry wasn't there, so I unpacked. When he wasn't home by ten, I texted him. I heard the ping and found his phone. I turned the phone off so it would stop pinging. When he wasn't home by midnight, I went to bed. He still hadn't come home when I woke up, so I called the police to report him missing."

Jo nodded, as if agreeing, and watched Laura relax.

"It must have been really tempting to have his phone, to be able to confirm whether he was cheating. How did you feel when you read the texts from Damon?"

"Who's Damon?" Laura couldn't keep the anger out of her voice. Her hands twitched, her breathing sped up, and she shifted forward in her chair.

Jo leaned in and spoke softly.

"Come on, Laura, we know you saw the texts and went to meet Harry at the park. What happened?"

Laura jumped up and swiveled toward the door. "I don't know what you're talking about." She fingered her hair.

"Your mother said you were angry and suspected Harry of cheating. You had Harry's phone. And a witness saw you in the elevator about eleven." Jo kept her voice conversational.

Laura spun and faced them.

"It was an accident. I was angry. He lied to me. He was cheating on me. And with a man." Her voice oozed hatred. "He was nothing but a dirty faggot. What if he exposed me to AIDS?" She began to pace. "When I got to the park, he was bloody and staggering, repulsive, like the cowardly filth he'd become." She sobbed. "I loved him. How could he do this to me?"

Griff moved to Laura's side.

"Laura Fleming, you are under arrest for the murder of Harrison Sanders."

"No, it was an accident."

She started for the door.

Jo intercepted her, herded her back to her chair, and handed her a tissue.

"Sorry, Laura, we have to do this to protect your rights."

Jo sat, and Griff issued the Miranda warning and, as required, had Laura sign each statement acknowledging that she understood it.

By the time she'd signed the last statement, Laura seemed more in control, and Jo stepped in again.

"What happened in the park?"

Laura twisted her hair around her finger.

"He insisted Damon was just a friend, and I lost it. I slapped him, then punched his chest. He screamed and backed away. I shoved him. He stumbled, his arms windmilled, and he toppled backwards onto that bronze sculpture, the fist. Blood spurted, but I thought I'd just knocked him out. I saw the rainbow flag draped over a fence, and it seemed perfect. I wrapped it around his neck and stuffed it in his filthy gay mouth, then I pulled down his shorts to shame him. I wanted to hurt him. But I didn't mean to kill him."

She buried her face in her hands and sobbed.

Love foiled by secrets and lies, self-hate and homophobia, a fucking Shakespearean tragedy. Jo thought about Max, about their love. Maybe it was time she was out and proud.

Laura dried her eyes on her sleeve.

"What happens now?"

Jo considered the question. Technically, Laura had killed Harry. But Wayne Harmon had played a role. And it really did seem like an accident. But she and Griff had done their job. Now the Medical Examiner and the ADA would have to sort it out.

"We'll take your written statement. After that, it's up to the District Attorney."

They left Laura writing.

Out in the hall, Jo extended her hand.

"Damn." Griff slapped a five into her palm.

Catherine Maiorisi lives in New York City and often writes under the watchful eye of Edgar Allan Poe in Edgar's Café near her apartment. Catherine's full-length mystery, *A Matter of Blood*, featuring NYPD detective Chiara Corelli, will be published in December 2017 by Bella Books. "Love, Secrets, and Lies" is Catherine's third mystery short story included in a *Murder New York Style* anthology of stories by members of the New York/Tri-State Chapter of Sisters in Crime—"Justice for All" in *Fresh Slices* and "Murder Italian Style" in *Family Matters*. Both Catherine's romance novels, *Matters of the Heart* and *No One But You*, and four of her romance short stories are currently available at www.bellabooks.com, Amazon, and Barnes and Noble. For information on appearances and a complete list of Catherine's publications, go to www.catherinemaiorisi.com. Catherine can also be found on Facebook and Twitter @CathMaiorisi.

BLOOD ON THE FLOOR

MARY MORENO

The door to Box 32 was locked. One of the new members of the custodial staff must have forgotten to leave it open for inspection after tonight's concert. Security chief Don Meachem rifled through his key ring and located the master. Something drew his eye downward: a dark red puddle of wine leaking out from under the door. It had collected on the marble threshold and was dripping down onto the red carpeting. Damn! The boxholders had obviously ignored the house rules governing Carnegie Hall audience etiquette.

He grabbed his radio and summoned Housekeeping.

ꝍꝍꝍ

"There will be blood on the floor if you don't know your intervals, girls!"

They say a good teacher inspires love in the heart of the student. Dr. Amanda Collier inspired mostly fear. What kept them coming back for punishment was her unique ear training and sight singing method. It enabled backup singers to walk into a recording studio and nail the vocal parts flawlessly the first time through— thus saving producers costly rehearsal time and earning themselves a six-figure annual income. Hence the hours of daily study required for success in Dr. Collier's musicianship course was a discipline they all practiced. And practiced. And practiced.

"Blood on the floor, do you hear me?" Dr. Collier slammed her Intervals textbook on the music stand and glared at Delores seated in the back row. "I don't care how much money you make singing background vocals for Paul Simon and Barry Manilow. If you make mistakes in here you're living on borrowed time. I won't have you taking up space in my studio at the expense of serious musicians who are willing to apply themselves to the work."

Delores felt her cheeks flushing. Just now she'd sung a major third instead of a minor. An unforgivable offense.

105

"So sorry, Dr. Collier, I just didn't move my eyes ahead fast enough."

Perhaps because they were tired from lack of sleep. Last night's recording session had gone until 2 AM.

"I'm not interested in excuses. I expect perfection. Anything less makes you a second-rate musician."

"Yes, ma'am."

Delores wiped away a tear with the tissue offered by the student seated next to her. She stared at her score, wishing she could make herself invisible. She thought she heard a giggle coming from the other side of the room.

Thing is, she *knew* her intervals—the numbers that identify the distance between notes of the scale that make up the essential building blocks of music. She spent a minimum of two hours a day, seven days a week, on her homework. She took a private lesson once a week with Dr. C in addition to the weekly sight-singing class. So Delores really *shouldn't* be making mistakes. But whenever she had to sing in Dr. Collier's presence, nerves took over. She felt more insecure in here than she did in a recording session with James Taylor.

For the balance of the class, Delores kept her mind on the music. She willed herself to relax and concentrate. She managed to ignore the icy stares the teacher continued to send her way. And she performed flawlessly. Like Pavarotti hitting his high C. Like Horowitz sailing through a tricky piece by Scriabin without missing a note. Yet she still felt inadequate.

As she packed up her music after class, she overheard several of the students making plans. They were heading out to their usual supper with their teacher at the Russian Tea Room, conveniently located next door to Carnegie Hall and across the street from Dr. Collier's studio in the Steinway Building.

Anna, who had offered the tissue earlier, asked, "Would you like to join us tonight, Delores? You look like you could use a drink."

Surprised at the invitation—the students in Dr. C's inner circle had never extended friendship—Delores considered canceling out on her dinner with Michael, but only for a moment.

"Thanks so much, Anna, but I've made plans."

From behind her, Dr. Collier inquired, "Seeing the boyfriend, I suppose?"

"Well, yes."

"I hope you're not letting him get in the way of your music, Delores. Musicians can't have a personal life if they want to be world class. I divorced my husband forty years ago when he made it clear that he expected me to do his laundry and iron his shirts!"

Delores was afraid to tell Dr. C that she'd been doing Michael's laundry since they'd moved in together three years ago. Fortunately, most of his wardrobe consisted of cotton tee shirts, so there wasn't much ironing involved.

000

"I don't know why you put up with this abuse," Michael said over dinner. "You're already in demand in the studios. What do you need her for?"

Delores hated to cry in front of Michael, but she hadn't been able to stop the flow of tears since she'd left the Steinway Building and made her way over to China Song, a favorite hangout for musicians on Broadway and 52nd Street.

"I don't want to spend the rest of my life singing backup for other artists," she said, blowing her nose. "And I'm tired of being known as a jingle singer. I feel like I'm selling out every time I sing, 'Fly the friendly skies of United,' even though the residuals are paying for my lessons."

Delores's income paid most of the rent on their apartment, as well. Michael was famous for his badass tenor sax solos, and his band was always booked around town, but playing progressive jazz was not a high-income gig.

"There are plenty of other people who can teach you music without making you feel like a toad. You're too talented to let someone beat you up this way."

"I want to compose music. I want to feel more comfortable playing my songs on the piano. I want to be able to write arrangements and maybe someday even be a producer. Yes, Dr. Collier's a bitch, but she's the best musicianship teacher in New York. And she's giving me the skills I need to be more than just a singer."

Or *chick singer*, she thought, which was how male jazz artists often referred to female vocalists. To his credit, Michael never did that. At least not when she was in the room.

"Sounds like a bad love affair," Michael said.

"This has nothing to do with love. Except love of music."

"Speaking of love, give me your hand." Michael drew a little box from his pocket, removed a diamond ring, and slipped it on her finger. "I think it's time we made our situation permanent, babe. I hope you feel the same way."

Delores felt a tingle travel up her spine. Was it excitement, or was it fear? Could she really have it all and prove her teacher wrong? Or would she end up abandoning her dreams in order to be Michael's wife?

000

Over at the Russian Tea Room, Dr. Collier and three of her favorite students were settled into Dr. C's regular booth, enjoying their usual borscht, pierogies, and gossip.

"I overheard you invite Delores to join us tonight, Anna," Danielle said. "Whatever possessed you?"

"I felt sorry for her," Anna said, looking straight at Dr. C, who was busy squeezing a lime into her vodka on the rocks. "She only made one mistake."

Dr. C took a sip of her cocktail.

"That's one mistake too many, Anna. And she's done it before in class. If she does it again, I'm going to lose patience."

Anna reflected that Dr. C exhibited about as much patience as a hungry pit bull eying a steak at mealtime, but she held her tongue.

"You know," said Kate, "if we got rid of Delores, there'd be space in class for my roommate." A Broadway singer who'd been with Dr. Collier since before *A Chorus Line* opened, Kate always had a roommate who had trouble making the rent.

Danielle—the voice of Burger King—looked up from the soup she'd been slurping.

"Your roommate's a dancer. What we need is another

108

studio singer, someone who can get us booked on sessions."

"Delores could get us booked on sessions if we were friendlier toward her," Anna said.

"Relax, girls. I'll take the appropriate action when the time is right. And it may never come to that. Delores is all caught up with the boyfriend. Pretty soon she'll probably get married and get pregnant."

ooo

When Delores showed up at Dr. Collier's studio for her next private lesson, she was wearing her sparkly new engagement ring. She was also well prepared. Although she'd been caught up in making wedding plans for the past week, she had not neglected her daily practice. There would be no mistakes at this lesson. And there weren't, until she sat down at the piano to play her keyboard harmony exercises and Dr. Collier heard her fingernails clicking on the keys.

"Delores! Your nails are much too long."

"I'm sorry, Dr. C. I usually keep them filed down, but I wanted to let them grow a little so that I could have a manicure to show this off." She held up her left hand, her Princess Pink nails complementing the shine of the diamond on her ring finger.

"I suppose you're going to get married, then." Dr. C looked as if she'd just gotten a whiff of raw sewage.

"Yes, and I'm so happy."

"If that's what you want, you might as well kiss your career goodbye, honey."

"But Michael's a musician. He won't stand in my way. In fact, he's very supportive."

"I'd better meet your Michael, then. Why don't you bring him to our Boston Symphony concert next Thursday? I have two extra tickets. Miranda's going to be on the road with Tony Bennett and Jenny's singing backup with Carole King at the Bottom Line."

The idea of Michael and Dr. Collier spending time together conjured up images of a cat hanging out with a sparrow.

"Michael's band is playing at the Vanguard next Thursday, but I'd love to come."

109

Hopeful that the invitation meant Dr. C was beginning to soften her attitude toward her, Delores whipped out her checkbook.

ooo

On Sunday morning, Delores and Michael were enjoying their special ritual: breakfast in bed with lox from Zabar's and bagels from H&H, their Sunday *Times* spread out between them, Miles Davis on the stereo.

"I can't come to your gig on Thursday," Delores said. "I have a command performance at Carnegie Hall. Dr. C's invited me to join her and her star students for a concert, and if I don't show up, she'll probably kill me."

Michael reached for her over the cream cheese.

"I thought she was going to kill you because you don't know your intervals."

ooo

On Thursday afternoon, Delores had her blonde highlights refreshed and her shoulder-length hair plaited into a French braid. That evening, she took extra time with her makeup and chose her finest outfit: a black silk pantsuit with a white satin blouse. She splurged on a taxi. Entering the magnificent marble lobby, she felt a palpable sense of awe at being in a landmark building that was the cornerstone of New York's cultural history. She climbed the stairs to the second tier, savoring every step, and found Box 32 located directly across from the lobby bar. She could see Dr. Collier and the others already seated. Dr. C's mink stole was draped around the back of her chair. Intent on making a graceful entrance, Delores kept her eyes straight ahead and promptly tripped over the elevated threshold.

Danielle smirked.

"Heels a little too high, Delores? I hope you didn't hurt yourself."

"I'm fine," Delores said, attempting to collect her dignity.

Dr. C motioned for her to take the empty chair next to hers at the front of the box. Delores noted that she, too, had freshly blonded hair.

"I'm so glad you could join us tonight, dear. It's going to be a very special evening."

Excited as she was to be there, Delores felt out of place, like a gatecrasher at a private club. The girls gossiped among themselves, and Delores was conspicuously excluded from their conversation. Attempting to put her feelings aside, she opened her program and studied it. The first piece was Elliott Carter's Concerto for Orchestra, composed five years ago for the New York Philharmonic's 125th anniversary. The notes described the piece as "an incandescent blaze of musical poetry."

The orchestra assembled on stage.

"Pay attention, girls," said Dr. C. "Notice the non-traditional layout of the orchestra? Carter notated instructions on the score for the placement of the instruments. They're divided by musical range from high to low, with the various percussion instruments scattered throughout."

That kind of detail was why Delores continued to study with Dr. C. Where else could she learn this stuff?

The house lights dimmed, and a hush fell over the hall. Maestro Seiji Ozawa bounded onstage to a roar of applause.

Delores prepared herself for an evening she would never forget.

For the next twenty-two minutes she lost herself in the music. It was magnificent, transporting her from her physical surroundings to an emotional space where she responded to every nuance of the score. Thunderous applause at the end of the fourth movement awakened her from her trance, and she joined the others in a standing ovation. From the front of the box, looking down at the auditorium, she felt a bit lightheaded and took a step back. How easy it would be to take an accidental tumble.

During intermission, she bravely joined the others at the bar. Dr. Collier remained in her seat, waiting for Anna to bring a drink to her.

"How are you enjoying the concert, Delores?" Kate asked. "Did you like the Concerto?"

"I loved it. This is the first time I've heard it. And I'm looking forward to the second half. Mozart's Requiem is one of my favorites." She took a sip of her red wine. "How sad that it was the last music he ever wrote."

"I know," Kate said. "He actually worked on it on his deathbed, but he died before it was finished."

"Amazing that he had the strength and discipline to keep working."

Delores stared into her wine glass and contemplated how much the world had been cheated by Mozart's early passing.

Just then Danielle jostled Delores's arm, spilling red wine on her white satin blouse.

"Oops," she said.

Had she done it on purpose?

Delores didn't have time to respond. She headed for the ladies room to try to sponge it off before the stain set.

When she returned to her seat, the stain still an unsightly pink, she noticed that the others had all brought their unfinished drinks into the box. Apparently they didn't believe the house rules applied to them. In spite of the magnificent music, Delores regretted that she was spending time with this group rather than hanging out with Michael at his downtown gig. Oh well, they would be together later, and that thought gave her comfort.

The musicians returned to the stage and began to tune up.

"Girls," Dr. C said, "I want you to leave immediately after the last movement and run next door to the Tea Room. Make sure Boris has saved my booth for us. Delores can walk me over afterward."

She leaned closer to Delores and whispered in her ear.

"Did you notice that the Requiem is in D Minor, dear?"

"Yes, ma'am."

"That's always been known as the death key, you know."

Another arcane tidbit from Dr. C's store of music history. Interesting, but Delores did not like the mean, steely look that accompanied it. She should leave. Now.

But she stayed. She wanted to hear the Requiem.

ooo

The young woman from Housekeeping finally arrived, armed with rags and detergent. She knelt down and inspected the stain.

"This isn't wine, Mr. Meachem. It's blood!"

Meachem quickly unlocked the door and pulled it open. A body lay on the floor directly inside. The dead woman's blonde hair was matted with blood. So was the mink stole draped around her shoulders.

ϙϙϙ

Over drinks at the Vanguard, Delores and Michael held hands, happy to be together after an evening apart.

"So how was the concert?"

"More fun than I thought it would be."

"Is that blood on your blouse?"

Mary Moreno is a New York City author, composer, and songwriter. Her work has been recognized with fellowships and awards from the New York Foundation for the Arts, the National League of American Pen Women, and the Elaine Kaufman Table 4 Foundation. Much of her fiction combines her passion for music with her love of mystery. She is currently working on a mystery series set at the Metropolitan Opera, as well as a mystery novel that takes place in the eighteenth century and involves Mozart. Her short story, "Killerfest," is the first in a series of satirical thrillers featuring a protagonist who kills to get published. Although she's never actually killed anyone, Mary does wake up just about every morning thinking about new ways to commit murder. She also sings. Her website is www.marymoreno.com.

ME AND JOHNNY D

RONNIE SUE EBENSTEIN

C.C. Green squirmed in her sensible shoes. Her feet ached, but not half as bad as her face—it wasn't easy keeping a smile plastered in place all the live-long day. She checked her watch: time for her spiel.

"Hello, Passaic. You're a Jersey girl, right? And Sydney: G'day, mate. Who's from the heartland?" She cupped her ear. "Wichita, let me hear you say hello. I have twenty souls in my charge today. Let's stay together, and that means you, Kokomo. I'm serious. No stragglers."

Herding a gaggle of tourists around Rockefeller Center was not her dream job, but it was either trudge through the elegant canyons of Rock Center, out-of-towners in tow, or wait tables; her PhD meant squat. A hoped-for assistant professorship at Columbia or NYU had never materialized. At least her tour groups liked her patter; they loved that she called Rockefeller "Johnny D," and some of them even forked over a tip.

ooo

Charissa Concordia Green arrived at work every day with high hopes, home-brewed coffee, and a paper bag lunch. Johnny D believed: *Thrift is essential to well-ordered living.* She loved walking through the underground concourse linking the towering buildings. All subterranean roads led to Rock Center, her home away from home. But after her third tour of duty, she was happy to make her way to the crowded staff locker room and trade in the required black pants, red vest, and crisp white shirt for a uniform more to her liking: a consignment shop floral print dress and shapeless beige cardigan. Her oversized satchel held her post-PhD reading: *Claw Your Way to CEO: Success Strategies Your Cat Can Teach You* and *Fifty Ways to Leave Your Cubicle.*

She headed up and out onto the Plaza to inhale the sweet scent of the multicolored blooms gracing the Channel Gardens and to smile at the spouting fish fountains in the pools at the center of the Promenade.

Most people pictured Rockefeller Plaza filled with ice skaters, but on a summer day like today she looked down onto a sea of white umbrellas covering café tables where chic women were enjoying Cobb salads and iced tea, shopping bags splayed at their feet. She treated herself to one truffle from Teuscher Chocolatier and crossed busy Fifth Avenue to mingle with supplicants inside Saint Patrick's Cathedral. She put two dollars in the kitty, lit a candle, and asked forgiveness for past—and future—sins. Couldn't hurt. Next door to the venerable church stood a house of worship of a different kind, Saks's flagship store. That's what she loved about Rock Center: it sat at the intersection of faith and commerce.

Today, commerce was uppermost on her mind. As the first in her family to earn a college degree, let alone a PhD, the pressure to succeed rested heavily on C.C.'s narrow shoulders. Since she couldn't leverage her thesis, "John Davison Rockefeller, Jr., Master Builder, and New York's Dreaming Spires," into a teaching job, she would strive to become, if not billionaire rich like the Rockefellers, at least jaw-droppingly rich. Maybe one day she would even create something noteworthy, just like Johnny D. Of course, he was to the manor born. And she? Not quite a Rockefeller.

She returned to the Plaza and positioned herself before the granite slab, incised with Johnny D's quotes, overlooking the café below. Which of Rockefeller's inspirational messages would guide her today? She communed with the great man: *I believe in the sacredness of a promise, that a man's word should be as good as his bond.*

Perfect. A man should keep his promise. So should a woman. To her family and to her dreams, no matter what she had to do to make those dreams happen. Her gaze wandered beyond the Plaza's two hundred world flags waving in the warm breeze to the gilded bronze statue of Prometheus. A quote from Aeschylus, writ large behind the sculpture, read: "Prometheus, teacher in every art, brought the fire that hath proved to mortals a means to mighty ends." Could she light her own fire without setting her values ablaze? And did it matter?

Behind Prometheus loomed 30 Rockefeller Plaza, headquarters of NBC and other companies famous and not so, including RRP: Reality Romance Productions. An article in *The Wall Street Journal,* a source she found fascinating reading now that she was no longer immersed in scholarly monographs, said RRP was on a hiring spree. The company was raking in a fortune living by PT Barnum's motto: "Nobody ever lost a dollar by underestimating the taste of the American public."

C.C. knew RRP would be a good fit. As an undergrad, she had worked as equipment manager in her upstate SUNY school's Cinema Studies studios. She'd learned a great deal about what makes equipment tick and a few hard life lessons. The self-absorbed students had mostly ignored her, could never remember her name. The one exception: the film school standout. He'd invited her to his room for pizza to thank her for all her hard work, showed her a new camera he had bought, and convinced her to prance around half naked. He'd told her she didn't know how beautiful she was. She was so flattered—until she found out he had shared the images with his friends. They all had a good laugh. For C.C., it was total humiliation. Did she report the incident? No. She'd traded the studio job for slinging hash in the cafeteria.

Still, her stint in the studios did teach her to parrot industry lingo like a pro. Rockefeller Senior, Johnny D's dad, once said, "I always tried to turn every disaster into an opportunity." That's what she would do at RRP if hired. And she was smart enough to dumb herself down, if that's what it took to get a leg up.

000

Sally Goldman clicked through the résumés flooding her inbox. She needed to find an assistant for Kevin Hansen, RRP's Creative Director. The ideal candidate: an innocent who would be happy to work for long hours and little pay, a girl too dumb to cry harassment every time a predatory producer pinched her ass or a stoned account exec "accidentally" brushed up against her boobs in the hallway.

As VP for Business Affairs, a title that included HR duties,

116

Sally answered to everyone in the executive suite. And where she fell most short of expectations was the job of hiring. She didn't have to do much firing; quitting in tears was more the norm. Whether young women left to join the circus, a convent, or run back to mama, Reality Romance couldn't keep staff. Sally vowed to choose a plain Jane for Kevin this time—less chance of a quiet mouse being hit on and clearing out her desk before she even had a chance to decorate her cube with pictures of cute kitties and the family back home.

The *Journal* article had brought a host of overqualified candidates to Sally's attention. She deleted the polished *curricula vitae* of a slew of desperate MBAs. Next up was a résumé with selfie attached, emailed on a cloying pink background. Who does that? Sally stared at the young woman in a tour guide outfit cradling a scrawny cat. With horrifying hair that made Medusa's writhing mane look good, glasses draped around her neck like Aunt Bea in the old Andy Griffith Show, and a smile that had never seen an orthodontist, Ms. Green was the grown-up version of every middle school lunch table loner. Even her name was goofy. No one would want to hit on Charissa Concordia. Not even Kevin. Not even after three dirty martinis.

Now to convince the horn-dog marketing maven to greenlight this hire.

ꝯꝯꝯ

Kevin entered his 30 Rock office, *Wall Street Journal* in his backpack. He buzzed for coffee, forgetting he had no assistant. Again. Damn. No one was in but Sally. He smiled to himself. That one was a panther in a pantsuit. And a tiger when the pantsuit came off. Too bad they had decided to cool it. Way too much at stake.

He walked into her office, sat down, and slung his cowboy boots onto her desk. He nodded at her copy of the *Journal.* It was open to the second article the newspaper had run on the company this month. *Bloomberg Businessweek, Forbes,* and a host of Internet sites were also covering RRP's rise in the profitable world of schlock TV.

"So what do you think? Are we going to be filthy rich?"

117

"You may have to trade in your backpack for a briefcase and put on a suit and tie once in a while."

He drained Sally's coffee, put down her empty mug, and slithered up behind her. He massaged her shoulders, lifted her hair, and reached over to kiss the back of her neck. Old habits die hard.

"Did you see the *Journal* called me 'the bad boy with good ideas'?" he murmured. "I was the one who leaked RRP's financial growth updates to a 'friend with benefits' at the paper. That's what I call a very good idea."

"You're so modest."

"Of course I am." He rolled his eyes and made a mock retching sound as he peered at the résumé on her screen. "Who or what is that?"

"Your next assistant."

Kevin groaned.

"Come on, I'll behave. You can do better than that."

"She's perfect for you," Sally said. "She's a tour guide, and you're about to become a guide yourself. Jeff wants you to give potential backers the VIP trek around Rock Center. Show them we're a classy outfit in a classy environment."

Kevin made a paper airplane and aimed it at Sally's head.

"Why can't Jeff do it?" he whined.

"Our fearless leader has better things to do," she said, tossing the airplane back at him. "And he wants you, Mr. Charming, to—"

"Charm the pants off them?"

"Pry open their wallets."

ooo

"Mr. Hansen's office. May I help you?" C.C. put on her chipper phone voice.

"Hi, it's Henry. I have a plum assignment for you." The tour office supervisor encouraged C.C. to work on weekends when big shots needed a tour. "You know way more about this place than all the rest of my guides put together. What did you do, memorize the training manual?"

C.C. laughed.

118

"Who needs my enlightenment?"

"There's a VIP tour for your company on the schedule. What's VIP about your sleazy outfit, I ask you? Their shows are awful. My girlfriend watches *Housewives Abducted by Sex-Crazed Aliens*. Garbage.*"*

"I guess we get star treatment because RRP is expanding," C.C. said. "We're taking over a whole floor."

Three months working at soul-crushing RRP, and C.C. actually missed the tourists. But her plan to make enough to repay her student loans—and support the hard-knock-life family that had filled her head with tales of the Rockefellers—was falling into place. All thanks to her smarmy co-workers.

"Gotta go," she said as Kevin strolled over to her desk, yawning.

"Hi, C.C. Sorry, late night. Did I miss anything important?"

Moving in too close behind her, he rubbed her back with one hand as he went through his messages with the other. She tried not to flinch. Even managed to give him a smile.

"I'll answer my emails, then we'll map out what's left of the morning."

C.C. took out her journal, checked her watch, and made a note: *10:45 AM. July 15. Mr. Hansen inappropriately touched me, gave me an unwanted back rub.*

The pages were filling up. She had noted six marks against Kevin for inappropriate behavior and ten for sexist comments he and others made when she took notes in meetings. She even had an ever-growing audio file featuring Jeff Norman, the company president, spewing gems like "look at the ass on that one" and "the tits on the blonde are as fake as her hair color." To the men in the RRP boys' club, C.C. was invisible. Did they also think she was deaf? And dumb?

The unkindest cut: Sally saying to Kevin, "You could always put a paper bag over her head."

C.C. couldn't get that humiliating phrase out of her head. Somehow, another woman joining men in treating her like a piece of meat—or laughing at her—felt like ten times more of a betrayal.

When she came back to work after hours to retrieve her copy of *The Art of War* by Sun Tzu, she heard thrashing and

119

moaning coming from Kevin's office. Something was going on. She crept up to the door and cracked it just enough to see Sally straddling Kevin. *On his desk.* C.C. pressed a button on her eyeglasses, took a photo, and quietly closed the door behind her.

ooo

Thank God tomorrow's Friday, C.C. thought. The company had a summer hours policy wherein lower life forms worked 9 AM to 7 PM Monday through Thursday to merit the half-day TGIF.

She found Sally in her office hanging pictures.

"Anything I can do for you before I go?" she asked.

"I'm giving my executive suite an upgrade," Sally said. "Good artwork. A few throw pillows. Personal touches. I want investors taking meetings here to know I'm a big player. Image is important." She gave C.C. a slow once-over. "Just a little hint."

"Is that how you got your promotions? The right *image*?"

"Plus brains and hard work."

Sally adjusted pictures of herself skiing and sailing, attending an art auction, sharing champagne with her beautiful friends. Juggling a hammer and a tape measure, she handed C.C. an 8x10 photo.

"Hold onto this while I make sure the picture hook is in the right place."

C.C. stared at the picture in her hands. Her head filled with water. Her feet stuck to the floor. Her lungs failed her. She was drowning on dry land.

"Earth to C.C." Sally's voice softened as she reached for the beautifully framed photo. "That's my younger half-brother Jason. Handsome, right? And so talented. Francis Ford Coppola said he showed great promise. But he had no discipline. He always went too far. Too many pranks, especially with girls. I tried to cover for him, but some of his stuff was so funny. He died before graduation. A tragic accident. They said it was an equipment malfunction. He was lighting a set, and he was electrocuted."

She looked at the stricken C.C. clasping the photo.

"Here, give it to me."

She pried the picture from C.C.'s clammy hand.

120

"I know. Awful. He was so beautiful. Even girls he never would have looked at fell in love with him."

ʘʘʘ

Sally, Kevin, and the creative team took Fridays off to work with Jeff Norman at his Hamptons hideaway. No glamorous sojourn for C.C. She was heading via subway and PATH train to Hoboken, NJ, where she transferred to yet another train for the thirty-minute ride to Clifton, followed by a twenty-minute uphill walk in the unbearable July heat to the Little Sisters of Charity nursing home on traffic-clogged Hazel Street.

It was the highlight of her week. And this week she needed a highlight.

"Hello, Dr. Green. Your grandmother is sitting out back in the rose garden."

"Thanks, Sister Grace. How is she doing today? May I take a look at her chart?"

C.C. had never bothered telling the staff she wasn't a *medical* doctor. It kept them on their toes as they looked after her beloved Grannie.

"Still adjusting to life here, but she seems content."

C.C. had moved her grandma from the small upstate New York town of Grantham to this low-budget but well-meaning place after her own mother died. She smiled. Feisty Grannie was rarely described as content by those who knew her well. And the "rose garden" consisted of one scraggly bush near the Dumpster. She guessed nuns, like everyone else, were guilty of the sin of embellishing the truth.

Sister Grace waited for C.C. to finish reading.

"There's just one odd thing."

Here it comes, C.C. thought.

"She insists her last name is Rockefeller."

ʘʘʘ

There would be no Hamptons weekend for Sally either. She went to sleep on Thursday night with a blinding migraine, and the next

121

morning pounding temples and flashing lights behind her eyeballs signaled a tough day ahead. Hours lying in the dark, a few doses of Fiorinal, supplied by one of RRP's pillhead techies, with a chaser of double espresso, and she almost felt normal by Saturday morning. She avoided doctors with the zeal of a Christian Scientist—maybe because her Jewish mother kept trying to marry her off to one—but she had an appointment with a neurologist next week. Kevin and Jeff kept telling her to stop looking up symptoms on the Internet. But what if it wasn't a migraine? What if it was a brain tumor?

Still a bit wobbly, Sally wanted out of her apartment. With nothing to do, no one to see—only losers stayed in the city on a summer weekend—why not go to the office and tie up some loose ends?

More than worry about headaches was troubling her. She walked over to C.C.'s cubicle. For all her polite, naive demeanor, Sally had the feeling the girl was whip smart. She knew the type. After all, Sally herself had started at this very same desk five years ago. She rifled through C.C.'s top drawer. Pens, pencils, herbal tea bags, granola bars. Nothing of interest.

The large bottom drawer to the left of the kneehole opening was locked. She used the master key she had kept when the office furniture was delivered and took a look-see.

Nursing home folders. A genealogy guide, bookmarked to the section labeled "Rockefeller." And a letter from the bursar at Warren Wheatleigh University, addressed to Charissa Concordia Green, PhD, regarding a still-outstanding student housing bill.

Sally stared at the letter. *Doctor* Green? A PhD? WTF? Immersed in the letter, she didn't hear the door open, didn't see C.C., who had come in hoping to ferret out info about the company's finances, lurking behind a giant poster for *Bikini Babes & Bikers: The Naked Truth.*

Sally didn't see C.C.—or the naked hatred in C.C.'s eyes.

000

Early Monday morning, Sally entered Kevin's office with two cups of coffee and no thought of hanky-panky.

"Can you believe she has a PhD?"

"So she likes the Rockefellers," he said. "And she has a doctorate. So what? You have a bad case of degree envy."

"But why take *this* job? I checked. Her doctorate is legitimate."

"And I have a nephew with a PhD who's driving a cab. What does that prove? Besides, wasn't it your job to vet her?"

"If it wasn't for your idiot behavior, I wouldn't have to waste my time trolling for losers. I contacted her last boss, the tour guide wrangler, and he said she was an exemplary employee. How far back am I supposed to investigate just to fill a lousy assistant position?"

"*Doctor* Green does her job, and she hasn't quit yet, so give it a rest. She'll tell us about her PhD if and when she wants to."

Sally couldn't let it rest. Jeff Norman had scheduled another VIP tour, this time with potential investors from Hong Kong. Sally signed on to serve as shepherd and asked the Tour Office to have C.C. serve as guide.

"You don't mind, do you, C.C.?" Sally asked.

"Of course not. When is the group coming, and can you give me a list of who will be attending?"

"Thursday, so you have two days to prepare. But you shouldn't need to prep. I understand you're an expert on the Rockefellers," Sally said sweetly, looking for a reaction. "Why do you need the names?"

"Just being thorough. They like it when you know where they're from and show an interest in them."

Pleading an upset stomach, C.C. left work early. She made a call to her cousin Caleb and took a detour to the tour office before heading home.

"Hello, C.C. What are you doing here?" Henry Longstreet asked. "I'm sorry RRP stole my *numero uno* guide."

"I miss you, too, Henry, but I'll see you in a couple of days. In the meantime, I think I left something in my locker. Can I check?"

"Sure, sure."

She made for the area where the audio tour headphones were stored. She swiped two sets, stuffed them in her tote, and left.

That night C.C. did her homework on three fronts. First, she checked the professions of the VIP attendees on her tour. Not an engineer, computer geek, or medical doctor among them. Good.

Second, she pulled out the family tree Grannie Charissa had created years ago and turned to the entry she had read hundreds of times: *Charissa Concordia Green, unacknowledged half-sister of John D. Rockefeller, Sr.* Didn't that connection, however remote, entitle Grannie, a great-great-niece of America's first billionaire, to at least a tiny piece of the Standard Oil fortune?

Johnny D had never touched alcohol. C.C. poured herself a glass of wine and drank it as she scanned the letter from the lawyer who had taken Grannie's case on a contingency basis. The verdict: "No claim possible" for purported Rockefeller relatives born on the wrong side of the sheets in the nineteenth century. The unsigned letters Grannie cherished from Johnny D's grandfather to C.C.'s great-great-aunt were not sufficient proof. Although an analysis of the paper and ink made the timing correct, they could have been written by anyone.

C.C. had promised Grannie to follow through on the elderly woman's dream until her PhD research led to the discovery that the long-departed Charissa, a seamstress who lived for a time in the same upstate New York town as the Rockefellers, had a profitable sideline servicing a multitude of local farmhands and miners. Her "baby daddy" candidates were legion, a fact C.C. never shared with Grannie.

Time to close the book on Grannie's Don Quixote quest—or should she say delusion? She wiped away tears and finished the bottle of wine. No use crying over broken promises and spilt billions. Still, if C.C. had an ounce of Rockefeller blood in her, she'd strike it rich. Maybe not in oil exploration, but via the oily people she now worked for. She called her pit-bull attorney, who had become wealthy championing lost causes, and they discussed strategy that would work in the here and now.

Next, C.C. knocked on her cousin Caleb's bedroom door. Of course he was in; he rarely left their shared basement flat. An MIT grad, unsung inventor, and hacker extraordinaire who never met a conspiracy theory he didn't embrace, Caleb had been following C.C. like an obedient puppy since they were kids. And he remained silent whenever one of their harebrained schemes imploded. Or worked too well.

C.C. handed him the headphones she had stolen from the tour guide office and the piece of jewelry he had asked for. She had already explained what she needed, and she fell asleep while he tinkered. By 5 AM, he'd thrown out the first headphone set he had tested, was happy with the second version, and woke his cousin.

"Here it is."

He demonstrated how to use the doctored equipment and handed her the remote control.

"Be careful, C.C. This isn't a toy, not like those 'spyglasses' I gave you."

"If they work half as well as the glasses, I'm in business. But I don't want to blow up Rock Center."

"Hey, I'm a microengineering genius, remember? This beauty is just powerful enough to do the job. Too bad I can't get funding for any of my inventions."

"Why don't you go on *Shark Tank*?"

"It's not about the money, cuz."

Yes, it is, C.C. thought. In the end, it's most definitely about the money.

After anxiously examining the headphones, she turned her attention to three nano-fuses scarcely wider than a human hair—the trigger mechanism—that now sat nestled inside an elaborate flea market brooch she would attach to the front of her white shirt. Against the rules to embellish the uniform, but what the hell.

"Don't worry, C.C. I tested this baby on a cantaloupe. There was no exterior disfigurement, so the fruit lived to be eaten another day. Actually, I just ate it, with the cottage cheese you keep in the fridge. Tasty. I hate to waste food."

000

Sally Goldman came early for the tour. She looked as sick as she felt. Henry was alarmed by her appearance.

"Ms Goldman, right? You're here to meet C.C.? Can I get you a cup of coffee or something? We have tea too. Are you

125

feeling OK?"

She clung to the wall for balance.

"Coffee would be great. Black, please."

What the hell am I doing here, Sally wondered. Stupid idea. Another migraine, if that's what it was. What could she learn by following C.C. around?

C.C. handed out audiophones. The tour started. Because part of the excursion was conducted outside in the busy, noisy Plaza area, the group couldn't hear the guide's narration without the headsets. Top of the Rock, the Rainbow Room, Atlas, Radio City Music Hall, NBC's Today Show studios. C.C. shared every possible fact, pontificating at length on the most esoteric construction minutiae as she watched Sally tire and falter.

By the time the long VIP event ended, Sally's group was worried about her. They asked if she was all right, urged her to take a seat on a bench and rest.

No one was more solicitous than the charming, caring, and erudite C.C. Green.

Finally C.C. led her group back toward 30 Rock and asked everyone to focus on her favorite sculpture. As she proclaimed, "Prometheus brought the fire," she gently pressed the fake ruby centerpiece of her brooch.

Sally Goldman clutched her forehead and dropped to the pavement like a stone. C.C., the first to arrive at her side, bent down to help her fallen comrade. In the confusion, she traded Caleb's doctored headphones for a normal set.

After seeing Sally into an ambulance, C.C. tossed the brooch into a restaurant Dumpster, where it was buried amid an avalanche of leftover General Tso's chicken, double cooked pork, and scallion pancakes. She looked at the restaurant's name—Good Fortune. Would Prometheus and his fellow gods find her guilty of hubris for seeing the name as an omen? She entered and ordered takeout for Caleb. The cousins had planned carefully. Nothing left behind. Nothing connected to C.C.

ooo

Sally's death merited a footnote in *The Wall Street Journal.* Rising female executive. An aneurysm: an explosion in the brain. Her problems with headaches, which had grown more severe of late, were known to everyone who cared about her. So was her penchant for self-medicating and refusal to see a doctor.

Following their religious dictates, her Orthodox Jewish family, whose religious faith she had barely acknowledged, refused an autopsy and insisted on immediate burial. Everyone at Reality Romance Productions attended the funeral.

The following Monday, C.C. took her place at Sally Goldman's desk.

Kevin arrived at work looking even worse than usual. He stopped short when he saw her.

"What are you doing?"

"I'm taking Sally's job, of course."

"Who said?"

"I assumed I'd take over. I can do everything Sally did."

Except you, she thought.

"You assumed wrong. Her body's barely cold. Jesus. I think you should pack your bags. I'm calling Jeff Norman."

As soon as Kevin was out of earshot, C.C. placed a call to her attorney.

"Gloria Alfonso, please. Gloria, this is C.C. Green. It's time to make our move."

That afternoon, the techies and sales force, creatives and accountants, still reeling from the death of well-liked Sally Goldman, wondered why lowly C.C. Green was in a meeting with company president Jeff Norman, Kevin Hansen, and a slew of lawyers. Gloria Alfonso's booming voice carried through the conference room door.

"Sexual harassment of this nature is a serious crime, gentlemen. Don't you ever read the newspapers or watch any TV other than your own troglodyte shows? Talk about a hostile work environment. You might understand the magnitude of your problem if you had any female lawyers on retainer. Mr. Norman, I've shared just a few details of what's in Dr. Green's journals. You've been treated to a taste of the shocking audio and video of you good old boys in action. Come on, C.C. Let's go."

That was C.C.'s last day at RRP. Two months later, her massive settlement came through. Her savvy lawyer went after not only RRP, but also the deep-pocketed investors who had bankrolled the company's expansion. C.C. opened RRE, Rocky Road Enterprises, in the former RRP space. Johnny D said: *Every right implies a responsibility—every opportunity an obligation.* So she filled out the ranks with PhDs who couldn't find work in their chosen fields and issued a press release touting their unusual hiring practices. As wily Rockefeller Senior said, "Next to doing the right thing, the most important thing is to let people know you are doing the right thing."

RRE raked in millions creating content for women free of both sexism and treacle. C.C. hired a publicist and a personal stylist, and the transformation led to her new status as a sought-after TV talking head on issues facing women in the workplace. She bought a co-op overlooking Central Park that she shared with Grannie and a lovely aide who had no problem calling the old lady "Mrs. Rockefeller." Cousin Caleb received an allowance, though he elected to stay in his basement apartment. He said NSA listening devices couldn't penetrate the walls.

C.C. still began every day with a cup of coffee from home, standing before the engraved quotes of John D. Rockefeller, Jr. overlooking the Plaza. *It's you and me, Johnny D*, she whispered, lifting her coffee in a toast to her unlikely hero. Her gaze traveled past Prometheus and up to the thirty-fifth floor of 30 Rock, to the windows of her office suite, where she kept a photo of Grannie and Caleb in a silver frame hiding the photo of Sally's half-brother Jason, the promising SUNY theater student, which she had stolen from Sally's office. Too bad about that lighting accident.

Her own set of sayings from Johnny D and his billionaire father were inked in gold leaf inside her now beautifully bound PhD thesis. Her very favorite came not from her beloved Johnny D but from his father, John D. Rockefeller, Senior: "The way to make money is to buy when blood is running in the streets."

Ronnie Sue Ebenstein is the co-author of three beauty books, including a #1 *New York Times* bestseller. In her past life she scripted public service announcements and short films extolling the virtues of household products and enjoyed ten years as creative director for a major cosmetics company. While serving as assistant Beauty Editor at *Cosmopolitan* during the reign of the legendary Helen Gurley Brown, she wrote features for *Cosmo* on topics ranging from snagging a man to setting up an aquarium, and her byline has also appeared in magazines as diverse as *Family Circle* and *Penthouse Letters*. A member of Sisters In Crime, Mystery Writers of America, the Authors Guild, and the National Arts Club, Ronnie Sue's hobby is devising ingenious ways to murder her noisy neighbors and other Manhattan miscreants.

LEGENDS OF BROOKLYN

TRISS STEIN

I wonder if Parisians stop noticing the Eiffel Tower and Romans the Coliseum? Do long-time DC residents look up at the Washington Monument each time they pass it? Probably not. I work near the Brooklyn Bridge, but I don't think about it or even notice it every day. It takes an event to make me stop and see, again, its beauty and grace and to remember, again, its history.

The most recent event was an announcement at the Brooklyn History Museum, where I work, that the 150th anniversary of the groundbreaking for the bridge was coming up soon. Not as significant as the date of completion, fourteen long years later, but we would have an exhibit to mark it and a number of events. They would need lots of planning. Preliminary research was one of my assignments. I would spend the next weeks digging up depictions of the bridge in legend, art, and literature. Not everyone's idea of fun, but it was mine.

I could have started in our extensive library, but instead, I went for a walk.

There it was, that soaring arc of stone and steel, thrown out across the water like a rainbow. It's not the magic it seems, though. Men died in its construction. When it opened, people were so nervous about whether it would hold that elephants were borrowed from the circus and paraded across to prove it was safe. Now crowds of people walk across it daily, marveling at the vastness of the river, the harbor, and the sky.

Back in our library, I tackled our massive collection of files.

Numerous visual artists could not resist that grand span and those pointed Gothic arches. Eisenstadt. Stella. Georgia O'Keefe, who painted the bridge long before she painted giant flowers.

There was great writing too. Hart Crane's "The Bridge." Walt Whitman, Brooklyn's most famous poet, wrote "Crossing Brooklyn Ferry" before the bridge was built. It's a ferry crossing, not a bridge crossing, but I would sneak it in somehow. Perhaps his words could be labeled as a prophecy of the bridge to come? I spent days searching out the best of the best. Some were famous, some were well known only to specialists.

Late in the afternoon, just before I wearily stacked up the file folders on my desk, I found a clipping from the lamented *Brooklyn Eagle*, the borough's own newspaper for more than a hundred years. It was a poem, "From My Window," an ode to the bridge by one Karl Muller, and it took me right back to my school days. I knew it well. It had been a poster in many classrooms and recited at many assemblies. The clipping in my hand was noted as "first publication." Reading it for the first time in decades, I saw that its jazzy, syncopated rhythm and delicate images mirrored the bridge itself with its delicate designs in indestructible steel.

I couldn't find a thing about the poet. How strange that was. It seemed that Karl Muller had not existed. We had no files on him. He was not in any reference work. He did not seem to have published anything else. I spent a lot of time I really didn't have. His name turned up just once, online, in a letter from a minor inhabitant of a famous Brooklyn Heights house.

That house on Middagh Street had once held the most unlikely collection of talent under one roof in Brooklyn. Or anywhere. Ever. W.H. Auden, Carson McCullers, Benjamin Britten, and Gypsy Rose Lee, of all people. Quite a few other famous and obscure people passed through, including Richard Wright, Paul and Jane Bowles, and Erika Mann, along with various longtime lovers, one-night stands, and sailors from the nearby Navy Yard. To say that the inhabitants enjoyed a freewheeling lifestyle would be an understatement. The house, only a few blocks from where I sat, disappeared long ago in the construction of the Brooklyn-Queens Expressway, but in photos I could see the bridge soaring above the vanished building.

In a letter from one of the obscure inhabitants, I found, "We have a new housemate named Karl Muller, who lives in the attic and cleans for his rent. Our own Cinderella! He's a delightful fresh young Iowa farm kid who rode the rails all the way to New York. George brought him home from the magazine one day. Poor little dear, he wants to be a writer. But can he clean! Wystan is thrilled to have a proper, tidy home at last."

George would be George Davis, who had leased the house. He was the fiction editor of *Harper's Bazaar* and published McCullers and many other friends. Wystan, of course, was W.H. Auden, who tried hard to impose familial order on his unruly housemates. A copy of that page went with the poem into the file for Sharon, the curator and my boss. But I continued to wonder about young Karl, the aspiring writer who had vanished from the records.

I hadn't taken my research beyond scrawling notes on a pad when my boss called me into her office.

"Mr. Parker," Sharon said, "this is Erica, one of our researchers. Please tell her what you just told me."

Mr. Parker was elderly and dressed in shabby but once elegant clothes. When I glanced at the Ivy League ring on his hand, he seemed to shrink into his ancient, fraying winter coat.

"I read that you are doing an exhibit about the bridge," he said, "and I may have something for you. I found it in a carton from an old family business. I wondered if it could possibly be of value." He seemed unable to look at us as he said, "The truth is, I need the money."

With shaky hands, he drew from his pocket a single sheet of notebook paper scrawled over in pencil. It was my Brooklyn Bridge poem, "From My Window." Small edits and comments in the margin were written in two different hands and two different shades of ink. One set was signed "W.H.A." The other was "Carson." On the whole, both had liked the poem.

I stopped breathing. I'm sure I did.

Sharon's face was turning an excited pink as she said carefully, "Please tell us how this came to be yours. Do you know what it is?"

"I have a pretty good idea," he said. "My grandfather managed properties in Brooklyn Heights. When he died, as much as I can piece it together, his children put his business records into storage. I remember my father and uncles dealing with it, but it looks like this carton kind of got lost. The company found it recently, doing some clearing out, and contacted me." His smile was sad. "I'm the only family member still around. The contents are mostly garbage but for this. I can guess who they were, the people who wrote on it, so it looked like, well, like something. What do you think?"

Like something? I'll say. This is the kind of discovery historians dream about. A first printing Declaration of Independence hidden behind a worthless painting in an old frame. The rare early Native American blanket folded up at the bottom of a box on the back porch. The Civil War letters found by a thrift shop worker in a box of donated household items. All right. Maybe it was not quite in that category, but it was both valuable and of historical interest, and not just to me. Or it might be.

"We'll have to have it authenticated before we can tell you anything," Sharon was saying. "You'll have to leave it with us. Locked up, of course." She took a deep breath. "We would love to own it, but we would also have to do some work to find a way to buy it from you." She smiled sweetly. "I don't suppose you'd be interested in donating it? We are certainly the place where it belongs, and there could be great tax advantages for you."

"A generation ago, maybe, but there's no tax benefit to a man with not much income." He shrugged. "Ironic, isn't it, that all the family real estate investments were unloaded as Brooklyn went downhill? They'd be worth a fortune now, but there's nothing left."

My sympathies were limited. Being a product of blue collar Brooklyn myself, I was pretty sure that when his family was living in posh Brooklyn Heights and sending its children to Princeton, my forebears were underground, working for the subway system and lucky to have the job.

"Have you shown this to anyone else?" A sharp question from Sharon that I would not have thought to ask.

"There are other people interested, yes. Private collectors. I would be happy to see it here, given the long family history in Brooklyn Heights, but I can't afford to give it as a gift, and I can't make you any promises."

"Nor can we. But do give us a little time." She smiled again.

When we asked for his address, he gave us a PO box, explaining that where he lived, mail was not secure. And he said he had no phone; he used a nearby pay phone.

133

As soon as he was out the door, Sharon was planning a special event around the find. It would be great publicity for the anniversary. In the next weeks, we had experts in and out, handwriting people and materials science people. Did the signatures match authentic letters? Could the paper be tested for age without destroying the whole page? And if it all came out as Mr. Parker said, could the museum raise the money to buy it? What would it be worth, at, say, an auction of valuable signed documents? The director of development began approaching our best supporters about a special gift.

Then one day I went over to Brooklyn's huge central post office to return an ill-judged late-night purchase I could not afford. Without thinking, I started to say hello to someone I recognized as he pushed through the lunchtime crowds. But he walked right past me. Where did I know him from? My daughter's school? Work? Had I seen him give a lecture somewhere? An actor I'd only seen on television, causing me to confuse real life and show business?

I didn't realize until I was on the way home that it had been Parker, the man with the poem. He'd said he used a post office box for his mail. But how could that be the same man? The man at the museum had been elderly and timid. Beaten down. His clothes had been neat, but they'd been gentlemen's business clothes, however ancient and faded. This man had shoved through the crowds aggressively, without even an "Excuse me." And he'd worn a spiffy leather jacket and jeans. Of course the midday post office lines could turn anyone into an aggressor. But something was not right.

I had no one to give me advice, because Sharon was out on unplanned medical leave. No one else at work had even met this man. Back at the museum, I shoved the rest of my work aside and pulled out his file. In our search for proof of provenance, we had requested a receipt from the storage company. I made a copy of the receipt to take over there.

It was close enough to walk, down under the approach to the expressway, a shabby old brick building with no signs of renovation in this gentrifying neighborhood. I smelled dust and mold as soon as I entered. When the young receptionist finally understood what I was asking, she shouted into the back. A muscular, balding middle-aged man appeared. He demanded to know my business there.

I summoned some Brooklyn attitude to give back to him.

"We have this receipt in our files." I stabbed at the line with my finger. "Do you know the guy who signed off on it?"

He squinted at the paper.

"Hell, no. That's not even our form. Not my signature either, here, and I sign them all."

It took me a few seconds to make my voice work.

"Could you please say that again?"

"Yeah, and then I get back to work. That. Is. Not. Our. Receipt. Susie can show you one of ours before you leave."

He disappeared into the back again, but Susie had a pad of forms to show me. When I asked to take one with me, she said, "No problem. We don't hardly even use them, ya know. We mostly do it all on computer."

The business name matched, and the format looked the same, but the typeface was all wrong. I asked how long they'd been using this form.

"Forever," she said. "I been here four years but we have old ones going back and back. Half a century, maybe."

That was not what I had expected. I'd come in expecting someone to say, "Sure, I remember that 'cause we were clearing old junk. It was an old guy, skinny. We gave him his family's misplaced carton."

I walked back with a massive headache, pondering what made no sense. In fact, I felt sick to my stomach. Sharon was too ill to be bothered with this problem, at least until I was sure it was as bad as it looked. Something was very wrong here, and I felt responsible. I'd been there at the beginning.

If Parker had no mailing address, he must check his post office box often. And I'd seen him there at lunchtime. I had to do something. I waited at the post office for four uncomfortable and boring lunchtimes, when it was most crowded and noisy and filled with grumpy, impatient people. I had to find a corner near the rental boxes and actually stay alert the whole time. Did I know what I'd do if I saw him? Nope.

By the fourth day, I was thinking it had been a bad idea. He probably varied his pickup time. I'd give it one more day. On the fifth day, I saw him. He removed some envelopes from a PO box, locked the box, and turned to leave. This time, I got a better look. Oh, yes, it was Mr. Parker, looking disturbingly energetic and dapper.

I followed him through busy, crowded streets. No reason I should not be there or he should object. The challenge was to keep up with his brisk movement through the crowds. I thought I'd lost him when he went into one of the nicer apartment buildings nearby. I was close enough to hear the doorman say, "Here's a package for you," and to greet him by name. And the name wasn't Parker. My heart was beating very fast as I walked away. The doorman was not likely to tell me anything about a resident, and I did not have a way to trick him into it.

In the end, I didn't have to. My quarry found me.

He bumped into me as if by accident when I was leaving work. It was courtly, shabby Mr. Parker. He gallantly offered to walk me to the subway. I was glad to accept. It was my opportunity at last. As we crossed a busy street, he put a hand on my arm for guidance. And then his hand became much tighter, painfully tighter.

"What are you doing?" I squeaked.

He twisted me around to face him. The street was crowded with a river of workers from the nearby courthouses hurrying home. Not one person noticed.

"What do you think *you* are doing? I saw you follow me to an apartment building. What the hell?"

The polite elderly man had transformed into a bully.

"Isn't it your building?" I tried to sound puzzled rather than intimidated. "The doorman knew you. He gave you a package. And I know that warehouse receipt is a fake."

"Not your business, Nancy Drew."

His grip on my arm hurt, and I could not pull away.

"If that poem is a fake, it is certainly my business."

"You only know George Parker, not me. If you keep quiet, everyone wins. Museum looks good. You look good."

"No! We all look like crooks."

I finally jerked my arm from his grip and tried to punch

him. At that, he pushed me hard, wheeled, and forced his way away through the sidewalk crowds. I was shaking but angry, scared but safe.

First thing the next morning, I told our security director the whole story. He was not happy. He told me all the reasons I should have come to him sooner.

"Looks like a con to me. No phone in this day and age? And you believed that? Yeah, right!"

So it went to the police. The discreet fundraising stopped just in time to prevent major embarrassment. Later, the expert reports came in, indicating the paper and ink were right but there were some questions regarding the handwritten comments.

Mr. Parker vanished. He walked away from the nice sublet apartment he had rented under the name of Hogarth, gone without a trace under both names.

I felt stupid but relieved that it had stopped there. As Sharon said, making a big event out of a fake document would have been a disaster. I redeemed myself in career terms by finally finding the missing poet. Karl Muller, at least, was a real person. A diligent search of Iowa records and the US Census turned him up in the obvious place, his hometown, where he had married and lived for many decades. In time, we found a great-nephew who remembered him fondly. Sadly for us, he had no samples of Karl's handwriting, so we could not determine if the handwritten poem Parker had given us was a forgery or the real deal. But he was able to complete the story.

Young Karl had been diagnosed with tuberculosis in New York and went back home to die. Only he didn't die. When he was still around after a few years, he got up off his deathbed, stopped talking about Whitman and Auden, and married a childhood friend. He took up farming and never published another poem.

Was he happy? Sad? Did he miss writing? Did he miss New York? Or did thinking he would die young make him question all his early choices? That, we never learned, and I still wonder.

Of course I also wonder about Parker, or whatever his real name is. Who the hell was he? A swindler, certainly, and a forger, possibly. But why? He knew enough about the literary history of the time and place to create a convincing con. Why not use that productively? Could this kind of scam be that lucrative? In the odd procrastinating moment, I search the Internet for stories about similar swindles. hoping to find him again. So far, I haven't, but I keep looking. He's the only con man I've ever met personally. And this is Brooklyn, after all, where con men are legendary for selling a whole bridge. Repeatedly.

This new swindle will never be public, but the famous old one? It will be part of our exhibit. You can bet the Brooklyn Bridge on it.

Triss Stein is a small-town girl from New York State's dairy country who has spent most of her adult life living and working in New York City. This gives her the useful double vision of a stranger and a resident for writing mysteries about Brooklyn, her ever-fascinating, ever-changing, ever-challenging adopted home. She is inspired by its varied neighborhoods and their rich histories, and her urban historian heroine, Erica Donato, has reasons to ask questions all over her native borough. In the 2017 book, *Brooklyn Wars*, she witnesses a murder at the famous Brooklyn Navy Yard and finds herself drawn deep into the story of the Yard's proud history, slow death, and current revival.

WILDLIFE IN NEW YORK CITY

FRAN BANNIGAN COX

The bad feeling I wake up with in my stomach every morning was no different on Thursday.

I stopped at my mother's bedroom, cracked the door. There was an unfamiliar male face on the pillow next to hers. I backed away. Whatever.

In the kitchen my twin sister, Lily, munched a bagel. I washed down takeout dumplings with a cup of last night's cold coffee.

"Come on, Lily. Let's get out of here before Mom's new what's-his-name invades the kitchen." I stuffed six granola bars in my backpack. "Ready?"

"I'm not going, Maggie. I'm wiped out from bad dreams."

I came up behind her and swept her strawberry blonde hair off her neck. Careful not to pull her hair, I made a long flat braid. My own hair is brown and curly. Even though we're twins, Lily and I don't look anything alike. I suspect we're the result of some crazy IVF experiment my parents tried along with rolfing, juice fasts, and LSD.

"Baby girl, you can't stay in junior year forever. Teshawn is waiting for us in the park."

Lily is lucky her friend Teshawn wants to help her write her paper. He's a whiz kid with five colleges trolling for him and a Black Community Scholarship.

"I don't care about the paper," she said.

"You will if you have to live with Dad and go to school in the sticks."

That got her moving.

I buttoned my jeans jacket over my old binoculars. I pressed Lily to take a pair of easier lightweight binoculars.

"You'll need them to spot the wildlife in the park. Then you'll have something to write about."

I wished I didn't have to mother her. I'm only eight minutes older than her, and I have a hard enough time getting my own life going. But I love her to pieces.

She groaned.

"Why can't I just write about something that lives in our apartment? Like, you know, wildlife in the Central Park Apartments."

"Get real, sweetheart."

"We could buy some goldfish and I could watch them, maybe feed them too much and watch what happens when they die."

She looked hopeful as she pulled at the ribbons on her peasant blouse. We've never dressed alike. She's all girly, and I dress practical. And I've never been a procrastinator.

"Lily, Teshawn is going to a lot of trouble for you. He's got a crush on you."

"I'm too young for him," she said, grumpy.

"Right! Eight months difference makes him an older man."

"Morning, Miss Maggie and Miss Lily Two Steps Behind. Can I get you a cab?" Mr. McCarthy, my favorite doorman, held the door open with his shaky hand. "You're up early."

"We're going birding in the park," I said.

"How many times I gotta tell ya? The park's no place for girls until it's crowded. Safety in numbers."

"We're meeting some other kids. We'll be fine," I assured him.

"Well, okay," he said, with a quick grin. "I'm just sayin'."

I slipped him a couple of bucks.

"If we aren't back by midnight, call the cops."

"Sure thing, Cinderella."

I loved Mr. McCarthy, my rent-a-parent.

My mother never worries about us. She says worry is a negative energy. I left her a note we were with Teshawn. In her eyes, he can do no wrong.

"Why aren't you more like him?" she's asked me a hundred times.

"He's a boy, Mom," I've told her. "You and Dad made girls. Why didn't you just abort me and Lily and tinker with new eggs until you got a boy?"

Teshawn waved when he saw us coming along Central

Park West. He had cow eyes for Lily but barely said hello to her. He's so shy.

She didn't notice. I nudged her. She can't turn Teshawn off, because then I'd have to write her papers and get her into senior year.

She waved to him, a small wave with no energy behind it.

"The birds won't wait," Teshawn said, adjusting his explorer's vest. It had at least twelve pockets that his mother had stuffed with sandwiches and trail mix. "You two need a snack?"

He offered Lily a doughnut, gazing at her hopefully through thick navy blue glasses he's lost without.

"Okay. Thanks."

A smile lit Teshawn's handsome face. He's a little heavy but not fat. I've reminded Lily he's waiting to hear from Harvard.

"Okay, then," he said. "Follow me."

I looked back to see my sister trailing behind us.

"Dammit! You're wearing flip-flops. We're going into the woods. What were you thinking?"

I took her arm, trying not to pull.

"Sorry," she said.

At West 72nd Street he led us into the Ramble, thirty-eight acres next to the Belvedere Lake in Central Park, right smack in the middle of New York City. In the spring, birdwatchers come to the Ramble from all over the country. With four kinds of habitat, the Ramble attracts many kinds of migratory birds: waterfowl, birds that perch in the tree canopy, birds that forage on the ground, and raptors and owls.

We passed the Marionette Theatre and came to the small curved iron bridge that leads over a tributary of the Belvedere Lake into the rocky entrance to the Ramble.

"There!" Teshawn lifted his glasses to his eyes. "Look across the promontory. Those crows are mobbing."

I looked through my binoculars.

"Look at the big pine," he directed. "Go to four o'clock on the trunk. There's an owl. The crows don't like owls anywhere near their nests."

I saw twelve black crows dive-bombing the owl.

"See that, Lily?"

"I can't get these to work." She was fiddling with the focus. "Here, take mine."

Teshawn gently pulled her in front of him and helped her site the glasses.

I re-focused hers.

Lily screamed. She fell backwards into Teshawn, who lost his balance and grabbed for a tree.

"Lily, what's going on?"

She dropped Teshawn's glasses in the leaf litter. Her teeth chattered, and she stared, pointing toward the pine.

Deep in high grass, just fifty yards away, a man's head and upper body appeared as he confronted a dark-haired woman. He held a knife aloft. As I watched, he plunged it down into the woman's chest. The woman screamed. I looked at the others. We all heard it.

"OMG! Did he kill her?" Lily broke away, running toward the man with the knife. "No! No! Stop!" she shouted.

I grabbed at her arm.

"He'll kill us."

She stumbled and fell.

"OMG. My ankle. I can't stand."

"Get down," Teshawn said in a hushed voice. "Damn. We can't let him see us. We have to get out of here."

"I can't leave Lily," I whispered.

She scooted behind a rock, using her hands and her butt, and I tucked leaf litter around her so she was invisible.

"Please, don't dare move, Lily," I said. "We'll get out of this."

"If we're lucky," Teshawn whispered, "that creep thinks there's only one of us."

"You go back across the bridge," I told him. "Call the cops. You'll have to lead them to that poor woman, if she's still alive. I'll take care of my sister."

He took off, crouching low.

I crawled about twenty feet away from Lily before I stood up. The guy was still on the promontory, searching for the person who had screamed. I knew it was crazy, but I had to keep him away from Lily. I waved my arms to attract his attention. When I

142

was sure he'd spotted me, I brought my glasses up and looked back. His face was red. He had dirty blond dreadlocks and a silver front tooth. My glasses are the best, able to magnify even the color of a beak. They didn't fail me now.

He raised his finger and swept it across his neck like he was telling me he planned to cut my throat. He started toward me.

I froze. Then I ran as fast as I could away from where Lily was hiding toward the rocks lining the path to the bridge. I felt like one of those mother birds that leads the fox away from her chicks. Once I got past the rocks, he couldn't see me. I couldn't see him either. But I could hear him crashing through the trees, slapping trunks as he passed. He'd be on me in no time.

I jumped down into the muddy bank at the base of the bridge. A black-crowned night heron fluttered up from the shallows. I must have frightened it. Under the bridge, I crawled behind a clump of sedge grass. Pulling my hoodie up to hide my face, I pressed my body into the bank. It smelled of rotten weeds and duck poop. I hoped the heron wouldn't give me away.

Boots landed on the bridge above me. The slasher stomped around looking for me. The startled heron was still fluttering around. He leaned over the bridge to see what had disturbed it. I held my breath.

A siren sounded in the distance. I prayed it was the police on the way to the Ramble.

The police car screeched to a halt at the entrance to the bridge. I heard Teshawn hailing them. The slasher was trapped. His boots landed in the mud near me, splashing my arm. His vest was covered with mud. I watched from behind my leaf cover as he slogged over to the strut of the bridge opposite me. He tucked himself into the metal corner where the strut met the walkway. If I hadn't seen him do it, I'd never have spotted him. He held his knife down by his trouser leg.

Now I had to make sure he didn't spot me. The last thing I wanted was to be a hostage. I could hear Teshawn yelling at the police to follow him.

"Stop!" the cop shouted. "Get down on the ground," he ordered Teshawn.

"Not me," Teshawn yelled. "Over there. The guy has a

knife. He killed a lady."

I was amazed to see the slasher shove his knife into the mud and climb up from under the bridge.

"Officer," he yelled. "That boy attacked me."

He must have pointed to Teshawn. OMG. Could he get away with blaming the murder on Teshawn? Who would the cop believe—black kid in a hoodie or a white guy? I couldn't let that happen. I pulled myself out of the muddy bank with the help of a bush and climbed up to the bridge.

"Officer. Over here."

It seemed to me the policeman didn't know where to point his gun.

"Nobody move," he said.

His partner, crouching low, gun extended, came to the end of the bridge.

"Hands in the air. What happened here?"

"That guy," I told him, indicating the slasher, "killed a woman in the woods. I saw him do it."

"Don't listen to her, sir," the slasher said. "I admit this is a pot deal gone bad, but she and her boyfriend nearly killed me. Those two are dangerous."

"Oh, yeah?" I said. "I don't even have a weapon. And I don't and never did have any pot. He," I jerked my chin toward Teshawn, "doesn't either. He's my friend. Anyway, why would that guy admit to dealing pot? He must have something worse to hide."

Both officers tried to watch all three of us at once.

"I know where he hid the knife he used to kill the woman," I said. "Under the bridge."

"The bitch is lying."

I thought the slasher looked scared.

"I'm telling the truth," he yelled.

Another police siren wailed in the distance.

"Keep your hands up. Move forward. All of you," the cop instructed. "You first, young lady."

"Maggie," Lily called.

She emerged, limping onto the path between the rocks, supporting the dark-haired woman we'd seen stabbed. The woman staggered but managed to lift her arm, pointing to the slasher. Blood dripped from her fingertips.

"He did it. He hurt me," she said.

Then she collapsed against Lily, who staggered under her weight.

The slasher turned, alarm in his eyes. He rushed past me, elbowing me against the iron bridge rail. I saw the rage in his eyes—one blue and the other brown.

I grabbed at his vest. I had the satisfaction of dislodging his water bottle and a birding book. But I didn't stop him.

He ran straight at Lily, ignoring the cops, who were yelling for him to stop. He shoved her out of the way and pushed the woman she was supporting against the rocks. Her head made a cracking sound like an egg being broken for an omelet. She crumpled to the ground. A shot hit the rocks just above the slasher's head, and sparks flew into the air. The slasher disappeared into the Ramble.

One cop ran past me after him.

The other cop rushed over to the injured woman. He called for backup and an ambulance. Then he helped me lift Lily.

Lily clutched her ankle.

"Maggie, go look. Tell me that poor woman is okay."

I didn't want to alarm Lily. But the woman was bleeding a lot. Her eyes were closed. She was deathly white and gasping.

"You really helped her, Lily," I said.

A cop car and an ambulance arrived with sirens blaring.

The EMT workers looked grim as they administered shots and hooked up IVs. The spot by the rocks was so tricky that it took them awhile to move the woman onto a gurney and into the ambulance. She remained unconscious.

Teshawn, Lily, and I drank bottled water the EMT crew had given us as we answered the plainclothes detectives' questions. The older one, Detective Sergeant Sellers, told us he was in charge of the investigation.

"The Ramble's not safe this early in the morning," he said.

"Sir, early is when the birds feed," Teshawn said.

"Yeah? Well, sonny, you caught yourself a great wacko bird. They're known to kill and eat kids."

145

He patted his gun.

The second ambulance arrived.

"We'd like to get going now," I said. "My sister's ankle needs to be looked at."

The EMTs slammed the doors of the ambulance shut behind us.

"Hey, can I write my biology paper on what just happened?"

"Not a chance," I told her.

We had to wait a long time in the ER. Lily's ankle wasn't as important as a heart attack and a gang shooting.

Teshawn and I used the time to search the Internet for information about Lester Holbrook. I'd made a note of the name in the birding book I'd shaken loose on the bridge before I'd handed it over to the cops.

"Maggie, my ankle hurts a lot."

"I'll see what I can do, Lily."

I spotted one of the EMT guys from our ambulance. He was on a break. I asked him how soon they'd take Lily. He told me the gunshot wounds came first.

"I'll see what I can do for your sister," he said, patting my arm.

I took a chance.

"What about the woman who got stabbed?"

"Unconscious. But don't say I told you."

We found Lester Holbrook's Facebook page, but there was no photo. We also learned he was running for president of a club called the Avian Society of Manhattan that had just received a large financial grant to study endangered bird populations in the city. He was scheduled to give a lecture tomorrow on identifying birdsong. In case he hadn't figured it out for himself, we left a message for Detective Sergeant Sellers, who'd given us his number.

We left the hospital relieved that Lily's x-ray revealed no broken bones. She had a badly sprained ankle. They bound it with an Ace bandage and gave her Tylenol for the pain.

When we got back to the apartment, we found fifty dollars on the kitchen counter with a note.

Go to the Café Buddha on Broadway. They have a new vegan platter that will be good for you, dears. Love Mater.

I settled Lily on the couch with enough Tylenol to make her smile and ask for something to eat. I put the channel changer near her. I know she loves to channel surf.

"Rest up, baby girl. You were great today."

Teshawn and I went to our favorite pizza place on Columbus Avenue. We promised Lily some ice cream.

The next morning, my usual anxiety was eased by a mourning dove's soft coo drifting in through the open window. Cool May sunshine brushed the bird's soft grey feathers. A loud rush of wings slammed into the dove as a red-tailed hawk grabbed her in its claws and lifted her off her perch on the fire escape. An explosion of feathers burst into the air and floated untethered down to the street below. I wondered if the slasher would attack us if we went to confront him.

Later, when I met Teshawn on the corner of West 79th Street and Central Park West, I asked if he thought we should be scared.

"You want to catch him, don't you?" He looked around. "Where's Lily?"

I told him she was afraid to come.

"She's been having nightmares about the slasher."

"No. No. That's not right. I'll go get her," he said to my frowning face. "It's not fair for her to miss catching the guy. Besides, catching him will stop her nightmares."

"We're not sure it's him," I shouted.

But he was already hailing a cab.

I took the elevator to the basement of the Museum of Natural History, where the Avian Society lecture was taking place in a room set aside for community events.

The guard directed me to a corridor lined with a display of community pottery on pedestals, to the left of the elevator bank. I slipped into a darkened room and found an empty folding chair in the last row, to the right of the bald guy who was working the slide machine.

"This is the last one, folks," the bald guy said. He made a long low-pitched gurgling sound. "The call of the American bittern."

Someone in the audience whistled in appreciation.

Everyone clapped, and the lights came up. The moderator asked Mr. Holbrook to come forward to answer audience questions.

He was staring at me from behind the slide machine. Was he the slasher or wasn't he? He was bald, but one eye was blue and the other was brown. It was him. He must have shaved his dreads.

As I stood up, he jumped back, eyes darting around.

"Mr. Holbrook, I saw you in the Ramble," I said.

"The hell you did," he said.

He ran toward the exit behind him.

I ran after him.

Holbrook grabbed a hefty pot from the corridor display. He threw it at my head.

I ducked and ducked again as he threw two more. When I looked again I didn't see him. Then I felt his arm around my neck and saw the glint of light on the blade in his other hand. His hot onion breath brushed my neck.

"Drop it," the guard yelled from the other end of the corridor.

The slasher dragged me backwards, bumping into a pottery stand and sending another pot crashing to the floor.

I kept up as best I could, my heart pounding and my feet slipping as we moved backwards.

He headed for the doorway to the elevator bank. Suddenly he crashed backward, dragging me on top of him.

I heard the knife clatter away.

Teshawn and Lily leaped from the doorway onto his arms. I rolled off him and jumped on his legs. We held him down.

"You two," I said. "You're amazing."

Lily and Teshawn had hidden on either side of the doorway to the elevator bank and tripped Holbrook when he backed through. Lily had used her crutch.

"The woman you stabbed talked," I told him, lying for a good cause.

"I planned to return the money to the club treasury," he whined. "She wouldn't listen. She wants to ruin me so she can get

148

the presidency for herself. Damn her."

The elevator doors slid open. Sergeant Sellers stepped out.

"Get off him. I've got this."

More cops arrived, slamming the stairwell door open.

They gathered around the slasher like crows mobbing an owl. They got him to his feet, cuffing his arms behind his back.

As we watched them get into the elevator, Lily pointed her crutch at the slasher.

"Maybe my paper should be titled, 'Predators, Human and Animal,'" she said.

"Lily, you have the courage of a lion," I said, hugging her.

"You too, Teshawn," she said, reaching for his hand. "I wish I could write about this."

Fran Bannigan Cox is a visual artist and writer. She holds an MA from Hunter College in New York. Her art work has been exhibited in one person and group shows in New York, Boston, and other major cities. Fran Cox is the co-author of *A Conscious Life*, published by Conari Press in Berkeley, California. Her short stories have been published in the anthologies *Murder New York Style* and *Fresh Slices* as well as the e-zine *Mysterical-E.* She holds a five hundred hour teaching certification from The Yoga Alliance. Yoga keeps it all together.

MURDER IN CONEY ISLAND

STEPHANIE WILSON-FLAHERTY

So it was one of those sultry, humid, breathe-through-a-damp-washcloth kind of days in Brooklyn when I was hanging out at my kitchen table loading donated pencil cases, crayons, and other school supplies into brand new backpacks for needy kids. And since it was already August, I knew I was behind schedule. Then my kitchen wall phone rang. Okay, okay, don't say anything. Believe me, I know I'm a dinosaur.

I grabbed the receiver, wondering who would call in the middle of a Friday.

"Yo, Aunt Sadie. It's me."

"Jayden," I said, surprised. "Is anything wrong?"

Although I'm not really Jayden's aunt, I am the closest thing he has to a responsible relative since his grandmother died. He had a rough childhood in spite of all my friend Lorraine's love and care. I promised her I would see her grandson graduate from college and do my best to keep him out of gangs if I could. He'd been going to Kingsborough Community College for a while now, and I remained hopeful that Lorraine's wishes would come true.

"Is everything all right at school? You're not working too many hours, are you?"

"Everything is fine at school, and I only work enough hours to get by." He sounded slightly exasperated with me. "I don't forget how important school is. And I never forget what you and Grams have done for me." He took a deep breath. "I was just wondering when you planned to come and see me, that's all."

Hmm. Never had children of my own, but I've had plenty of experience with them in my life. When he was little, he eagerly called me up all the time to find out when I'd come to visit. But he'd been mostly making his own way since he'd turned fourteen. Right now, he was reminding me of my nephew when he was ten and only called my sister "Mommy" when he was sick.

So I knew what to do.

"Funny you should ask about that, because I was just

thinking that a trip to Coney Island would be a great idea in this weather. I was going to call you tonight to suggest a visit tomorrow. As a matter of fact, I was just putting together a little care package for you right here on my kitchen table." I can fib with the best.

"Okay, then." He sounded relieved. "How's noonish?"

"Sold," I said.

I bundled the school supplies off my kitchen table into a couple of boxes to deal with later. I had a higher priority at the moment. It was time to crank up the air conditioning and sit down to make a list of what I could bring Jayden. Number one item? Plenty of homemade chicken soup. Not that I make it myself. I do very little in the kitchen except use the table for my projects, but I know who makes the best in the borough.

I packed a small rolling suitcase with my care package for Jayden, better than lugging shopping bags to the subway in Bay Ridge. I boarded the train to Coney Island and then scooted a few more blocks to Jayden's apartment, if you can call dragging a suitcase filled with chicken soup and other treats scooting. I gave him a big hug at the door, quite the exercise in agility for both of us, as he is way over six foot tall and I am, ahem, considerably shorter. Then we retreated to the kitchen, where I set my rolling suitcase on a chair and proceeded to unpack my goodies.

"So, Jayden, what's wrong?" I handed him a six-pack of athletic socks and a package of T-shirts, extra long. I believe in giving out the practical as well as the delicious. "I know something's up. We both know you don't call me up for a visit much anymore."

Then I waited.

He looked uncomfortable.

"I'm not sure what to say, Aunt Sadie. I'm not sure how wise it is to involve you."

Okay, this was not going to be about a bad grade in one of his classes. This was going to be serious. Time for me to get serious too.

"Jayden, remember how I always brought you goodies when you were young? Pounds of licorice sticks and gigantic containers of chicken soup? Remember how much your

151

grandmother loved that I brought you the soup but hated all that sugar? Well. I bribed you then to get what I wanted, and I'll bribe you now, if it'll get you to talk to me." I patted the rolling suitcase. "You know I didn't only bring you socks and underwear."

He smiled a bit sadly.

"Oh, Aunt Sadie, of course I remember your bribes. But my troubles were just kid stuff then. Now I'm talking about real trouble. You know how it is around here. I didn't want to talk about it on the phone. Don't pretend you don't know what I'm talking about, Aunt Sadie. Gangs and drugs."

Oh, crap. Jayden had just twitched one of the biggest nerves in my body. While it's true that most gang and drug violence was confined to the rivalries of the gangs in question, random bullets and innocent victims of those random bullets were a fact of life in the projects. And no one knew that better than Jayden and I. Both his mother and his grandmother had been victims of driveby shootings.

"Don't tell me you're doing drugs," I said. "And if you say you've joined a gang, I just won't believe you."

"I try to stay far away from all that," he said. "But that's sometimes harder than you'd think. Do you remember Rafael Cortez?"

"Your friend Rafael? Sure, I remember him. He seemed to be a charismatic kid, a real leader, the life of every party, and a nice enough kid."

He came to every birthday party for Jayden, back when all the kids went to every party so they could eat cake and have fun. Back before race and turf defined their priorities.

"Well, he's not nice anymore, and he's certainly not a kid. He's taken the shortcut to money and power that too many have taken around here. Either you're with him or you're against him."

Holy crap. My pulse started to speed up.

"And that affects you how?" I asked.

"All I know is that I am not with him."

I took a deep breath.

"Okay. What can I do for you? How can I help?"

"There's nothing you can do, Aunt Sadie. I just wanted you to know in case anything happens. I had no one else to talk to."

"Ah, honey. You know I've always got your back."

Inside, I was almost crying. Outside, I went over and gave him a big hug.

ooo

"Aunt Sadie? I'm in trouble."

My heart took a nosedive.

"Okay, Jayden," I said as calmly as I could, "what's up?"

" I need help. They've arrested me for murder."

My heart went from merely diving to scraping the soles of my shoes. No. For a moment, all I could think was, No. Okay, deep breath. I could only help him if I stayed calm. It was time to regain some balance.

"Okay, Jayden, tell me what happened."

"I don't even know the guy who died. They say it was a gang-related revenge shooting. You know, last week one of their guys shot one of the other guys, and this week, vice versa."

Did you give in and join the gang? I wanted to ask. Was the pressure too much for you? Did Rafael get to you? But I knew I couldn't ask him any of that, and he certainly couldn't answer, not while he was in police custody. I suddenly realized I must be his one phone call. It made me want to cry.

"What makes them think you had anything to do with it?" I asked, but then I realized he couldn't answer that either, and so did he.

"Aunt Sadie, I need a lawyer."

I gathered together my last bit of composure.

"I know, Jayden. I'll get you one. Hang in there. I will not let you down. I'm on the case."

With that, I hung up the phone and cranked up the air conditioner. If I had thought it was hot before, now I was in a virtual steam bath. I grabbed a kitchen towel and wiped my sopping brow. Jayden had my confidence. Lorraine could rest easy in her grave, because Sadie was about to make a few phone calls and raise the heat in Coney Island. If it had to get as hot as Hades, so be it.

My first call had to be to my favorite attorney. I called and

153

called until his wife picked up. Then I made her drag him out of the shower.

"Leo? I need a favor."

"Sadie, you're killing me. Every so often I need some paying clients so I can actually make a living. Every time you ask for a favor, I'm not making the money I need to put my own kids through school."

"Chill, Leo, even though it is a thousand degrees out there today. You know I'll get you some clients that pay real bucks. You know I know a whole lot of people."

That is true. You can't be the know-it-all busybody in chief of half of Brooklyn unless you do know lots of people. And I'm a professional at what I do.

"Okay, Sadie, I know your word is golden. What's up?"

"It's about Jayden. You know, Jayden Williams, the grandson of my old childhood friend Lorraine Johnson. Apparently, there was a gang shooting, and he's been accused of murder, but I don't buy it."

"So, Sadie, what can I possibly do? I'm not a miracle worker, just a regular guy with a law degree who does the best he can."

"Exactly, Leo. You're my guy! I want to try to get to a certain gang leader in Coney Island. I need to see if he'll talk to me."

Indeed, I needed to know if Jayden was correct about Rafael Cortez.

"Sadie, I can certainly help with that, but those guys aren't pussycats. They're drug-peddling animals. Are you sure you want to meet those guys?"

"Absolutely. But it's not those guys, Leo. It's just one guy, Rafael Cortez. Hey, it's not as crazy as it sounds. I knew him once upon a time, and he knew me. I won't do anything if he won't agree to meet me, I promise. But Jayden is one of my people, and I'm determined to try and do whatever I can to defend him. Oh, and speaking of defense, Jayden needs a lawyer pronto. I know you do pro bono. It's a good cause, Leo. The boy is innocent."

It turned out that Leo knew some of the same people that I knew in the projects in Coney Island, and he knew a few I don't.

When people who've never been to Brooklyn think of Coney Island, they usually picture the Cyclone wooden rollercoaster, the Parachute Jump, Nathan's Famous hot dogs, the fabulous boardwalk, and the beach. For me, Coney Island was always the place you went on the cheap via the subway and the bus to the sandy beach to cool down, enjoy the family, eat home-packed peanut butter and jelly sandwiches, and get a wicked sunburn.

Later, the neighborhood declined, and the projects, gigantic multifamily racial ghettos, were built. More recently, there's been some renovation and redevelopment. But poverty is still embedded in the neighborhood, and to some people, crime and violence can look like a shortcut, the quick way out. These guys ruled the streets of Coney Island. Rafael Cortez was one of them, and with any luck, Leo was going to find me a way to talk to him.

It was a broiling day, the kind of day when you wish you could strip buck naked, wet down, and just loiter in front of a fan or air conditioner, by the time Leo found a way for me to meet Rafael. Three young guys I didn't know met me when I got off the train in Coney Island.

"Yo, you Sadie?"

"Miss Sadie to you."

They may rule the streets, but I have my dignity.

That guy laughed.

"Well, Miss Sadie, Rafael warned us you might be like that. He remembers you very well."

What a wonderful young boy Rafael had been. It had seemed like he could come to represent the best of his generation. But what a waste.

They crowded me. Big shoulders jostled me, making me all too aware of being physically small. I felt nervous as they hustled me along. But I couldn't afford to succumb to fear. After a blessedly short walk to a wooden bench on the grounds of one of the projects, they told me to sit. Deep breath. I didn't need to be told twice.

They disappeared around a corner and then reappeared a moment later in a formation similar to the Secret Service protecting the President. Rafael, all grown up.

"So, Aunt Sadie," he said, "you come to rescue your

155

Jayden."

Wow! He was just as handsome and vital a presence as I remembered, even more so now that he was a grown man.

"Yo, Boss," one of the goons said, "she said you gotta call her Miss Sadie."

"No, it's all right," I said. "He can call me Aunt Sadie. All the kids did at the birthday parties, right, Rafael?"

"*Si*, Aunt Sadie, I remember those birthday parties. I remember you coming all the way here to the projects to see Jayden and his *abuela*. And I remember how you brought Jayden a brand new backpack for school every year, with new pencils and rulers and whatever he needed."

"It was the least I could do," I said. "Lorraine was my friend. A simple thing in a complicated world. I treasured every moment that we had together. I loved her, and I love Jayden. So are you going to help us?"

"It is because of those birthday parties that you are here without a bullet hole in your body. You are Aunt Sadie. But what makes you think I can help?"

"Hey, Rafael, you must know that Jayden would never be guilty of this crime. He's a good boy. Never joined the gangs. Always stayed in school. Word is that your gang was involved in this. So you have to know he wasn't involved. And if he wasn't, why is he the primary suspect?"

"Ah," he said, "that is truly a good question. Why should Jayden be a suspect in a crime he couldn't possibly have committed?" He shrugged. "Maybe I wasn't sad to know that he happened to be in the wrong place at the wrong time. Maybe I don't care if he gets blamed for a murder he didn't commit."

"Why don't you care, Rafael?" I asked. "You two were good friends when you were kids. Is it because you didn't get the breaks that Jayden did? Would that really make you let him take the rap for this?"

He shrugged again.

"I deal in death every day, Aunt Sadie. In general, I don't really care about people. And specifically, I don't care much about my former friend. He has his life, and I have mine."

"I'm not asking you to give him an alibi," I said, "or

156

provide a better suspect. But if you really don't care about the outcome, am I free to try and get Jayden off the hook?"

He thought about it, wiping his brow on his sleeve. The heat and humidity were unbelievable.

"I wouldn't lift a finger to help him," he said. "However, I won't stop you from doing what you want to do."

For a moment, I was humbled. Here I was, a white woman of a certain age stumbling around a world that wasn't my own, and for a moment, this young man had connected with me, acting not out of the rage and hate he lived with every day but with the potential I had seen in him as a boy.

I wiped my own brow with my sleeve.

"Rafael, I thank you for giving me the opportunity to help Jayden. I think his grandmother would thank you too."

"And now I say goodbye, Aunt Sadie. My *compadres* will see you safely back to the train."

Oh, crap, I wasn't sure why, but now I felt like I wanted to cry. But I didn't. I let his *compadres* accompany me to the train, and I went home to my safer place.

ooo

The heat continued. I kept cranking up the air conditioner and working at my kitchen table on my school backpack project for disadvantaged kids. In the end, everything turned out for the best for Jayden. I contacted the NYPD and told them what I knew. DNA evidence eventually exonerated him, too. So I celebrated the outcome of the case. But every so often, I would think about Jayden's childhood friend Rafael. Only six weeks after I met with him, Rafael was killed in a drug war between gangs. You know, the kind of thing where last week one of their guys shot one of the other guys, and this week, vice versa.

So as autumn approached and I bundled up in sweaters, I decided to enlist my friend Leo to look into Rafael's background. I wanted to see if there was something I could do. After a while, Leo got back to me with the information that Rafael had a son—like himself, the child of a single mother.

So busybody that I am, I poked around the situation a bit

157

and talked to some social services folks I know. And Leo helped me arrange for small amounts of help for a boy in the projects— just a little bit here and there. Just enough to hope that he would feel that someone cared. I also made sure his school was on my list of those at which each child gets a brand new backpack at the start of the semester. You know, the kind that has the latest superhero on the back and is chock full of everything a kid needs for the school year.

It was the least I could do.

Stephanie Wilson-Flaherty is a member of Sisters in Crime, Mystery Writers of America, and Romance Writers of America. Her finalist entry was published in RWA's Golden Heart contest, earning a four-star review from RT Book Review upon its release. She has recently focused on writing short mystery stories with a humorous touch, set in her native Brooklyn, starring a busybody older woman sleuth. Two of those stories were published in previous anthologies of the New York/Tri-State Chapter of Sisters in Crime, and the second was also listed among the "Other Distinguished Mystery Stories" in *Best American Mystery Stories 2015*, edited by James Patterson and Otto Penzler.

EVERY PICTURE TELLS A STORY

CATHI STOLER

Tap.Tap.Tap. The museum guard's footfalls echo on the marble as he passes behind me. I can feel his eyes on my back each time he paces the length of the gallery. The old woman who's been sitting in front of the same photograph for hours. He's probably deciding if he should tell me to move along. Is she one of those crazy old ladies with nowhere to go? Senile? Dangerous even? I smile as the taps pass in the other direction. He doesn't recognize me. No one does. Not anymore.

They say every picture tells a story. But not the whole story. I should know. This one told mine.

It was so long ago you'd think the world would have forgotten about it, and him, by now. But the media still dredge it up every year on the anniversary of the day it happened. Those gossip rags love to remind people about the scandal. A great photographer, one of the world's most famous, accused of such a terrible crime. Their boldface headlines scream for attention just the way they did back then. They blamed Otto, but he wasn't the only one at fault.

000

A farm girl right off the bus from Iowa, I knew I was pretty, and I was young and foolish enough to believe I could make New York mine. I had big plans. I was going to become a model. Soon the name Chloe would be as well known as Twiggy's. *Glamour* and *Seventeen* were my window on what was happening out there in the real world. It was the Sixties, and everything was changing, especially fashion. Miniskirts, high boots, shoulder bags, big dangling earrings. All it took was a long neck and a sexy vibe to pull it all together. That would be me. Was me, I was certain.

I talked my way into a job at a little boutique on Eighth Street and moved into a tiny apartment nearby. A shared space with lopsided floors and cracked walls hardly big enough for one

159

was filled to bursting with three of us. The other two girls knew the city better, especially places to go to meet men with money. That's what girls did then. That's how I met Otto.

Selina, who worked as a secretary to one of the editors at *Vogue* magazine, had snared her boss's tickets to a preview of a fashion photography exhibit at MoMA and invited Maryann and me to go along. I slipped into my shortest mini, pulled on my go go boots, and headed out. No one would mind that we weren't famous. All they'd notice is that we were pretty.

The photos were beautiful, the champagne sparkling, and the photographers among the best in the world. Helmut and Richard were holding court, surrounded by the art world's glitterati, as well as a few rag tag fashion followers like us. I turned my head to look at a photo one of them pointed out, a dramatic image in black and white, all shadows and angles that gave the clothes and the model an ethereal look.

That's when I noticed Otto watching me. Some of my Iowa shyness still stuck to me. I felt my face blush red and lowered my eyes. When I brought them up again, he stood in front of me, just a short breath away. He took my hand and kissed it.

"I am Otto," he said. "Who are you, beautiful creature?"

"Just Chloe," I replied.

"No. You are my Chloe, and I will make the world fall in love with you."

That's all it took, and I was gone.

Otto was a force of nature. A swirling vortex that drew me in with power I couldn't resist. It's not that he was so handsome. His face was long and angular, with cheekbones sharp as a knife, a crooked mouth, and deep black eyes that slanted upward and drew attention to the silvery streaks at his temples. Individually, his features seemed exaggerated, but together, they were captivating. And I was. Captivated, from the first.

From then on, Otto and I were one. I was his muse, he told me. More beautiful than Shrimpton. More stylish than Penelope. More waifish than Twiggy.

Sassoon cut my hair. Mary Quant chose me to model her new line for her London show. Otto took the shots. *Vogue* featured them on glossy pages I viewed with awe and ran my fingers over as if they were the finest silk. We went to parties at the Factory, danced till dawn at Trude Heller's, and listened to music at Max's Kansas City. We met everyone who was anyone. Heady stuff for an eighteen-year-old. This was the life I'd always wanted. Otto and me. Me and Otto. Inseparable.

But life with Otto wasn't all glamorous openings and dinner parties filled with New York socialites. He could be arrogant and uncaring, often uttering scathing comments no matter how hard I worked to make his photos look perfect. I tried to ignore it, rationalizing that he was artistic and temperamental. I told myself he only wanted the best for me.

While I made myself overlook his tirades—I loved him, after all—his assistants couldn't. He treated them with a rudeness and disrespect that most couldn't tolerate. They came and went in a week or two. Then Otto would hire the next one, and after a few days, the abuse would start all over again.

Still, I was content. We were content. Until Jed came into our lives.

"The new assistant, Chloe. Jed."

Otto's voice boomed out our names as if we were miles apart instead of just a few feet away. He waved his hand dismissively. Impersonal. Detached. Rude. As if to remind him assistants were a dime a dozen.

Jed was tall and lean, with a face that would have been just as at home in front of the camera as behind. I watched as his sea blue eyes went hard at Otto's words and the corners of his mouth turned downward. Maybe this one would be different, I thought. He looked secure enough to stand up to Otto. When I looked again, his eyes found mine. They were filled with danger.

000

The space race was on. It was all anyone could talk about. America was determined to put a man on the moon before the Russians. They'd beaten us once with Yuri Gagarin and the first manned flight, but this time, we would win.

Even Otto, who hated politics and government, was obsessed with the lunar program. He decided to create a series of photographs to celebrate America's upcoming feat. I was to be its star, basking in the moonlight.

The studio became a whirlwind of activity. Prop, lighting, costume, and makeup people scurried around. Otto worked day and night to get the images exactly the way he wanted them. He shot hundreds of rolls of film, his Nikon clicking endlessly. Later, in the darkroom, he'd process the film and tear up most of the shots with maniacal utterings.

He lashed out at everyone. Jed bore the brunt of it. Otto blamed him for the slightest mistake. A shadow on my face, a prop slightly out of place, no matter what imperfection, it was Jed's fault. After each tirade, I'd look at Jed as he shucked off Otto's tantrums and fits, his abuse. I'd watch as he set up the next shot. He wasn't leaving, not anytime soon, and I knew why. Me.

It started over shared cups of coffee and chatting about work and life. Like me, Jed was from a small town, and it gave him a non-New York shyness that drew me to him. We talked about our childhoods, about walking to school on tree-lined country roads and hanging out with friends at the soda fountain. Discussing my life before New York was something I'd never done with Otto, who wasn't interested in the past.

Jed's dad had given him a Brownie camera for his eighth birthday. It had awakened his passion for photography. From then on he took photographs of everyone and everything. I told him I wished I'd known him then. He smiled and said if we'd been together, he would have taken thousands of photographs of me with every camera he owned.

Our work brought us together nearly every day. We couldn't help becoming closer. A look, a touch of a hand. I pretended it wasn't happening. I was terrified Otto would find out. Although there was nothing to find out. Not yet. We snuck glances when Otto's back was turned, brushed arms when we passed each other in the studio, and smiled over the rims of wine glasses at gallery openings. I thought I knew what Jed was feeling. I was feeling it too. It was seductive and demanding, this new sense of abandon that had me in its grip. It made me into someone different, a woman I didn't recognize.

The pictures were brilliant. In one, a huge moon with the slightest touch of blue beamed an undulating path on the ocean. I walked along the moon-path toward the shore dressed in a silver bikini and white space boots. In another, I was nude and curled around the top arc of the moon. Sparkling strands of diamonds dripped down the moon's face, then turned and floated up as lifelines to far-off astronauts. In Otto's favorite, he superimposed my face on the moon's and dusted us both with golden powder that trailed off into the sky.

There were fifteen shots in all. Otto's agent went wild—he knew MoMA would want them and made a fantastic deal to have them exhibit them all. The publicity would be huge and all but ensure Otto's place in history.

All the while, Jed and I had been sliding around each other. If you looked hard enough you could see the desire in our faces. I didn't plan to fall in love. I tried resisting Jed, but it was impossible. He felt it too and told me again and again how much he loved me.

There were stolen moments when Otto was in the darkroom and brief encounters in the studio's creaky elevator. We contrived secret meetings at Jed's apartment. I became adept at making excuses. Drinks with my old roommates, shopping for clothes, a desire to see a movie I knew Otto would hate, the words bubbled up from my mouth on the spur of the moment. Any lie would do so Jed and I could be together.

The three of us were at MoMA, supervising the hanging of the photos, when it all fell apart. Otto went off to speak with the exhibit's curator, and Jed and I were in each other's arms in a heartbeat. We didn't hear him walk back into the gallery. When we realized he was there, we pulled apart quickly, but it was too late.

"Otto," I began, "please—"

"How could you betray me like this, Chloe?" Otto shouted. "You were a nobody until I found you. Whore. Slut." Black eyes blazing, he slapped me across the face.

"Don't touch her!"

Jed was on Otto instantly, getting in between us and

163

pushing him away from me.

Otto laughed at him, pushing back.

"You smug little bastard, you think you can take her away from me? Never." He grabbed at my arm. "Come with me. Now, Chloe."

"No." The word flew out of my mouth. "I don't love you, Otto. I never did. I only wanted what you could give me."

I gestured toward the photographs on the gallery wall, a testament to the fame I'd come to enjoy. I lied. I did still love him, but not enough. It was impossible for me to stay with him. Not now that Jed and I had found each other. Otto stared at me, his face a mask of rage, his body shaking in fury.

"I'm in love with Jed," I said.

"This is not over, Chloe." Otto's words dripped with venom.

Then he turned and left the gallery.

I stood there for a moment, my resolve weakening. I didn't want it to end with such bitterness and hatred. I looked at Jed, then started after Otto.

Jed pulled me back.

"No. You stay here. I'll go speak to him and make him understand we're together now."

He touched my bruised face tenderly.

I let him leave me there, amongst all those images mocking me. I could hardly look at them. The moon, the diamonds, the glitter of gold. I saw it now. This was what Otto had offered me, what I had accepted so easily. My betrayal seeped out from the prints and poured over me like liquid fire. I had to get out of there. My thoughts were a whirlwind. Had Jed found Otto at the studio? Were they even now circling each other like gladiators? Had Otto refused to accept the reality of the situation? I walked for hours imagining the worst. That's what you do until you realize the worst is beyond anything you could imagine.

ooo

I called Jed's apartment and let the phone ring and ring. I tried the studio that had been my home as well as my workplace, but there

164

was no answer there either. I needed to collect my things and prayed that Otto had gone out. I couldn't bear the thought of another confrontation.

When I pulled up the old wooden door of the service elevator that opened onto our studio, the silence slipped over me like a shroud. I entered slowly, tentatively, barely breathing. I forced myself to move forward, one foot in front of the other, alert for any sign of Otto's presence.

I walked through the kitchen toward our bedroom at the back of the studio, feeling only relief that Otto wasn't here. Until I saw Jed. His body was on the floor, a pool of blood surrounding him. I flew to him, threw myself over him, screaming his name over and over. Otto had meant what he said. He'd never let Jed take me away from him. He'd slit Jed's throat and cut his beautiful face to ribbons.

Our neighbor, Anna, an artist who lived on the floor below, heard my screams. She rushed into the studio shouting my name. When she saw Jed's body and the state I was in, she called the police.

I was cradling him in my arms, but she finally managed to pull me away from him. She sat with me until the police arrived and held me close to her the whole time.

I tried to pull myself together. I told them I believed it was Otto who'd murdered Jed. I stammered my way through what happened at the museum and said that I'd come back to get my clothes. They asked me questions about Otto and about Jed. I answered through my tears, trembling with sorrow. They wanted to know if there was someone who could stay with me, and I gave them Selina and Maryann's phone number, knowing they would come as soon as they could. I agreed to go to the station in the morning and give them an official statement.

Hours later, after the police left and the coroner took Jed's body away, my sorrow and my guilt remained. For as much as I blamed Otto, I knew it was my fault as well.

The police searched for days, not finding even the smallest trace of Otto. Finally, a tourist walking along the ramshackle piers along the Hudson River found a camera in a case hanging from one of the pilings. It had Otto's name inside.

Everyone believed Otto had drowned himself, that he couldn't bear what he had done. Everyone but me. I knew Otto. He was too proud, too confident of his own invincibility to choose death. Otto was gone, escaped to some European city remembered from his childhood, where he could create a new identity. I hired a private detective to search for him, but his efforts proved futile. After a year, I gave up. We would never find Otto. And I would never avenge Jed's death.

000

The Museum of Modern Art opened the exhibition on July 21, the day after the moon landing and Armstrong's walk. The crowds that gathered were enormous, titillated as much by the moonscape photographs as by the murder. MoMA had a hit on its hands, and I had blood on mine.

After the exhibit ended, the museum would be permitted to keep fourteen of the photographs on permanent loan as long as they exhibited them once a year. The fifteenth, the one of my face over the moon's, was to remain in Otto's possession. Now it was mine, as I inherited everything that had been his.

Eventually, I gave this photograph to MoMA as well. I visit it once a year, as I am doing now. Like the moon itself, it beams over me, filling me with thoughts of a life that might have been. Instead, I sit here lost in time, an old lady with nowhere to go and nothing left to lose.

Cathi Stoler is the author of the three-volume Laurel & Helen New York mystery series, which includes *Keeping Secrets*, *Telling Lies*, and *The Hard Way*, as well as the novella, *Nick Of Time*. She has recently completed a new urban thriller, *Bar None,* a Murder on the Rocks mystery, and *Out Of Time*, a full-length sequel to *Nick Of Time*. She is the winner of the 2015 Derringer for Best Short Story for "The Kaluki Kings of Queens." Cathi is Vice President of the New York/Tri-State Chapter of Sisters in Crime and a member of Mystery Writers of America and International Thriller Writers. You can reach her at www.cathistoler.com.

THE FAMILY CURSE

MIMI WEISBOND

"So, how would you do it? You're the writer."

My brother Tom leaned towards me across the dinner table. He had rolled back his shirtsleeves, and his arms, covered in their thatch of dark hair, lay in harsh contrast to the white damask cloth.

"You must have loads of ideas," he said. "You always were the smart one."

He began to play with the wax that hung from the ornate silver candelabra. In the flickering candlelight, the Persian carpet, peach-toned walls, and polished silver took on an even more prosperous glow.

"You know me," I said. "I just write about skin care and sun goop."

"But you must have some thoughts on the matter. I mean, besides tossing the toaster in the bathtub."

"Who keeps their toaster in the bathroom?" my sister-in-law Lucy said.

"Or their bathtub in the kitchen," said Sam, my date. He wasn't exactly a boyfriend, but I called him every time I got invited to dinner at my brother's. And my brother had started to make some eyebrow-wagging innuendos.

Escorting me to dinner at my brother's was not all that onerous a task. His apartment was luxury incarnate. Perched on the penthouse floor of one of those pre-war buildings that line Park Avenue from midtown to Carnegie Hill, it had breathtaking views of Manhattan. His walls were lined with art, the furniture was sleekly modern, the floors were deeply carpeted, and seating was soft and comfortable. Add to that the delicious food and charming presence of my sister-in-law, and you could pretty much overlook any annoyance my brother served up.

"What would you do, Sam?" I said. "Empty a packet of cyanide into his drink?"

In an obvious show of giving this some thought, Sam shoved his own shirtsleeves up his arms, loosened his tie, and

168

rubbed his chin.

Dear Sam. His tie was loudly patterned, as was his shirt. As was, in fact, his sports coat, hanging from the back of his chair. Plaids and patterns were Sam's way of distracting the eye from the quality of the fabric.

"I wouldn't," he finally said. "Besides, poison's more of a woman's thing."

"Well, let's look at it from a different angle," I said, turning back to my brother. "Who is it you want to bump off?"

"No one special," he said, his eyes darting sideways.

I found that hard to believe. My brother usually had a long list of people he wanted to eliminate, for one reason or another.

"How about rubbing out that guy who's trying to outbid you on the Hamptons house?" I asked.

"That jerk. But he's not going to get it." My brother smiled thinly. "I made a call." Inspecting his nails, he added, "Don't ask."

"Well, what if we knock off that other friend of yours—the broker who sold you the stock that took that spectacular dive?"

"As it happens, your brother got back at him already," said Lucy. "Sold him our old Beemer. Turns out it had a cracked engine block."

"Who knew?" said Tom lightly.

Sam gave him an appraising look.

"I thought this was a party game."

"Oh, it is." My brother cast an innocent glance at each of us in turn. "To find out who among us is the grisliest. So, c'mon. Give. How would you do it?"

Sam frowned slightly before he said, "How about using that old taxidermists' trick and tossing the guy into a barrel full of carpet beetles? Nasty buggers will eat anything. Get your bones picked clean in a jiff."

"This conversation has stopped being fun."

Giving her husband an angry glare, Lucy got up and started to clear the table. There were a great many dishes, as my brother's wife enjoyed making what she called "small plates" and what my brother referred to as "a boatload of dishwashing."

I jumped up to help.

"What's up with Tom?" I asked, as we ferried load upon

load out to the kitchen. "This is an unpleasant topic of conversation, even for him."

Lucy's only answer was to shrug and say, "He's your brother."

"Well, I don't see how you can put up with him. You must be bucking for sainthood." I took a deep sniff of the air. "Something in here smells wonderful!"

Lucy's response was a melodious laugh that tinkled on for a little longer than need be.

"I made a little soufflé for dessert," she said with a smile. "It does smell good, doesn't it? Tom's favorite."

We returned to the dining room, where Tom was refilling everyone's wine glass.

"Could you pass me that platter, Tom?"

Lucy reached across the table, the stones in her rings and bracelets tossing out brilliant shards of light.

"Afraid it didn't sell so well, sweetheart. I could have told you so. No one likes truffles. They smell like feet. And why did you make so much of this puréed stuff? Did you happen to count the guest list?"

Lucy said, "Well, silly me. I just thought it might be fun to try something different."

"Another of your glorious misadventures. You can take away this little prizewinner, too." He shoved the remains of a deeply pungent broccoli rabe down the table.

Sam intercepted the dish and followed Lucy into the kitchen.

"How about some music?" I suggested, hoping to break the silence that had descended.

Tom touched a small silver button on the side table, and the strains of Mozart filled the air.

"Had to get rid of her insipid so-called music before I transcribed my classical treasures. Much easier this way. All on the cloud."

Lucy came back from the kitchen carrying four dessert plates.

Tom greeted her with an exasperated sigh.

"For heaven's sake, Lucy. Can't you keep yourself

buttoned up?" He stared pointedly at his wife's neckline, buttoned to what I thought was a modest degree. "Going around half naked when we have guests!"

With a sharp intake of breath, Lucy retreated into the kitchen.

"I'll see if I can help with dessert," said Sam, following her.

I turned on my brother.

"For heaven's sake, Tom. Aren't you being a little tougher than usual on Lucy tonight? She's worked hard on all this," my hand swept over the table, "and you're not being especially nice to her, to say nothing of grateful."

Running a well-manicured hand over the top of his head, he scowled.

"Now don't start in on me, kiddo. You're always taking Lucy's side. You want me to sing her praises? Okay. She's great. She cooks. She cleans. Keeps the place immaculate after working a full day down at the pharmacy. One in a million. I honestly don't know what I'd do without her. There. Now will you please get off my back?"

That's when we heard the crash of broken crockery coming from the kitchen, then a peal of laughter, followed by a low chuckle.

My brother started to rise from the table, then settled back down.

"Guess it's all under control," he said.

"Are you and Lucy okay?" I asked.

"Of course we are, kiddo. Right as rain."

At that point Lucy and Sam emerged from the kitchen, flushed from the oven's heat. Lucy bore in her mitted hands a spectacular soufflé—golden, fragrant, and rising high above its fluted dish.

Sam carried two small bowls, each heaped with velvety whipped cream.

"Voilà!" Lucy set the dish down with a flourish.

"Now what?" said Tom.

"What does it look like, darling? Your favorite. Grand Marnier soufflé." With a beatific smile, she began to dish out the

171

steaming dessert. "With your choice of whipped cream. Plain or almond."

"Almond?" Tom murmured. "I love almond whipped cream."

Lucy passed me one of the small bowls and, after a moment's thought, I gave it a careful stir and handed it to Tom.

"This one's the almond," I said.

My brother helped himself to such a liberal dollop that the rest of us had to content ourselves with the unflavored cream.

True to form, I thought.

The soufflé was perfect. Light as a cloud and richly flavorful. A grand finale by anyone's standards, making up for earlier social transgressions and culinary disappointments, and bringing a rather uncomfortable evening to a glorious end.

"Well, we hate to eat and run," said Sam, pushing himself back from the table, "but tomorrow's a workday, and it's closing in on 11:30. You want a hand with those dishes, Lucy?"

Lucy laughed and said no, she had everything under control, and got up to give us our coats and see us to the door.

"Now, don't be a stranger," she said, more to Sam than to me. Giving us each a peck on the cheek, she turned back into the apartment and closed the door softly behind her.

Sam seemed thoughtful as he walked me home. The night was clear and filled with stars, and we made our way silently along the quiet city streets.

"Penny?" I said.

"Just wondering," he replied.

"About what?" I asked. "All that talk about murder? That's just Tom being Tom. He likes to get people stirred up. You know that."

"I was wondering more about what was in that other little bottle."

"What other bottle?" I'd forgotten how perceptive Sam was.

"After we whipped the cream and she divided it into two bowls," Sam said, "Lucy added a couple of drops of almond extract to the smaller one, and I can't be sure, but it looked like she shook a few more drops into it, too."

"Why didn't you ask her about it? You were right there."

"My back was turned," he said. "I only saw her reflection in the window. Besides, I could be wrong. Cooking is more of a woman's thing."

ooo

I ran into Sam and Lucy at my mother's funeral. They had married not long after my brother's death. I had a feeling they would. Sam is kindness itself, and Lucy needs to have a man to take care of. My father had passed a few months before, and I was slowly adjusting to the finality of being completely alone in the world, the last surviving member of my family. Weak hearts had carried them all off, starting with my brother. It was beginning to look like a family curse.

"We're so sorry, darling," Lucy said, her hands clasped before her in a charming display of sympathy. "This must be incredibly hard on you. I don't know what I'd do if I lost my whole family within the year." I had never seen Lucy look happier. Her skin glowed, her hair shone, and her voice rippled with good will. "If there's anything Sam or I can do, you have only to ask."

"But we do want to thank you for your wedding gift," murmured Sam, shooting his cuffs to expose handsome gold links. "I don't think we ever did."

He took my hand and looked directly into my eyes.

"We wouldn't be married if it weren't for you," he said quietly.

I lowered my gaze and smiled a little.

He dropped his voice another notch.

"At first I thought it was an act of selfless generosity. Once I'd figured it out. But now—no, you don't have to say a word."

He looked at the room full of well-heeled mourners. My parents' neighbors, traveling companions, and fellow country-club members were as well dressed and coddled as my parents had been. Preserved in money, like insects preserved in amber.

Sam's smile was imperceptible to everyone but me. If anyone could be said to be my next of kin, it would be him. We love each other so well. And know each other so deeply.

173

As he held my hand, he raised his eyebrows slightly. I nodded gravely in response. Then I turned so the long stream of well-wishers could embrace me. As I returned platitude for platitude, I found myself thinking how well life can work out—given a little help.

Mimi Weisbond spent over a decade as Senior Copywriter at Clinique, where she learned more about what makes women tick than anyone would want to know. She lives in New York with her husband and a cat, and, like many New Yorkers, made a brief, brave foray into stand-up comedy. She is a member of Sisters in Crime and Mystery Writers of America.

I GOTTA BE ME

LINDSAY A. CURCIO

"And what I'm sayin' is," Johnny Monroe spits out, "if they don't want to obey the law, then they must go! That's it for today. Be careful, my friends, there are a lot of crazies out there!"

As always, these lines end his radio show with force. As he takes off his headphones, he looks at Masha, his producer, and Bart, his engineer, in the booth. Masha makes the thumbs up sign. Bart shrugs and picks up his crossword puzzle.

Red Rizzo, the station owner, opens the door to the studio.

"Johnny," he exclaims, "what a show! The phones were ringing off the hook the whole two hours! Your comments on illegal immigration really hit a nerve. Everyone is listening to your show! Latest numbers show you leading again in the Arbitron ratings."

"What can I say, Red? I just seem to know what America is thinking." Johnny takes a long sip from his water bottle and begins putting his notes into his tan leather briefcase. "After five o'clock already. I have to get ready for that awards dinner tonight at the Plaza. They asked me to say a few words."

Masha taps on the glass, and Johnny put his headphones back on.

"A guy dropped off a note for you earlier," she says.

Masha is from Novosibirsk. She has lived in Brighton Beach for twenty years with her husband, with whom she has a twelve-year-old son. Without a family, Johnny has enjoyed many holiday dinners with them, eating Masha's deftly made pelmeni and savory borscht while drinking hot tea with cherry jam and many glasses of vodka.

"A lot of guys drop off notes," says Johnny.

He puts on his Burberry wool overcoat and his U.S. Army veteran cap, a gift from the members of the American Legion post near the studio.

"This guy was different. He looked like he could be your brother."

"Meet me outside," Johnny says.

"Here's the note," Masha says when they reach the hallway. "He said his name was Stein. I'm sorry I didn't get his first name."

Johnny crumples the note without reading it and puts it in his jacket pocket.

"Hey, that might be important," says Masha. "I couldn't believe how much he looked like you. If I didn't know you were on air, I would have thought it was you!"

"Yeah, yeah, yeah, he's not me. Nobody's like me." Johnny stops and collects himself. "You want to come to the awards show tonight? There's a dinner. They got pretty good food at the Plaza. We could go to Bergdorf's beforehand. I'll buy you a new dress."

"Can't," says Masha. "There's a parent-teacher conference for Alex. Why not take one of your lady friends?"

"Lady friends. Don't tell me you're jealous after all these years."

Johnny shakes his head and smiles as he gets into the elevator.

ooo

The radio studio rents space in the Hotel Pennsylvania, across from Penn Station and Madison Square Garden. Every weeknight, there is a small crowd waiting for him after he finishes the show. As he walks through the lobby, fans call out to him.

"Great show, Johnny!"

"You tell it like it is, Johnny!"

"My grandpa says hi, Johnny! He fought for his country, just like you."

"Say it, Johnny, will ya? I want to tape it for my ringtone."

A teenager holds his cell phone up to Johnny, and Johnny obliges: "Be careful, my friend, there are a lot of crazies out there!"

Johnny shakes some of the fans' hands and nods to others as he makes his way to the revolving door.

"Hey, Robbie! How's your daughter doing at Parsons, Susan? Good to see you, Sam. Glad you're feeling better."

176

Johnny tells his inner circle that the fans are kooks and characters, but really, he is grateful for them.

As he stands at the corner, waiting for a taxi, he puts his hand in his pocket and fingers the note. It shocks him that Stein has been in the building until he remembers that everyone knows where to find Johnny Monroe. He's famous: radio personality, Vietnam veteran and war hero, awarded the Silver Star, badges for marksmanship, high school football All-American, heard on more than two hundred radio stations throughout the United States, broadcast live from bustling midtown Manhattan five times a week. But Stein is not supposed to seek him out. Why? Why now? What does he want? For a moment, he forgets he is headed to his apartment in Tribeca to change into a tuxedo before a car arrives to take him to the dinner at the Plaza.

He has not thought of Stein in years. But he knows how to reach him if he needs to. Along with many other homeless people in the city, Stein gets his mail at the main post office on Eighth Avenue, just below 34th Street, in the name of Stein Larsen.

Johnny reads Stein's note in the cab taking him home.

Have to see you, it says. *You have something I need back. Meet at Rudy's. Your pal, Stein*

No time for this tonight. His public is waiting.

QQQ

Two weeks later, Johnny Monroe has put Stein out of his mind. He has just finished up another successful show. He's feeling good about himself. Over the years, his on-air persona and his show have become more and more abrasive. People seem to like it. Controversial topics—immigration, pro-life vs. pro-choice, gun control, climate change—those are the subjects people want to discuss. Everyone has an opinion, and a seemingly endless line of people call in every day to tell him theirs. His show brings in more revenue than any other show the station has ever produced. His national speaking tours are fully booked. His motivational books become bestsellers. He's even awarded an honorary doctorate in letters from a prominent university. When Johnny takes the time to think about it, he has to admit that's not bad for a guy who dropped out of grammar school.

Johnny gets into the elevator contemplating a steak dinner with the lovely Lila, followed by box seats at the Rangers game at the Garden and later, well, who knows what else. He greets a group of fans in the lobby and steps outside. On the sidewalk, a man in a torn ski jacket and dirty wool cap falls into step with him.

"Hello, Johnny."

Johnny looks around quickly. For the moment, no one is watching him. The rush hour pedestrians all have their eyes fixed on their phone screens. Johnny keeps walking, and Stein keeps pace.

"I waited for you at Rudy's," Stein says, "but you didn't show. I need it back, Johnny. It's a matter of life or death for me."

Johnny looks at his watch.

"Okay, we'll go to Rudy's now," he says. "I don't have a lot of time, but we can talk there."

Just two guys having a couple of beers, nothing unusual about that. If anyone were to look at them, really look at them together, they would see two men of similar height and weight with blue eyes and thick white hair who could be twins. One is well dressed, about sixty-five years of age, tall, still broad shouldered like an athlete, with expensive but understated clothing. The other's jacket and jeans are worn, and he could use a visit to the barber. The blue eyes are a little faded, but really, they look like twin brothers.

They walk west to Ninth Avenue and turn right. Johnny walks fast, head down, but passersby still call out.

"Hey, Johnny!"

"Great show, Johnny!"

Stein and Johnny walk in silence to 44th Street, where a six-foot-tall pink fiberglass pig marks the entrance to Rudy's. Entering the bar, Johnny signals Stein to go find them seats in the corner. Customers turn to acknowledge Johnny. Johnny is polite to everyone but doesn't stop to chat. He orders a pitcher of Rudy's Blonde and carries it and two glasses over to Stein, who is sitting at a small table in the corner.

Stein says, "Look, Johnny. I need it back. I need Medicare. I'm sick."

"Sorry to hear you're not well." Johnny takes a sip of his beer. "There must be some kind of benefits you can get in New York City."

"My social worker says I'm entitled to treatment at the VA, but I can't get anything," Stein says, almost crying. "I can't prove anything. I don't have the right papers. I know we said this was forever, but I can't do this anymore. I'm sick. I can't afford my room." He coughs into a cotton bandanna. "And you, you've got this great life. You've got my life."

"You made your choice years ago," Johnny says, "when you came back from Vietnam. It's too late to do anything about that now."

"You can't let me suffer like this! I'll tell the radio station if I have to!"

"Nobody would believe you," Johnny says. "What difference would it make, anyway? I'm the one who got famous. I'll send you some money, general delivery."

He leaves Stein sitting at the table. He hails a cab to the Garden so he won't be late for Lila and the hockey game.

000

Stein's notes continue. Johnny thinks an offer of big money may end this and agrees to meet him at Rudy's two weeks later. At 8 AM on a Tuesday, the bar is empty except for some customers who have just finished their night shifts. Stein looks a little better. Maybe the social worker got him some help, Johnny thinks.

They have a pitcher of beer, then another. Johnny means to come to terms with Stein about the money and get out of there fast, but with the dark bar and the alcohol, he gets nostalgic.

"You remember the old days in Brooklyn? I was living with my aunt and uncle in Bay Ridge and working on the docks. They took me in when I jumped ship. I took the Bible my mother gave me back in Oslo and left my passport by my bunk. I loved this city the moment I saw it! Times Square! The Garden! The beautiful women! You ever seen such pretty girls? I never looked back."

Stein pours Johnny another glass of beer.

179

"You think it was easy for me?" Johnny says. "I had no education, no identification. When I went out for a night in Manhattan, people made fun of my accent. I went to free English classes to sound more American. I knew there was something better."

"We all want something better," Stein says. "Remember how everyone in the neighborhood thought we were brothers? Yeah, like brothers. Remarkable. Everybody said so."

"But I worked, and you turned to drugs," Johnny says. "We just looked alike."

"I went to war," Stein says, "and you stayed home."

"I remember the night you walked into the Three Jolly Pigeons on Third Avenue," Johnny says," just back from Vietnam. Everyone greeted you like you were a hero. You *were* a hero."

"You don't know what it was like." Stein shakes his head.

"You became a druggie," Johnny says. "Your sister threw you out of her place. When I saw you standing in front of her building, glassy eyed, your belongings scattered in the yard and on the sidewalk, I wanted to help you."

"Yeah, you helped me. Took me to Coney Island Hospital and checked me in. Later I realized you took my veteran's ID, all my papers. And that's how Stein Larsen became Johnny Monroe and Johnny Monroe became Stein."

That reminds Johnny why they are here and what he has to lose.

"We shouldn't have met. Look, I'll talk to my accountant, figure out a way to get you money every month."

"Money won't fix this!" Stein yells.

But Johnny is already out the door.

000

Johnny puts that morning at Rudy's out of his mind and goes to work each day. For a few weeks, notes from the real Johnny Monroe—*Need to see you. Your pal, Stein*—continue to appear at the studio. He does not reply, and the notes stop. Yet he thinks he sees Stein everywhere: on the street, at a bar, in a restaurant, at a Nets game, at the gym. Maybe it's his guilty conscience. Years

180

ago, he was threatened by some listeners, and the station decided he should have a gun. He has a permit, but he has never carried the Ruger with him. Now he does.

Six months pass. After a great show, Johnny is walking down Seventh Avenue. Someone taps him on the shoulder. It's the real Johnny Monroe. He looks better. His hair is cut like Johnny's, and his clothes are clean. He has a nice coat on.

"Not here," Johnny says, "we'll go to Rudy's."

It's cold as they walk to the bar. Johnny's got his hands in his pockets. He tucks his neck and head as far down into his wool coat as he can. He hopes no one sees them together. The real Johnny Monroe is wearing gloves.

They push their way into the bar, full of the after work crowd. Some young men in suits with ties loosened see them, recognize Johnny, and offer them their table.

"We'd do anything for you, Johnny!"

"I'm a big fan, Johnny!"

Now, sitting quietly off to the side, a beer in front of him, the real Johnny Monroe pleads with him.

"Give it back."

"I can't do that," says Johnny. "We've gone too far."

"I wouldn't bother you," says the real Johnny Monroe. "I don't like this New York life. I'm thinking about going to Jersey."

"I'm sorry. Too much time has passed. I'll give you anything else. What do you want? Money? I've got plenty of money. I can get you an apartment. I can get you the best doctors. Anything you want."

"Look," says the real Johnny Monroe, "I never was too good at school, but I remember that line from Shakespeare about stealing my good name. I thought you were helping me, but really, you only helped yourself. I don't want your money. If I could show who I am, I could get treatment at the VA. I could get a better place to live. I told my social worker—"

"You did what? You told your social worker about us? Are you crazy?"

"I'm desperate. I got no safe place to live. I need medicine. I'm walking around the city all day waiting for the shelter to open, and I see your face on the cover of the *Post* on the newspaper stand. Famous. Successful. Healthy. Living in a ritzy place downtown. What are you on, your third marriage now?"

"Fourth," mumbles Johnny, "but we're separated, it's not going well."

The real Johnny Monroe gets louder.

"That could have been me!"

People are starting to look. Johnny sees a tourist aiming her phone at them. He downs his drink, grabs the real Johnny, and walks him out of the bar. The real Johnny is yelling about honor and the old Brooklyn neighborhood.

"Too much to drink," Johnny says.

Johnny has to think fast. He grabs a cab on Ninth Avenue and shoves the real Johnny in first. Real Johnny is still talking, but now he's crying. The cab pulls up to the curb at Duane and West Broadway. Johnny thinks he might take the real Johnny up to his apartment, calm him down a little. Maybe there is something he can do to stop this. But if some social worker knows the whole story, it might be in the *Post* before sunrise. Real Johnny is still crying and talking as Johnny wrangles him out of the cab and onto the sidewalk. Johnny tips the driver heavily, hoping he won't mention this scene. The driver doesn't even look at him. He might not have realized who was in the cab.

Johnny starts to guide the real Johnny towards the apartment building, but real Johnny staggers off. It gets dark early in December, and the streets are slippery with black ice. Johnny slides a little but catches himself. The real Johnny runs on ahead into the alley behind the apartment building, and Johnny follows.

The real Johnny Monroe lunges at him, screaming, "Give me my life back!"

What can Johnny do? The alley is empty, but the streets are full of people. A celebrity chasing after a man who looks a lot like him will be noticed. He can't heft the real Johnny onto the fire escape and into his apartment twelve stories up. Johnny pulls back his coat, reaches for his gun, and says a quiet prayer.

The real Johnny Monroe, authentic Vietnam vet and war hero, sees the shiny metal of the gun at Johnny's waist. The real Johnny Monroe sees an opportunity. The real Johnny Monroe moves fast. Twisting Johnny's arm, he wrests the gun away and points it at Johnny.

"I want it back," he says. "I want it back now."

Johnny backs away slowly.

"Come on. Don't do this to your old pal. I'll take care of you. I'll set you up in a condo in Arizona. The weather will be good for you."

The shot rings out, and Johnny falls. Dead.

The real Johnny Monroe reaches into Johnny's pants pocket for his wallet, quickly finds a driver's license. His license. He takes his keys too. Within moments, squad cars pull up, sirens wailing. Police officers on foot come running too. He can hear them speaking into their radios.

"Hey! Hey! Look who this is!" says one officer. "Sarge, look, it's Johnny Monroe!"

Johnny leans back against the building and closes his eyes for a moment as the police converge on the area. It's good to be back, he thinks.

"Oh yeah, Johnny Monroe! The guy on the radio. My wife loves you, man!"

Later that evening, the reporter from the *Post* asks, "Were you scared, Johnny?"

He smiles.

"Ah, you know, there are a lot of crazies out there."

Lindsay A. Curcio is a lawyer who writes about all facets of immigration law. Her short story, "We All Have Baggage," appeared in *Family Matters,* the third volume of the Murder New York Style series. You can follow Lindsay on Twitter @lindsayvisa.

THE COUSINS

ANITA PAGE

When Ellen's father said he didn't want her going to the candy store with Michael anymore, she said they always looked both ways before they crossed, thinking that's what he was worried about. That had nothing to do with it, he said.

They were in the tiny kitchen of the bungalow, she and her father the early risers in the family. He was pouring sweet cream over his Rice Krispies, his open newspaper at his elbow. Outside the window above the sink, the cloudless sky promised a good beach day, which he was now spoiling by putting her in a bad mood.

"Then why?" she demanded, in the tone of voice she knew he didn't like.

"Because I said so," her father said. Of all the words she'd ever heard in her ten years, those were the ones guaranteed to make her furious.

When her mother appeared in the doorway a second later, little Annie trailing behind, Ellen saw her parents exchange a look that meant her mother knew what was going on. In Michael's family, if his mother said he couldn't do something, he'd say, *but Papa said I could*, and that would end up with his parents yelling at each other and Michael doing whatever he wanted. In her family, her parents stuck together like glue.

Now Ellen's mother said that she didn't know what the fuss was about, there was a whole bag of Hershey's Kisses in the cupboard. As if that would make Ellen feel better. She didn't care about the candy, she just liked the way it felt, walking down the sandy street without any grownups, her and Michael running an errand for his parents, but she felt stupid saying that, and anyway, they wouldn't understand.

"That is so not fair," she muttered as she stormed out onto the porch, letting the screen door slam behind her. She sat down on the top step to watch for Michael, the sun warm on her bare legs. Early as it was, some people from the bungalows were already on their way to the beach carrying towels and blankets, the kids with their pails and shovels, wanting to get a spot close to the ocean before the weekend crowds came.

Just then her oldest cousin, Arthur, on his way to the beach for his morning swim, called out from the sidewalk in the teasing way he had.

"Hey sourpuss. Watch out or your face is going to freeze like that."

He didn't have a shirt on, and she could see the crooked scar on his chest. Once, when Michael asked how he got it, Arthur said it was a souvenir of the war. That didn't make sense to her or Michael, but that's all he would say. Now she thought about asking Arthur if she could go with him, but that would mean telling her parents, and she wasn't planning to speak to them for the rest of the day.

ooo

Every summer the families rented bungalows on Beach 25th Street in Rockaway, Queens, a long block that ended at the boardwalk. This year, they'd taken five bungalows, one for Ellen's family, one for her grandparents, and three more for the great-aunts and uncles.

Other summers she'd had her cousin Ruthie to play with, but this year Ruthie's family had decided to go to the mountains, so the only friend she had was Michael. Her sister Annie was four, too young to jump the waves with them or to spy on teenagers kissing under the boardwalk.

For years the families had left their hot Brooklyn apartments for the cool breezes of Rockaway. Ellen had heard the story of how, after her parents got married, her father didn't want to rent a bungalow because for one thing he didn't like the beach and for another he liked his wife's family, but in small doses. Then one day he came home from work and Ellen, who was a baby, was lying in her crib sopping wet with sweat, and her father said, okay, they'd get a bungalow. Since it would take too long to get to his office in Manhattan from Rockaway, he stayed in Brooklyn during the week and joined them on the weekends.

It was clear to Ellen from the time she was old enough to

185

notice such things that her father didn't fit in with her mother's family. For one thing, they all talked in loud voices, not because they were angry—it got loudest when they were laughing at one of Grandpa Saul's jokes, told in Yiddish so the kids couldn't understand—it was just the way you had to talk to be heard in this group. Her father's family, on the other hand, always spoke quietly. Even when they laughed it was in a quiet way. For another thing, when the men were playing pinochle on her grandfather's porch, her father was usually reading *The New York Times* on their porch.

ooo

She spotted skinny Michael in his red T-shirt and blue swimming trunks way down the block. Even though he was younger, he was almost as tall as she was, with light brown hair that turned blond in the Rockaway sun. They didn't see each other much the rest of the year, but in the summer they got to be friends. He was a bad kid who got in trouble a lot and laughed when he got yelled at or hit. His mother, her great-aunt Flo, hoped that Ellen would be a good influence on him, but so far that hadn't worked out.

Once they were spying on two teenagers and saw the boy pull the girl's top down. When Michael yelled, "Nice titties," the boy chased them, screaming, "You're going to die, kid." Ellen was scared, but Michael laughed so hard he fell down in the sand. Another time, when they went to the boardwalk by themselves to get ice cream, they stayed for an hour, taking rides on the bumper cars with money Michael had stolen from his mother's purse. When they got back and his mother asked where they'd been, Michael told her they'd gone on the bumper cars with money they found in the sand. Then his mother asked Ellen if that was true, and she said it was.

Now he sat down next to her on the step and handed her a 3 Musketeers bar before he tore open his Snickers. The candy bars were the tips they got from Michael's parents for giving Willie, the candy store owner, two dollars to bet on a horse. Since she hadn't gone to the store, Ellen hadn't expected the tip.

When she told Michael that, he said, "My mother said it's

186

not your fault that your old man's on his high horse and that I should still buy you candy."

Then Ellen asked what a high horse was, and Michael said it meant that her father didn't like Michael's mother sending them to place bets with Willie. Now the injustice of not being allowed to go made her even madder. Michael was the one who gave Willie the two dollars and the little piece of paper with the horse's name. All she ever did was pick out a candy bar. This was what she hated about being a kid. The grownups made rules you had to follow even when you knew they were unfair.

ooo

After lunch, Ellen said her stomach hurt so she didn't want to go to the beach. Her mother immediately felt her forehead to see if she had a fever, and her father wanted to know when she'd last had a bowel movement. It embarrassed her when he asked that, and she said she didn't remember, another lie. She'd lied about her stomach hurting partly because she was still mad and also because she liked the idea of being alone in the cool, quiet bungalow, reading her book, nobody telling her to get her feet off the couch.

Soon after her parents and Annie left, the Saturday afternoon pinochle game started on her grandparents' porch. Ellen, stretched out on the lumpy brown couch with her book, could hear the men through the open window but didn't pay attention to what they were saying. She'd brought her Louisa May Alcott books to Rockaway, old books with hard covers that felt like cotton when you ran your fingers over them. She'd finished *Little Women* and was reading *Eight Cousins* again, imagining she was Rose, with a kind uncle for a guardian and boy cousins who did whatever she told them to do.

When the voices from next door got louder, Ellen thought they were arguing about the pinochle game, but then she heard her father's name, Ben, and put down her book. It felt funny, hearing them talk about him when he was still at the beach. Listening, she figured out that everyone was mad at her father except for her grandfather, who was taking his side. By the time her grandmother came to the door to ask in her loud voice if the whole street had to

187

know the family's business, Ellen understood that they were mad at her father because of something he'd done to Arthur.

ooo

At the beginning of the summer Ellen had felt shy with Arthur because he'd been in the army and she hadn't seen him since she was little. After he started teasing her, not in a mean way, they became friends, and he sometimes took her and Michael to the boardwalk arcades.

Once, when Michael couldn't go because he was being punished, Arthur took just her, something that annoyed her father when she mentioned it the next weekend. Why, her father asked her mother, would a grown man want to spend time with a ten-year-old girl? Her mother, who was clearing the table after Friday night supper, said something about the war and that Arthur was having trouble finding himself. Then her father said the war had been over for two years and that maybe Arthur wasn't looking hard enough.

"Why doesn't he just look in the mirror?" Ellen had asked. She was trying to be funny but nobody laughed.

ooo

The pinochle players lowered their voices for about two minutes, but then Arthur's father, Ellen's great-uncle Morrie, started yelling, calling Ellen's father a cheap s.o.b. for not helping Arthur out of his jam, especially since he had more money than the rest of them put together.

Ellen was trying to figure out what an s.o.b. was when her grandfather slammed his hand on the table and forgot about keeping his voice down. First of all, he said, you don't count someone else's money, and second of all he didn't blame Ben because how many times was the family supposed to bail Arthur out? Then her uncle Morrie, sounding to Ellen like he was almost crying, said, "For the love of God, Saul, you know the kind of people we're dealing with here. Birdie is worried sick."

When he said that, Ellen remembered the time Arthur had

188

taken her and Michael to the boardwalk to play skeeball and this man came into the arcade and asked Arthur, not in a friendly way, to step outside with him. When Arthur came back in he said they had to go home even though they'd only played one game. Now Ellen wondered if the man was one of the people her uncle Morrie and aunt Birdie were worried about.

By the time her parents and sister got back from the beach, the pinochle game had ended. Ellen wanted to ask her father why he wouldn't help Arthur with his jam and if it was true that they had more money than anyone, but realized if she did that he'd know everyone was mad at him so she didn't say anything.

ooo

That night, soon after she went to bed, she got up again because she needed to pee. As she crossed to the bathroom, she heard her parents talking at the kitchen table. Her mother was saying that she didn't blame her father for not giving Arthur money again, but still it was upsetting to have the family angry at them. Her father said that this whole business was putting him in a very uncomfortable position and maybe the best thing was for them to go back to Brooklyn. Ellen, listening to this from the doorway to the bathroom, wanted to yell, *Not fair.* Why should they have to leave Rockaway before the summer was over just because her father wouldn't help Arthur?

The next day, Sunday, she was worried that her parents would say that they had to pack up and leave, but instead she learned that her father was going back to Brooklyn that night instead of Monday when he usually went. He said it was because he had an early meeting Monday morning, but Ellen wondered if the real reason was his uncomfortable position.

ooo

Early the next morning, with her father gone and her mother and Annie still asleep, Ellen let herself out of the bungalow. She and Michael liked to go down to the beach to look for money and bottle caps in the sand before anyone else got there. That morning she waited in front of the bungalow for a while and then decided to check the boardwalk because he sometimes waited for her there.

The sky was gray but in a foggy way that meant it might turn sunny later. No one was out on the street except for two fathers who were getting into their cars to go to work. At the end of the street, she went up the ramp to the boardwalk, which was also deserted. After a few minutes and still no Michael she thought about going back but then heard a familiar voice coming from the beach below.

Moving closer to the railing she saw Arthur a short distance away talking to two men. She thought the skinny one looked like the man who'd come to the skeeball arcade but couldn't be sure. Arthur was facing her but didn't look up and see her.

She went down the wooden steps onto the beach, her sandals leaving prints on the sand, still damp from yesterday's rain. As she approached the group, the skinny man turned and saw her and said, "Who the hell is this?"

She expected Arthur to say, "She's my cousin," but instead he said, "Go home, Ellen," as if he owned the whole beach. His voice sounded different, and he had the same worried look he'd had that night in the arcade. Even so, she didn't like being bossed around in front of these two strange men.

"It's a free country," she said, her hands on her hips, looking at Arthur but not at the men. When the other man said maybe she'd like to go for a nice swim, Arthur grabbed her by the arm, and with two hard wallops on the behind for emphasis, said, "I *told* you to go *home*."

She'd never been hit before, and tears of humiliation and rage blinded her as she struggled to free herself from his grip. When he let her go, she stumbled and then ran, slowed down by the sand, turning when she got to the boardwalk steps to scream that she hated him and hoped he'd die, but he wasn't even looking at her.

She ran down the street, the tears still coming, and brushed the sand off her feet before she tiptoed into the bungalow. She went straight to her room, dropped her clothes on the floor, put on her pajamas, and slipped into bed just as Annie was starting to stir.

She pretended to be asleep for a long time so that she wouldn't have to talk to her mother or to Annie or to anyone.

000

The next day, Tuesday, Michael had a sore throat. He was allowed to go outside but had to stay on the porch and not run around. Ellen was told she had to keep him company so he wouldn't drive his mother crazy. They were playing Chutes and Ladders when Morrie and Birdie and, a couple of minutes later, Ellen's grandfather showed up. They went straight inside, taking no notice of her or Michael. Ellen, sitting close to the open window, heard enough to figure out that Morrie and Birdie were worried because Arthur hadn't come home the night before.

At the mention of Arthur's name, Ellen felt her face burning. She wondered if he'd gone away with the two men, but she couldn't say that to Morrie and Birdie without telling them the rest of what happened. Then her grandfather said, "What do you think, a young good-looking guy like that is going to sit on his behind all summer with the old men? He went out to have some fun."

That seemed to make her uncle Morrie feel better because he said in a jokey way, "At his age, it took me ten minutes to have fun, and it takes him all night?" But her aunt Birdie, still sounding worried, said, "I'll laugh when I see my son walking through the door."

000

Early Wednesday morning, Ellen was wakened by voices coming from the kitchen: her mother, who sounded like she was crying; her father, who was supposed to be in Brooklyn; her grandfather, who at that hour was supposed to be in his own bungalow.

She got dressed quickly and went to the kitchen where Annie, eating her cereal, said, "Mommy's crying," as if Ellen couldn't see that for herself. The grownups were talking half in English, half in Yiddish, so Ellen understood there was no point in asking what was going on. Instead, she ate her cereal, then slipped out of the room and out of the bungalow without anyone but Annie noticing.

Michael's parents, in their kitchen, also looked as if they'd been crying, so she didn't say hello but went straight to Michael's room. He was taking clothes out of the bureau drawers and piling them on his unmade bed, an open suitcase on the floor. He told her everyone was going back to Brooklyn because they were too sad to stay in Rockaway, but they couldn't go right away because the police were coming back to talk to them.

He said all this as if she'd know what he was talking about, but she didn't know anything, not even what questions to ask. She'd gone to sleep the night before with everything in its right place and woken up to a big confusing jumble. When she said that, Michael told her that someone had shot Arthur and now he was dead and that the police had come in the middle of the night to tell Birdie and Morrie. His voice sounded funny when he said that, like he was going to cry any second, so she knew he was telling the truth for once.

She asked where they shot Arthur, meaning where like on the beach, but Michael didn't understand and said he thought they shot him in the head. Then she asked why the police were coming back, and Michael said he didn't know. She was shivering now even though her face was hot and she felt like she was going to throw up.

Ellen went back to her own bungalow and shut herself in the bathroom waiting to throw up, but nothing happened. Sitting on the closed toilet seat, she thought about Arthur, the good one who'd teased her and taken her to the boardwalk and the other one who she hated. She felt sad about the first one, but not about the second. It was as if the bad Arthur had killed the good Arthur, and then he got killed too.

When she came out of the bathroom, Annie asked if she would play with her, but Ellen said no. She wanted to ask her parents, who were talking in their room, if it was true that they were going back to Brooklyn.

She was about to knock on their door when she heard her father making strange noises. At first she thought he was sick and then realized he was crying, something she'd never heard before in her life.

Then she heard her mother say, "Ben, please, it's not your fault," and she understood that her father was crying because he hadn't helped Arthur with his jam and that was why he got shot in the head.

She knew it was her fault too because she'd screamed at Arthur that she wished he was dead, so maybe she'd given the jam guys the idea of killing him. She wanted to say that to her father, but if she told what Arthur had done to her on the beach, it would feel as if it was happening all over again, and then she would wish she was dead too. She knew she could not say those words ever, not even to make her father feel better.

000

Her parents spent the rest of the morning packing and loading up the car. Her mother, tearful the whole time, kept saying that she couldn't stop thinking about what a sweet little boy Arthur had been. Then to Ellen, "He was so crazy about you when you were little."

Ellen knew what was coming, the story about how she fell and broke her tooth the summer she was two while running down the street to Arthur, who picked her up and cried when he saw her bloody mouth. Ellen wanted to say please don't tell that story anymore, but she didn't.

Her father got sandwiches from the grocery store because the kitchen was all packed up, and they ate these on the front porch, waiting for the policemen. When Ellen asked why they were coming, her father said the police probably wanted to know when they'd last seen Arthur. When he said that, Ellen again felt sick and asked her father what if she didn't remember. He said, "Then that's what you say when they ask you."

The two policemen arrived a few minutes later and they all went inside. Ellen's father brought chairs in from the kitchen, so the small living room felt crowded. Everyone sat except Ellen, who stood next to the couch where her parents were sitting with Annie on her mother's lap.

The old policeman did most of the talking, asking the

193

question Ellen's father had predicted he'd ask, while the young one wrote down what they said. Ellen's mother said they'd seen Arthur that past weekend and her father said the same.

When they said that, Ellen remembered Arthur teasing her when she was sitting on the steps waiting for Michael. She knew that was Saturday morning because her father had come back from the city the night before, so that's what she told the policeman. When he asked if Arthur had talked to her, she said he'd said hi, but didn't mention that he'd called her a sourpuss. Then the policeman asked if she was sure that was the last time she'd seen him, and she said yes. Her heart was beating fast the whole time she was talking, but she knew from watching Michael that the important thing when you lied was to sound normal and make your face blank. At the end the old policeman smiled at her and said she'd been very helpful.

Looking out the car window a short while later at the people walking to the beach, Ellen thought it was unfair that for them it was an ordinary day while for her family it was goodbye to Rockaway. She'd heard her mother say that to her father as the car pulled away from the curb and understood that she meant they were never coming back.

In a few years she would realize that Arthur had saved her life on that foggy morning, but as the car turned off Beach 25th Street, she blamed him for the end of the summers she'd thought would go on forever.

Anita Page's short stories have appeared in a number of webzines and anthologies, including *Family Matters*, a Murder New York Style anthology which she edited. Other publications include the MWA anthology *The Prosecution Rests* and, most recently, Level Best Books's *Windward*. Her short story "'Twas the Night," published in *The Gift of Murder*, received a Derringer Award from the Short Mystery Fiction Society in 2010. She has a story forthcoming in *The Paterson Literary Review*. Anita Page's crime novel, *Damned If You Don't* (Glenmere Press), is set in the Catskills, where she worked as a freelance feature writer for a regional newspaper. She currently reviews classic crime films for the webzine *Mysterical-E* and blogs occasionally at anitapagewriter.blogspot.com.

78841079R00125

Made in the USA
Columbia, SC
13 October 2017